BLIND EYE

ALSO BY JOHN McLAREN

Press Send

7th Sense

Black Cabs

Running Rings

BLIND EYE

John McLaren

SIMON &
SCHUSTER

London · New York · Sydney · Dublin

A VIACOM COMPANY

First published in Great Britain by Simon & Schuster UK Ltd, 2004
A Viacom Company

1 3 5 7 9 10 8 6 4 2

Simon & Schuster UK Ltd
Africa House
64–78 Kingsway
London WC2B 6AH

Simon & Schuster Australia
Sydney

www.simonsays.co.uk

A CIP catalogue record for this book is available
from the British Library

ISBN 0-7432-0290-2

Typeset by M Rules
Printed and bound in Great Britain by
Mackays of Chatham plc

for Jeremy Black

Acknowledgements

My thanks must go first to my editor Suzanne Baboneau, to Ian Chapman, to my agent Jonathan Lloyd, to Sir Jeremy and Lady Black, to Ken and Phyllis Lemberger, and to Madeleine Milne.

Researching this book has enabled me to spend much time in the company of members of the Royal Navy. I am lost in admiration for their professionalism, skill, and dedication. I hope they will allow me to remain a friend. Many of them gave an extraordinary degree of help in my efforts to make the text authentic. These include the First Sea Lord, Admiral Sir Alan West, Commander in Chief Fleet, Admiral Jonathon Band, Vice Admiral Mark Stanhope, Rear Admiral Tim McClement, Rear Admiral Charles Style, Commodore Richard Leaman, Commodore Anthony Rix, Captain Alistair Halliday, Lieutenant Colonel Ben Curry, Lieutenant Commander Kevin Fincher and Lieutenant Commander Chris Mahony. I also received important help from HMS *Ark Royal* – especially the captain at the time, Rear Admiral David Snelson, and the commanding officer as I write, Captain Adrian Nance, and Commander James Humphreys and Commander Gordon Graham, from HMS *Invincible* – especially Captain Trevor Soar and Commander David Elford, and from HMS *Torbay* – Commander Mark Cooper, Lieutenant Commander Ryan Ramsey, Lieutenant Steve Keeley, and Lieutenant Rosco Tanner. My warmest thanks too go to Commander John Parris R.N.R., Lieutenant James Blackmore, Nikki Lightly, and Wendy Shaw. (I hope all the Navy personnel will forgive me for omitting their decorations. Including them would have extended this section by several pages. Their titles are, I hope, accurate at the moment this text was finalised, but doubtless many will have gone on to higher things in the interval before publication date.)

On cultural matters, I received extensive, invaluable and most thoughtful guidance from Theresa Akwaboah and Dr Joanna Lewis, and also from Akosua Annobil-Dodoo, Moira Bennett, Angela Foster, Alistair Sommerlad, and Mohamed Sumani.

Other good friends gave their time generously as critics or enablers, including Graham Baker, James Baker, Angie Barrow, Manfred Bischoff, Charles and Pascale Clark, Bertrand Coste, Sir Clement Freud, John and Jenny Gild, Larry Gross, Darren Henley, Edward Hill, Dr Martin Hirsch, Freya Jonas, Jacqueline Koay, Stan Lawrence, Tracy Long, Margaret McLaren, Sir Peter Michael, Andrew Mitchell, Paul O'Neill, Teruko Sado, Nina Sadowsky, Tomoko Sakuma, Ben Samuelson, Anne Smith, Diane Stidham, Stewart Till, Hidenori Tokuda, John Weston, Christopher Whalley, Nigel Williams, and Peter Yao.

I would be lynched, rightly, if I did not acknowledge the immense help and encouragement I have received from my colleagues in the Barchester Group, in particular David Charters, Colin Clark, Lorne Forsyth, Roger Lewis, Steve McCauley, Karen Mistry, and David Young.

Finally, I offer profuse thanks to everyone at Little Good Harbour, a gem of a hotel in Barbados, especially the proprietor Andrew Warden, Andrea Greaves, Arlene Thomas, and the elegant taxi driver, Kareen Harris. Above all, to Helen Edwards and her marvellous company Essential Detail for finding such an idyllic perfect place to write a book.

If you would like to learn more about the Navy, there is a wealth of information about the Navy at
www.royalnavy.mod.uk

The two jets screamed on through the white. Five thousand feet below them were sodden stretches of rock and peat and the heaving, flecked mass of the chill South Atlantic. A few more minutes and they would be getting low on fuel, and it would again be time for the pilots to head back and wrestle the evil crosswinds, fighting to land tidily on *Invincible*'s bucking, Teflon-faced runway.

The radio crackled into life.

'Satan Two, let's try one last time lower down. Descending to three thousand feet. Over.'

The reply came back with a mild twang in the accent.

'Roger, leader.'

Back in *Invincible*, the Commander Air sat on a tall metal stool in Flyco, the flight-control centre next to the bridge. He gazed abstractedly at the activity down on the deck as he listened to the exchanges of the pilots with each other and with the fighter controller in the Ops Room six decks below him. Today had been unusually quiet. Not a single inbound threat to intercept. It was as if the Argies were having a day off.

'Jesus, leader, did you see that?'

The urgency in the voice ripped the Commander Air's reverie. He stared intently at the little loudspeaker as the leader's voice came back.

'I didn't see anything. Over.'

'*Invincible*, this is Satan Two. I flew over a gap in the cloud. There was a swept-wing aircraft on the runway. Over.'

The Commander Air was already on his feet as he heard the fighter controller responding.

1

'Satan Two, did you get a photo? Over.'

'Not sure if I got it. Permission to attack? Over.'

'Negative. Return to mother. We need to develop that film right away. Over.'

'It has to be an Étendard, and if it takes off now, we won't have a base to return to. Repeat, request permission to attack. Over.'

'Unless we send in a whole squadron, you'll be cut to pieces. Return to mother. Do you read me, Satan One and Two?'

'Roger. Over.'

'Thank you, Satan One. Satan Two, do you copy? Over.'

'*Invincible*, I seem to be having a radio problem. Can you repeat that? Over.'

'Return to mother immediately.'

'Still can't hear you. Was that a go? Over.'

'No, it was negative. Do you read? Over.'

There was nothing but static.

'Satan One, if Satan Two's got some sort of problem, we're looking to you to guide him home. Over.'

'I've lost him. The cloud's too dense. I'm descending to two thousand feet to try to find him. Over.'

The Commander Air grabbed a microphone.

'Satan Two, if you can hear me, do not attack. Repeat, do *not* attack.'

There was no reply. He cursed and swung round to the Lieutenant Commander standing next to him.

'Prepare to launch Satan Three and Four. And we'd better get some Sea Kings airborne. If that bloody idiot attacks, he won't have a cat in hell's chance of making it back here.'

*

The Argentinian lieutenant sitting in the tiny control tower looked at his watch again. After an eternity, the engineers had finally fixed the problem with the fuel nozzle. Now the fuel was pumping into the plane from the tanker truck. The pilot of the Étendard supersonic bomber had been growing increasingly agitated. The navigator kept walking under the wings, checking the mountings on the twin Exocet missiles. If they could get close enough to either one of the carriers *Hermes* or *Invincible*, these sleek beauties could win the war at a stroke.

They had good reason to be nervous. The ground radar had picked up blips from two enemy jets. At times they could hear them. Thank Heaven for cloud cover. The lieutenant willed the Étendard to be airborne and off his watch.

The voice of his radar operator broke in: one enemy jet at five hundred metres, range seven kilometres to the south. It looked like an attack pattern. The lieutenant barked orders to his batteries to prepare to open fire. The Étendard pilot cursed and raced back to the steps beneath the cockpit. The navigator was inches behind him as they climbed up, and he gestured angrily to the tanker crew to pull the nozzle clear so they could start the engines. As the whine of the turbines began, they heard through their headsets that the enemy was four kilometres away and closing. The pilot was desperate to get his machine back to the start of the runway and the hell out of there.

The lieutenant had to force himself to wait till the range was right. Three kilometres, two and a half, two . . . He issued the order. The clouds flashed bright with fireworks, and the control tower windows rattled fiercely as the whole structure shook. At the far end of the field, the Étendard was approaching the end of its bumpy taxi and starting a tight turn, its engines winding themselves up to catapult the craft forward. He glanced up at the eastern sky; he couldn't see the enemy yet. The Étendard was beginning to gather pace. Another six hundred metres and it would be airborne. Go, *go*.

*

The Harrier jet was bathed in the hail of tracers, and 35mm cannon shells were exploding all around. The pilot knew he would only get one chance.

He felt a sudden vibration. The engine must have taken a hit. Alarm lights started flashing all over the panel. Don't eject over land. Try to get back out to sea. He thrust the stick forward and the plane hurtled down in a steep, screaming dive. Any moment now he would be clear of the clouds and into the eye of the firestorm. The fuselage shuddered massively as a huge explosion nearly sheered off the starboard wing. The engine was alive with flame now. Five seconds more, down, down, down.

And suddenly clear of the cloud. The g-forces assailed him as he levelled out. He could see the flashes from four batteries. Where was the runway? *There*. He flicked up the switches to arm the SNEB rockets and waited till the Étendard came into his sights as it streaked down the runway and began to lift off. *Now*. He pressed the red buttons, and twin missiles fell clear of the wings, ignited and fizzed forward.

As he tried to pull back up, another shell rocked his plane and his front screen crazed. He could see nothing, except the hills on the port side below him. He tried to look round to see what was happening behind him, but only caught glimpses of fire and black smoke. He could feel his back getting very hot.

He barely managed to coax the dying machine to bank as more cannon shells began to tear it apart. Time to Mayday.

No good. The radio was gone.

He was too low to eject. At this altitude he would crash like a stone into the water. The Harrier vibrated horribly as he tried to get the nose up. The heat was becoming unbearable. Was the back of his flying suit on fire? Try to hang on.

He managed another few miles before the heat became too intense. Better drown than burn alive. He reached under to pull the lever. The twisted remains of the canopy flew up and he was wrenched skywards, blacking out.

Three hours later, the Commander Air paced around, trying to cling to the threadbare remnants of his temper. The pilot, his neck in a brace, stood to attention, staring stiffly ahead of him, waiting for the thunder to start rolling again. It didn't take long.

'You're blowing smoke up my arse, Cameron. Your radio never malfunctioned.'

'Definitely did, sir. Wish the engineers could check it.'

The Commander halted in his tracks. 'It's at the bottom of the bloody ocean. Do you have any idea how much a Harrier costs? . . . You're suspended from flying pending an investigation. If we prove you lied, you'll be court-martialled and drummed out of the navy . . . Yes . . . What the hell *is* it?

The young officer who had knocked politely looked taken aback.

'Cloud cover's cleared over Port Stanley, sir. We've got a decent high-altitude reconnaissance shot.'

'Show me.'

The lieutenant pulled the picture out of the envelope and handed it over.

'Looks like the aircraft has sustained major damage to its port wing and fuselage. It's definitely an Étendard, sir, and if you look at that little white shape coming out from under the starboard wing just *there* . . . it has to be an Exocet.'

'Hmm. Okay.'

The Commander waited till the steel door had clanged closed.

'Cameron, you're still suspended.'

'Yes, sir.'

'This is the worst case of insubordination I've ever seen in eighteen years in the navy. It's a miracle we didn't lose more aircraft rescuing you . . . Listen, I know this is no exercise. If that photo's telling the truth, it's possible you may have saved the fleet – even this ship – from a major attack. If you were acting on orders, you'd be in line for a medal. But you weren't.'

He paused and ran his hand through his hair.

'This isn't the first time I've had to speak to you. You're only twenty-two. Some people think you're quite clever, in spite of your constant efforts to prove the contrary. Your leader thinks you're a half-decent pilot. You could do well in the navy. When you get too old for flying you could drive ships, you could go all the way. But not if you go pulling stunts like this. This is your last chance. Never pretend your radio's not working when it is. Do I make myself clear?'

'Yes, sir.'

'The captain wants to see you. Right away.'

Cameron was making his way back to the cabin he shared with another young pilot. Christ, his neck hurt. The captain had given him another bollocking, but he'd delivered it more quietly, chosen his words more judiciously, and it had far more effect.

As he slumped down on the bunk, his cabin-mate came in, looking concerned.

'You all right, Chris?'

Cameron nodded.

'How did it go with the captain?'

'Not much fun.'

The cabin-mate's face registered surprise when Cameron pulled a slim chocolate bar from his pocket.

'You didn't get that from the captain, did you?'

'Yeah. After he'd ripped me to pieces.'

'Jesus.'

It was the strangest, but one of the more successful, means of motivation in modern navy history. The captain had once given a young sailor a Crunchie bar for something remarkable he had done. Word of it spread like wildfire through

Invincible, and soon it became institutionalised. Crunchies weren't hard to find: they had them by the gross in the ship's little store. But buying one for yourself wasn't the same thing.

Cameron went to tear open the wrapper. The other guy looked horrified.

'You're not going to eat it, are you?'

Cameron studied it carefully for a moment and smiled. 'On second thoughts, maybe not.'

1

More than forty years after it had first startled the world, the liquid coupé form of the E-type Jaguar still turned heads. As the gunmetal shape drove down the wintry streets, it drew eyes away not only from humdrum Fords, Volvos and VWs, but from the grander BMWs and Mercedes. Tiny rear lights came on in a dab of brakes, the Jaguar snaked round another roundabout and sped on towards Portsmouth.

Apart from the music on the radio, the pair had driven in silence since they left Lymington. He could not work out what she was thinking. She was often withdrawn on the day he was leaving, but had never been as uncommunicative as this. In fact, throughout his month's leave, she had been uncharacteristically quiet. Even when they made love that morning, she had seemed somehow unreachable, and as soon as it was over she had rolled away and lain on her side, staring out the window while he showered and packed.

As they slowed for a red light, her hand hovered politely over the volume knob, waiting until the Sheryl Crow ballad cadenced to a close before switching it off.

'You realise this is the second year running you've missed my birthday.'

'I'm sorry. You know I'll be back for Christmas.'

She looked out of the side window. He touched her hand.

'Come on, Charlotte, please don't be like this.'

She closed her eyes for a moment. 'I sometimes think I must have been genuinely mad.'

'What d'you mean?'

'Throwing away what I had.'

He swung his wrists neatly left and right. The road was one roundabout after another. He accelerated out of it and changed up to fourth gear.

'This is the last time I'll be away. Then we'll be able to spend much more time together.'

'Doing what? Trundling on, with me never knowing from one week to the next how long it will last? You're not a child, Chris. You're forty-four. If you could commit, you'd have done it by now . . . What's the longest relationship you've ever had? Four years? Well, we're past three already – unless you deduct all the time you've spent at sea. How long before you trade me in for a newer model?'

'You know that's crap . . .'

'Is it?'

'Charlotte, I *have* committed to you, in my own way. But if we did what you want, it would just be an extra burden, and a greater sense of failure if it didn't work.'

She shook her head sadly. 'I suppose I feel it most when Christmas is coming. Every bloody card seems to show a happy family gathered round the hearth.'

'Come on – your kids are coming to us on Christmas Eve, aren't they?'

'Yes. And if I'm really lucky, they'll stay past the stroke of midnight, so we can all pretend they spent part of Christmas Day with me. Then they'll go to their father's. For all three of them that's still the real family home.'

'Why don't you tell me what's going on in your head? I know this isn't just about Christmas. What is it? Are you thinking of going back to Tim?'

She snorted. 'You think he would take me? After the way I – and you – humiliated him?'

He glanced sideways. 'But if he would? Would *you*?'

'I don't know. I don't know anything any more.'

The last miles passed in brooding silence. Just short of the Unicorn Gate, he pulled over and turned to her.

'I'll get out here.'

9

'Don't bother. You can park inside while you're away, can't you? I'll take a taxi back to the flat.'

'What *are* you talking about?'

She looked him hard in the eye.

'Chris, I'm not sure I'll be around when you get back.'

He took her hand. 'Please, Charlotte, you've said things like this before. You don't mean it, do you?'

'The tragedy is that I love you like I've never loved anyone before.'

She kissed him on the cheek, reached for the door handle and climbed out. She was already fifteen yards away, almost round the corner, when he called out.

'Charlotte, wait. I've got something.'

He rummaged around on the metal-ribbed rear shelf, unearthed a small, elaborately wrapped box, got out of the car and began to carry it towards her.

She stood her ground. 'What is it?'

'It's for your birthday . . . A necklace.'

She shook her head. He was about to take another step forward, when something in her eyes stopped him. He glanced down at the little box in his right hand as if it held the answer, and when he looked up again, she was gone.

He walked slowly back to the car, tossed the box onto the passenger seat, lowered himself in and drove up to the security gate. The guard recognised him and smiled.

'Good afternoon, Captain Cameron.'

When he'd been waved through, he drove out of sight of prying eyes and let the car roll gently to a halt. He lowered his head, so it rested against the steering wheel. After one minute, he composed himself, and the Jaguar went back into gear, the rasp of the exhaust bouncing off the Georgian brick buildings on either side. To his left he caught a glimpse of Nelson's flagship, HMS *Victory*, before driving on to the north-west wall where, beyond many frigates, destroyers and lesser naval craft, he could already make out the towering shape of *Indomitable* jutting up against the grey winter sky.

10

The sight always thrilled and inspired him. Today the big ship didn't immediately cast her full sensational spell.

Parking opposite the carrier, he yanked the lever to open the hatch, and took out two large canvas bags. He pulled on a dark blue jacket with heavily braided cuffs, and walked the few yards over to the gangway.

From among the welcoming party, the Commander, the ship's number two, took a step forward and saluted with a smile.

'Welcome back, sir.'

'Good to see you, Tom.'

A seaman moved smartly to take the bags, and followed in their wake as they made their way briskly down narrow passageways and up skinny, near-vertical ladders. They passed a succession of officers, petty officers and seamen, who drew back and stood to attention, receiving in return nods, smiles and the occasional friendly word from the captain. As they passed the main communications office they saw a short-haired girl of perhaps twenty-four talking with a barrel-chested leading seaman in his late thirties. The girl looked pale and had bloodshot, dark-ringed eyes. Cameron grinned at her.

'Big last night in port, was it, Seaman Moore?'

She nodded. 'Bit *too* big, sir.'

Cameron swept on, exchanging a smile with the man.

'How're the kids, Leading Seaman Ward?'

'Terrible, sir. They take after their mother.'

There were only two more ladders to climb and they were at the captain's harbour cabin. His yeoman was waiting there holding the handsome oak signal board with over a hundred sheets of paper held by a clip. A steward provided a cup of strong black coffee for Cameron to sip as he flicked through the signals. Satisfied, he handed the board back, and walked to a briefing room where the sloping-shouldered Commander, Tom Hitchens, was waiting with the officer commanding the marines and the key heads of department –

11

the Commander Air, the Operations Officer and the Weapons Electrical Commander.

Hitchens ran through a number of routine matters, including a minor problem with one of their four engines and a delay in patching part of the surface of the flight deck.

'And that's more or less it, sir. Morale on board is sky high. Everyone aboard can't wait to get to the Med and pit their wits against the Americans. We sail in two hours at high water. As soon as we're past Nab Tower, aircraft will start landing on. Wings, can you run through the complement?'

The Commander Air, Chris Butler, known to all as Wings, bluff, solid, forty-one, nodded. 'We have eight Harriers and ten helos – six Merlin and four Sea King, sir.'

Hitchens gestured towards Captain Colin Dewar, the tallest and toughest-looking man present. 'Colin is commanding half a platoon of marines, who are here primarily to practise amphibious landings as part of the exercise. Otherwise, it's pretty much as usual. Apart from the marines, headcount will be three hundred and eighty-four air group, and six hundred and seventy-six general ship's company.'

The Captain nodded. 'When do we rendezvous with our escorts, Tara?'

Lieutenant Commander Tara Wynn, the Operations Officer, was slim and tautly attractive, her short auburn hair framing fine features.

'In four days, sir, on December sixth. They'll be waiting for us just east of Gibraltar. Two frigates, two destroyers and the Royal Fleet Auxiliary *Fort George*. Before that, we're planning to test some of the new electronic systems we've had fitted. Once we hook up with the escorts, we sail east and meet up with the Americans near Crete . . . There's one more thing we'll be picking up at Gibraltar . . . Robert, would you like to explain?'

Robert Young, the Weapons Electrical Commander, had an infectious, open enthusiasm which made him seem younger than his thirty-six years. He had volunteered to take on media liaison.

'Corporate Communications are inviting the *Daily Post* to send someone to cover the exercise, sir. They think this will be an exceptionally good platform, and as we all know, with the defence budget review coming up, they think it's important that the navy gets some positive press. The general public seem to have very little idea what we're here for.'

The Captain smiled. 'Wonderful. Well, I hope you can keep him under control, Robert . . . Okay, navigator's report, please.'

*

Jason Carvill had just celebrated his thirtieth birthday. He'd gone through the motions of bemoaning the passing of his youth, but it was all pretty phoney. He was still young and cool enough not to feel out of place even in the hippest club. His carefully groomed casual look helped. He'd also got automatic respect from his mates for working on a national like the *Post*. A few of his liberal pals mocked him when he was made deputy defence correspondent, but he didn't care. It was promotion.

He leaned back, his black suede shoes resting on his desk, the telephone nuzzling his neck, and smiled.

'When will the official letter come? . . . That's great. I owe you one. Talk to you soon.'

He pushed back a few inches so his feet fell to the floor, and banged the receiver down in the cradle.

'Fan-fucking-tastic.'

Debbie, the twenty-five-year-old at the next desk, looked up curiously. Even in the six months since she'd joined the paper, Debbie had grown conspicuously blonder and a couple of pounds heavier, but with a figure like hers, she could probably afford it.

'What's so great?'

'Never you mind.' Jason grabbed his unstructured Armani jacket from the back of his chair and marched off across the broad open-plan office. Debbie watched as he negotiated his way over to Grace. There were three black women in the room, but it wasn't hard to pick out the one truly striking face. Grace looked up as she heard his steps.

'Let's get some lunch.'

'I can't. I've got to finish this feature on Mariss Jansons.'

'Do it later, I've got something to celebrate . . . Come on, Grace, this is a big deal for me. We'll go to Marco's.'

She nodded, wrote one last sentence, and pressed the key to save her work.

In the run-up to Christmas, every restaurant and bar in Canary Wharf was packed, and if people from the *Post* weren't such regulars, the maître d' would never have fitted them in. As it was, they had to accept being shoehorned between two tables stuffed with loud bankers. Heads swivelled as Grace walked towards the table. With her model height, sculpted medium-length straight hair, long legs, lithe figure and easy elegance of movement, she was always an attention magnet. Depending on his mood, Jason could be gratified or irritated by that.

They clinked when the glasses of champagne arrived, but Jason's quick explanation on the way over hadn't got through. Grace was still looking puzzled.

'Even if the guy at the Ministry of Defence who's fixed this is your pal, how can you be sure the editor won't send Peter? You're only the deputy defence correspondent.'

'Whoever gets chosen has to fly down to Gibraltar on Wednesday, and go on board first thing on Thursday. That's the day Peter's wife goes into hospital for her cancer op.

'You sly bastard.'

Jason grinned. 'I wish I could take credit, 'cause there ain't nothing wrong with trying to get on, but actually the timing was a total fluke. The navy doesn't love me *that* much.' They broke off for a moment as their starters arrived. Jason dug hungrily into his insalata Caprese. Grace took a wary sip of her steaming minestrone.

'When will you be back?'

'Can't quite remember. By Christmas, anyway.'

'What about our weekend in Paris?'

Jason shovelled in another mouthful of mozzarella. 'You can get us a refund from Eurostar, can't you?'

As Grace took another spoonful, she looked down at her plate a little too long.

'If you're going to give me a hard time over this . . . *Jesus*.'

She looked up. The bankers on her left had broken off from their own gossip to tune in. Jason didn't care.

'We can go to Paris any fucking time. Surely you can cope on your own for a couple of weeks?'

Grace couldn't let that go. 'Oh, I can cope. Don't ever doubt it.'

Jason pushed his plate away. 'I've lost my appetite. Let's get out of here.'

He swung round and put up a hand to call for the bill. Grace had to stretch to pull his arm down. As she did, one of the bankers noticed with mild disappointment the tiny diamond on her wedding finger.

'I'm sorry, darling. I didn't mean to spoil your big moment. Come on, tell me more about it.' She got no response but tried again. 'What's the carrier doing in the Mediterranean, anyway?'

Jason forked a slice of tomato and chewed it slowly.

'Joint exercises with the Americans.'

'What's it called, by the way?'

'*Indomitable*. And it's not an "it", it's a "she".'

*

Manoeuvring an aircraft carrier in the confined space of Portsmouth harbour is not simple. Two or even three tugs are

15

normally needed to help defeat the caprices of winds, currents and tide as the leviathan casts off, nudges delicately aft for three or four hundred yards, and then executes a one hundred and fifty degree turn in a channel only twice her own length. If the captain gets too close to the east bank, he risks ramming one of the destroyers moored there, and if he veers too near the west side, he might crush some of the many tethered pleasure craft.

The navigator's report had indicated that there would be a maximum wind of ten knots, and he conservatively recommended attaching two tugs. Cameron brought a wicked grin to the man's face by mentioning that the admiral, whose seamanship had never attracted widespread admiration, might be observing, and suggesting that they show off and make the manoeuvre unassisted.

Along with the navigator, pilot and the Commander, Cameron went up to the roof of the bridge. From there, the carrier felt like a skyscraper in a village high street. As she began to slide away from the jetty, he glanced down to the flight deck where the entire ship's company was arrayed.

For the next few minutes he concentrated intently as the ship began to swing sideways into the turn, the waters beneath it getting whipped into frothy fury. Only when they stopped turning and the bows settled south did he relax, and enjoy the last mile of stately progress to the mouth. His vantage point was so high that he could peer down the funnels of frigates and destroyers as they passed them. Then he gazed ahead to the Round Tower ahead of them, where hundreds of husbands, wives, lovers, parents and children were waiting. If the carrier had been going to war, all their emotions would have been ratcheted sky high. Even when they were only leaving for exercises, some tears would be shed on the walls. As the ship approached, a forest of flags and arms began to wave, and each man and woman on board tried to spot their own loved ones. All too soon, though, the moment was over, and as the water began to widen, the crew hastened back to their posts. Minutes later, the captain turned to the navigator.

'Course one eight five, half ahead. Revolution six zero. Ready to take the ship?'

'Ready to take the ship, sir.'

'You have the ship.'

They sailed down the Solent until they had enough sea-room and the right level of westerly wind for jets to land safely. To the north-east the sky began to rumble and the first of the Harriers hove into view. The mission was underway.

Three hours later *Indomitable* had slipped past the Isle of Wight, and was steaming in open water at fifteen knots. The sea was calm, the evening sky clear. The aircraft had all landed on while there was daylight, and were now safely tucked up in the immense hangar beneath the flight deck.

The wardroom was packed with officers, all dressed in 'Red Sea rig' – formal trousers, white open shirts with epaulettes and cummerbunds embroidered with *Indomitable*'s insignia, except the airmen, who wore their own squadron's crest. They enjoyed a drink in the vast bar before going through to the dining room with its long refectory tables. The decor in both was Formica functional, softened with hunting prints and chintz lampshades.

Christopher Cameron was dining alone in his sea cabin. This was not only because this was the norm – a carrier captain only dines in the wardroom occasionally and when invited; tonight he was glad not to have to make small-talk. He reached for his phone and tried one more time to reach Charlotte. On both her mobile and at the flat he got voicemail. He kept wondering why she brought this to a head now. She knew this was his last mission in *Indomitable*. Had she picked this timing deliberately to make sure he couldn't interfere or talk her out of it? He tried one more time. The same. She had never refused a present before. If she was leaving him, why couldn't she just say so?

17

It would be hard this time, if their relationship was over. Charlotte had got under his skin. However many times he had been through break-ups, there was nothing that would take away the long chilly months of emptiness. Being at sea would help him through the first weeks; most of his waking hours would be brim-filled with things to take care of. The gut-wrencher wouldn't come until he got back to Lymington, turned the key in the flat door, and found a large pile of envelopes on the mat, no lights on, the heating off. And the sharpest stab would come when he walked through to the bedroom, pulled open her wardrobe and saw only coat-hangers there.

Had he been a fool to risk losing her? After three years they still got on well. Wasn't this as good as it got? His few close friends, supporters of Charlotte to a man, had all given him up for lost. But even if he offered what she wanted, would she accept him now? And, if she did, how would *he* feel about it one year on? Why didn't she at least take his call? With a carrier to drive, he couldn't afford this distraction.

He got up and walked the few steps up to the bridge, where the officer of the watch stared out into the blackness, a tiny red beam tracked their progress on a paper chart and a girl of nineteen daintily held the tiny handles that steered the multibillion-pound machine of war.

2

The House of Commons was as much a rough house as ever. Another fifteen members jumped to their feet to try to attract the Speaker's attention. This time, behind the Government benches, it was the MP for Walsall who got the nod.

'Could my right honourable friend the Secretary of State for Foreign Affairs tell the House what action he intends to take following the expulsion of the EU's observer mission from Numala?'

The Foreign Secretary rose.

'Naturally the government deplores this action. I hope that President Nabote understands that in the absence of any external verification, the international community will form its own view on the validity of the result of the forthcoming election.'

He sat down quickly, hoping he'd got away with it. Having no more than glanced at the briefing on this subject, he was not well prepared. His luck was out. It was the Opposition's turn to speak next, and they saw the chance to press home an attack.

'Following on from the honourable gentleman's question, is the Foreign Secretary aware of the Numalan government's flagrant breaches of the rule of law? Several of my own constituents are among the foreigners who had their assets in Numala confiscated illegally and without compensation. Does the Foreign Secretary also realise that now many prominent members of the minority Lobu tribe are concerned for their safety? There are disturbing and widespread reports of brutality. A number of Numalan government ministers have made statements designed to inflame relations between the tribes there. Left unchecked, this could escalate to another Rwanda. Mr Speaker, I don't have to remind this House that Numala is a former British colony, which gives us a special responsibility. Is the Foreign Secretary going to turn a blind eye if this situation gets out of hand?'

The Foreign Secretary shuffled back to his feet. 'As I have told the honourable member for Sutton Coldfield on a previous occasion, we are monitoring the situation carefully. We share his disquiet about the reports of ill-treatment of Lobus, and as a mark of our concern, I have decided to recall our High Commissioner, Roger Fairfax, for consultations. However, I must remind the honourable gentleman, we do not have the right to interfere in the affairs of another sovereign state.'

The uproar took half a minute to settle. The Foreign Secretary stared stonily ahead, all too aware that the Chancellor, sitting beside him, would be enjoying his discomfiture. It was an open secret that they were the two most obvious candidates if the Prime Minister ever called it a day.

Half an hour later, during the short drive back to the office, he was still fuming. His Private Secretary listened with professional sympathy.

'Unbelievable. We've got another crisis looming in the Middle East, a stand off on trade with America, and all they want to talk about is bloody Numala.'

'Ridiculous, I agree, Secretary of State. But if the intelligence reports our submarine has picked up are true, things really could be getting worse there. I'm not sure that this will just go away. I wonder whether it's worth considering some sort of gesture to get the House off your back?'

'What could we do? Raise it in the Security Council?'

'I don't think Number Ten would appreciate that. Nor would we want to involve Brussels. What I had in mind was something that wouldn't need the consent of our allies. A brief naval presence in the region, perhaps. Provided, of course, the Defence Secretary is amenable.'

The Foreign Secretary laughed caustically. 'Oh, I don't think he will be much of a problem. The whole Cabinet knows he's out of his depth. Why don't you have a word with his private office and ask if the Chief of the Defence Staff could come and see me?'

'Of course. Should we first have a session with the Deputy Under-Secretary for Africa, to work out exactly what we might want?'

*

It had been dark for three hours and the wind-chill factor was rising, but whatever the weather, the Chief of the Defence Staff, Admiral Sir Alan North, was not one to summon his official car merely to cross Whitehall. He strode briskly down King Charles Street, past the main gates and on to the smaller entrance to the Foreign Office next to Clive Steps. Even in the camouflage of his grey suit and coat, any careful observer would have detected a bearing noticeably more erect than that of the two civil servants from the MoD who accompanied him. They paused while the messenger checked his list, nodded curt acknowledgement, and led the way round to George Gilbert Scott's great staircase. At the top of the stairs they walked the last few yards to the door to the private office. The discretion of those who worked within was underscored by the mural of the Sybil above the door, finger to her lips in an eternal hush.

As the door swung open, the messenger withdrew and began the plod back to his station. Inside the private office were four secretaries, three assistant private secretaries and the Private Secretary himself. He was on the phone but smiled in greeting and got to his feet to show that he would not allow this call to undermine basic courtesy.

Crispin Adair had already spent two years in what many thought to be the best job in the whole office. He was at the height of his suave powers, well aware that, in the absence of

21

any major setback, he should within the year be given a minor embassy to cut his teeth on before slipstreaming smoothly to Paris or Washington. As Private Secretary, he was in the eye of every storm. The strength of the role depended heavily on the nature of the Foreign Secretary himself. Some, over time, became genuinely well versed in foreign affairs and prided themselves on their cordial relations with their opposite numbers abroad. Others, like the present Foreign Secretary, Patrick Dawnay, arrived unburdened by knowledge and evinced only mild interest in rectifying that. As one of the great departments of state, the Foreign Office was traditionally awarded either to a Cabinet heavyweight on the way up or as a grand consolation prize to someone whose chance of the ultimate glory had eluded them. Patrick Dawnay was in no doubt which camp he was in. While it would have been idiocy to wear the ambition too obviously on his sleeve, he stamped hard on anyone who suggested that his political career had already peaked.

Adair finally put the receiver down, walked towards the door to the Foreign Secretary's office, and put his head round it.

'The CDS is here.'

They all trooped through. Dawnay was seated at the end of a long table by the casement windows. As he went over, Sir Alan glanced through the net curtains towards the blackness of St James's Park. Dawnay gestured with a hand at the two men seated next to him.

'I'm sure you know Toby.'

Toby Gordon-Booth, the Deputy Under-Secretary in charge of Africa, stood up and smiled. Dawnay left it to Gordon-Booth to introduce the head of the Central Africa Department. Sir Alan reciprocated with his own team, and they all sat down and looked towards the Foreign Secretary.

'Thank you for coming over at such short notice, CDS. You'll have seen the intelligence reports on Numala, and, as you know, a presidential election will be held soon. It'll be rigged, of course, and there's damn all we can do about that. Nor, in truth, does that affect any British interests, especially now that there are hardly any of our citizens left there. What we're more concerned about is what Nabote might do afterwards.'

The CDS nodded. 'I'm aware of his arms purchases, and I've seen the American satellite shots showing some sort of activity along the border with Zania.'

Gordon-Booth handed over a paper. 'I'm sure you've also seen that Nabote's appalling Presidential Guards have begun what looks like a systematic campaign of harassing Lobus.'

'Yes, but I don't understand what it'll achieve.'

'Two things, potentially. Now that he's succeeded in wrecking every company he stole from foreign owners, the low-hanging fruit has all been consumed, so he may have to reach higher up the tree. The Lobus own a lot of the better farms and businesses, and are generally better-off than the majority Gandas. There's a particularly big concentration of them in Talu, the second largest city. It looks like they could be his next milk cows. Nabote's other purpose is more crudely political. Since the economy nose-dived, the regime's popularity has plummeted. Nabote knows he can rig the polls, but if unrest becomes serious, even his dreadful guards could have trouble keeping control. So what does he need? One million scapegoats . . . Nabote's said nothing publicly himself yet, but he's orchestrating a campaign to lay blame for the country's woes at the door of the Lobus, as well as claiming that they originally migrated from further east, from what is now Zania.'

The Foreign Secretary leaned in. 'Provided this doesn't get out of hand, it's nothing for us to worry about. However, if he starts really persecuting the Lobus, or, worse still, launches some sort of attack on Zania, it's important that we don't look flat-footed.'

Crispin Adair smiled urbanely. 'We need to find a way to show Nabote that the international community's watching. A gesture which is powerful, but doesn't carry the risk of any actual involvement.'

The CDS held Adair's gaze for a second and looked back at the Foreign Secretary. 'What do you have in mind?'

'I'd like to send a carrier to patrol the waters just beyond the twelve-mile limit. Since Kindalu, the capital, is on the coast, it should be clearly visible.'

'And when would you want this?'

Dawnay deferred to Gordon-Booth. 'The election is on the twentieth of this month, sixteen days from now. If it was to serve any useful purpose – not least in mollifying some of the more vocal backbenchers – it would have to be before then.'

'The only carrier we have which could conceivably be deployed so quickly is *Indomitable*. She left Portsmouth two days ago to take part in the Omega exercise with the Americans. As you know, this is the biggest joint exercise we have mounted for several years. *Indomitable* is the only Royal Navy carrier participating, and detaching her would greatly reduce our contribution to the exercise, not to mention hugely disappointing her crew, who have trained for months for this.' He paused, hoping vainly to detect some flicker of sympathy. 'Her escort frigates and destroyers are already in the western Mediterranean. I suppose, if it was judged essential to redeploy her, the escorts could rendezvous with her at Gibraltar and sail south together.'

'Ahhh . . .' Dawnay fashioned a thin smile. 'Toby, why don't you . . .'

'We've thought about that very carefully. We're well aware that this is normal navy practice. However, we're concerned that sending an entire battle group might be interpreted as more than a gesture – it could be considered . . . *provocative*.'

Dawnay nodded vigorously. 'It could look like we actually mean to take action.'

Sir Alan made no attempt to hide his alarm. 'You cannot be suggesting sending a carrier there alone.'

Adair smiled reassuringly. 'HMS *Tenacious* is down there, isn't she?'

'Yes, but she's only gathering intelligence. Submarines aren't equipped to defend carriers against missile attack . . .' North looked hard at Dawnay. 'I have to tell you, Secretary of State, the captain of *Indomitable*, Christopher Cameron, will resist this strenuously.'

Something in Dawnay's expression changed. 'Is that the Cameron who commanded the frigate *Chatsworth* eight or ten years ago?'

'I believe so. Why?'

'Suffice it to say that he's not someone whose opinion should carry a lot of weight. Frankly, I'm amazed to hear that the navy have promoted him so far. He should simply be told.'

A silence ensued, broken by Dawnay himself. He had other things to attend to, and had limited patience.

'I had a word half an hour ago with the Defence Secretary. I'm glad to say he was supportive . . . Come on, we're not sending Cameron to war. His ship will remain in international waters. If *Indomitable* doesn't need an escort to Gibraltar, why should she need one for a jaunt off Africa? Are you afraid she'll get lost?'

The CDS did not grace that comment with a reply. Gordon-Booth, embarrassed, looked down at the table. Adair was rather amused. This CDS was well known for taking a robustly independent line, and it was entertaining to see him roughed up. However, Adair was too much of a professional to let the meeting end on such a sour note.

'In the meantime, as you'll have gathered, CDS, GCHQ will be working with the navy to intensify the intelligence effort.'

*

Long before dawn Simon Charters had left his mother's small terraced house in central Cheltenham and driven the few miles in his VW Polo to the doughnut-shaped complex of GCHQ – Government Communications Headquarters. He made himself wait until ten o'clock before pulling open the drawer on the left of his grey metal desk and viewing the little beauties. There were eight left out of the twenty-four-pack he'd bought at the weekend, and it was still only Wednesday. He picked one up, and thought for a second about denying himself the indulgence. His mother was always on at him about eating too much and exercising too little. She said he had no willpower. Well, the fact that he could seriously consider putting the bar back showed she was wrong. He bit into the chocolate as the phone rang. The display showed it was the director's secretary. He swallowed a large mouthful and picked up the receiver.

The sudden summons took him by surprise. In the two and a half years since he'd joined GCHQ, this would be only the second time he'd seen the director. He was ushered immediately into his office.

'Ah, Simon. Good to see you. Please take a seat . . . How *is* everything?'

'Fine.'

'Good, good. Thanks for dropping by. There's something I wanted to discuss with you. I know that you've studied a number of African languages including Mendé, but how closely do you follow events in Numala?'

Simon shifted in his seat. He was at GCHQ because it was close to where he lived with his mother, and because he liked languages. They gave him lots of time off to display his remarkable talent for picking up new ones. However, the fact that he worked for the government didn't mean he was interested in politics.

'I can't say I'm terribly au fait. It's one of our former colonies, right?'

'Yes.' The director looked at him icily. Simon thought he'd better try harder.

'And the President's not terribly nice.'

26

The director began fiddling with his cufflinks. 'That's a fine understatement. Yes, Nabote is a throwback – an old-style African dictator. He's had absolute power since he seized control in 1989. Now he's an embarrassment to the whole continent.'

Suddenly a flash came to Simon.

'But didn't I read that there's a presidential election coming up?'

'Well done. Yes, it was in the papers this morning. There was a fuss about it in Parliament yesterday. The EU sent an observer mission, but Nabote slung them all out when they didn't see eye-to-eye on monitoring methodology.'

Simon nodded. He was trying to work out where this was leading. 'So is there anything else the Europeans can do?'

'About the election, no. However, tiny little place that it is, Numala's suddenly become a priority for other reasons. The FCO is concerned about what else Nabote's getting up to. For the last three years he's had a group of North Korean military advisers helping him. We presume they get paid in diamonds. They seem to have helped him to get hold of some serious kit. Anti-ship missiles, fast attack boats, landmines, and so on. Of course, there are plenty of tin-pot dictators who build up an armoury, but the odd thing is he seems to have gone exclusively for defensive weapons. Yet his neighbours pose no threat. So whom does he want to deter and why?'

'What does our embassy think?'

'Since it's a Commonwealth country, technically it's a High Commission, not an embassy. Our High Commissioner, Roger Fairfax, has been recalled, so now it's down to three diplomats headed by Bob Tiernan, the chargé d'affaires, and a handful of local staff. Britain is not exactly flavour of the month, so it's hard for them to get access to the government. As the security situation has deteriorated, virtually all expatriates have left, including most journalists, and a lot of major countries have mothballed their embassies or arranged for Numala to be covered by their missions in neighbouring countries. That's what the Americans have done, for example. The net effect is that the usual sources of information have all but dried up, and that's why we need you to help find out what Nabote's up to.'

'*Me?* I know nothing about the place.'

'Evidently. But you're the only person we have who speaks both Korean and Mendé, which as you know is the main local language, along with English. In short, you're ideally qualified to listen in to any exchanges we can pick up between the North Koreans or among Nabote's henchmen, whatever language they use.'

'Hang on, you're not expecting me to *go* to Numala, are you?'

'Good God, no. With all the casual violence, you'd find life there very uncomfortable . . .'

A little colour came back into Simon's face.

'No, the plan's for you to be safely out of harm's way on board a nuclear submarine, HMS *Tenacious*, which the navy has quietly stationed down there for a while.'

Simon was still wary. 'So there wouldn't be anything physical involved? I was never very good at sport.'

The director smiled reassuringly. 'Think of it as a pleasure cruise.'

'I *will* be back for Christmas, won't I? My mother would never forgive me . . .'

'Of course.'

*

When the *Daily Post* first moved from Fleet Street to Canary Wharf, few of the staff had minded. The tube worked well most of the time, and the place had a decent infrastructure of shops, bars and restaurants. However, after 9/11 they were less sure how wise it was to be on the upper floors of one of the more likely terrorist targets in the country. A few people got spooked enough to leave, but the rest switched to gallows humour and got on with it.

Grace joined later, and the risk would scarcely have crossed her mind had it not been for the anxiety of her parents back in Birmingham. After the first few months, though, their worries were bested by their pride in their daughter's achievement. Every byline was a cause for celebration, and every article was expertly scissored out and placed tenderly like a flower in one of their growing set of leather-bound albums. They knew what Grace had overcome to get there, how tough life had been at her scruffy comprehensive. Being studious had been profoundly uncool, and resisting the constant siren calls to play truant and party had brought her contempt and isolation. At times the ridicule had driven her close to breaking point, but the experience had instilled a quiet determination to go her own way. She was one of only two pupils in her year to make it to university, and her perseverance stood her in good stead when it came to making her way in journalism. Not that adult life had freed her entirely from peer pressure, and she still had to endure haughty scorn and unspoken accusations of snootiness when she turned down invitations from black girlfriends to get involved in the reggae and hip-hop scene. Grace didn't look down her nose at exclusively black culture, but she did resent any sense of obligation to take part if she didn't feel like it.

This was only her third year at the *Post*. She had enjoyed her previous jobs in magazines, both in London and the US, but found work on a daily much more stimulating and exciting, and was determined to give it her best shot. As a feature writer, much of her time was spent out of the office, interviewing lesser or greater celebrities.

However, for her and the rest of the team, the editor's morning conference was the key fixture in their lives. Normally, Grace enjoyed it, but today, as she entered the room, she was feeling uneasy. She sat down and glanced over at Peter Mayhew. He looked grey and haggard. They all knew how he adored his wife, and what her illness was doing to him.

For the first twenty minutes they ran through the routine of current news stories. Grace found her attention had wandered and was lucky that no one asked her a question. She tuned back in to the flat vowels of the editor.

'Okay, that's enough of paedophilia, on to defence.'

Grace noticed Peter flash a glance at Jason. Did he know already? The editor picked up a piece of paper.

'I have a letter here from the Ministry of Defence. They're inviting us to send someone to the carrier *Indomitable* to observe a major exercise which will begin shortly in the eastern Mediterranean. Peter, obviously you're the natural candidate, but we all know the unfortunate reason why you can't go. But what's your opinion on whether we should take up the offer?'

Peter glared across the table at Jason. Even Grace flushed with embarrassment. She somehow felt part of a conspiracy. Peter turned back to the editor. 'I think you'd better ask Jason. I believe he's the one who's prompted this.'

Jason let the barb go. He waited for the editor to gesture to him to speak.

'Well, personally I think it's a great opportunity for the paper. An exclusive to cover the first chance for the Americans and the Brits to show what lessons they learned from the second Gulf War and to test the technologies and procedures they've introduced since. They'll be playing the mother and father of war games against each other.'

The editor didn't look too impressed. 'So what? How many copies will that sell, with no war in the offing?'

Jason leant forward. 'I really see this as no more than the topical hook for a much bigger story . . . The navy has ordered two new carriers, at a cost to the taxpayer of double-digit billions, including aircraft. But are these monsters still relevant in today's world? And what about the people who serve in them? Are the officers still chinless wonders poncing about while working-class oiks do the work?'

The editor nodded. 'So you think it's as much a human interest story as a pure defence piece?'

'Absolutely. I did a bit of digging on the ship's captain, Christopher Cameron, and unearthed weapons-grade dirt. Remember when that Tory MP Tim Creswell's wife, Charlotte, walked out on him in the middle of the general election? Just after he'd made a speech about family values. Well, guess who she left him for . . . ? Christopher Cameron. And it isn't the first happy home that he's wrecked, either. He has a son who's in jail in Miami for pushing drugs. The lad blamed it all on his dad for abandoning him as an infant. He really does sound a first-class shit.'

Peter stared coldly at him. 'I ran across him once and rather liked him. When you stitch him up, Jason, you might at least mention that he was decorated for what he did in the Falklands.'

'Come *on*. That was over twenty years ago.'

The editor raised a hand to end the exchange. 'To cut through this, Jason, you definitely recommend that we send someone?'

Jason nodded. 'It's a no-brainer.'

'Okay, I think I buy that. However, the situation has changed a little. Just before this meeting began, I got a call from the MoD. *Indomitable* won't be joining the exercise after all. Instead, she'll be deployed off the coast of Numala in the very vain hope of keeping Nabote under control.'

Jason went pale. 'You mean they've withdrawn the invitation?'

'No.'

'Good.'

'But with no exercises to observe, the defence side of the story is much weaker. It's now mainly political. Sadly, with two of our political team on maternity leave, there's no way they can spare anyone . . . Grace?'

She looked up in alarm.

'When you worked for *TIME*, didn't you once interview the Numalan opposition leader, Michael Endebbe?'

Grace could hear Jason's knuckles cracking under the table.

'I was just filling in for someone who was sick. I've always been a pure feature writer. I don't know the first thing about politics.'

'But you must have mugged up about Numala before seeing him.'

'Only a little, and I've forgotten most of it.'

'It still means that you know more about the place than anyone else here. Not only that. If Jason's right and this Cameron is some sort of womanising scumbag, you're more likely to nail him. Right, Jason?'

There were grins all around the table, not least from Peter. Jason stared at the ceiling.

'You'd better get home and pack. Your flight to Gibraltar leaves in five hours . . . Okay, everyone, that's it.' The editor snapped shut his folder of papers and stood up. Jason barged out of the room, with Grace rushing after him. As the room emptied, Peter Mayhew walked up to the editor.

'Thanks for that, John.'

The editor nodded. 'It was a pleasure.'

Grace was out of breath by the time she caught up with Jason, just as he sat heavily down in his chair. She had to glare at Debbie to make her pretend not to listen. She dropped her voice to a whisper.

'I don't know what to say.'

'Then don't say anything.'

'Come on, it's not my fault the frigging carrier's going to Africa. The last thing I want is to be cooped up in a tin can for days on end.'

'Then don't go.'

'What?'

'Tell the editor you can't go. Say your mother's sick or something.'

'He'd never believe me. Jason, if I refuse a straight order, he could fire me.'

'So?' He swung his chair round suddenly and looked into her eyes. 'If it was the other way round, and I was asked to take a big story away from you, d'you really think I would?'

'Come on, Jase, don't be a jerk. You know I have no choice.'

'So you're going to go?'

Grace nodded.

'Then we'd better both think about whether April the fifteenth is still such a good idea.'

It was to be the day of their wedding. Jason had ended the relationship once before, and it had devastated her. However contrite he was afterwards, however amazing the sex was when they made up, she never entirely forgave him. Without waiting for any further bidding, she quietly pulled the diamond off her finger and placed it carefully on his desk. It took him aback, but he was damned if he was backing down now.

'Where's my Eurostar ticket? I might want to go Paris myself.'

Grace walked to her desk, rummaged in a drawer, and marched back to him.

'There you are. Have both, in case you can't cope on your own.'

She grabbed her red coat from the stand and stalked off towards the lifts. He yelled after her.

'You let that cocksucking captain lay one finger on you and you're dead.'

Grace hardly broke stride as she gave him the finger.

Debbie waited till the lift doors closed.

'Do women often do that to you? The finger, I mean?'

'Fuck off.'

He kicked the stubby filing cabinet under his desk. Debbie smiled.

'Fancy a drink after work?'

'I'll think about it.'

33

3

Bob Tiernan tapped in the code next to the heavy steel door and went down the few steps into the registry. It was the one room in the High Commission local staff were not permitted to enter, where they kept all the files, the safe for any valuables and the communications gear. The building dated from colonial times, when security was less of an issue, but even if the architect had possessed 20:20 foresight, he could not have specified it better. It was right in the core of the building, a small room with no windows, and a few steps below ground level. It would take a very committed mole to tunnel in there.

Unlike his boss the High Commissioner, Tiernan liked Kindalu. Roger Fairfax was in the Foreign Office fast stream, and had once hoped to end up somewhere grand, with a knighthood thrown in for good measure. To be given Kindalu instead was offensively far below his dignity. His wife Victoria wore her rage at the affront even more visibly. They both hated everything about the place and weren't afraid to say so.

Tiernan was a hog in muck anywhere in Africa, but then his outlook on life was very different. Not being in the fast stream, he was on a more modest career trajectory. For his ilk the most ambitious final resting place would be as Consul General in Lyon or Milan, or head of a two-man mission in some country your dad had never heard of, probably ending in -stan. When he had graduated in the year his poly was upgraded to a university, Bob had never been further than Ibiza, so a first posting in Accra was an exotic adventure. There he'd met Alice, who was working for an aid agency, and ever since he had managed to wangle one African job after another, so that at thirty-seven he was already a veteran of Lagos, Monrovia and Dar es Salaam.

There was so much he loved about life in Africa: the big skies, the rich smell of earth after rain, the music, the vivid colours, driving a Land Rover instead of a Ford, wearing shorts more often than a suit. If he wasn't convinced he would ever truly solve the riddle of the African mind, he had made a better fist of it than most Europeans, and had come to understand that there was more than one view of life.

When he'd arrived two years before, his first impressions of Kindalu weren't too bad. The hotels and office blocks which German and Japanese groups had built looked impressive. The power supply worked more often than not. There were enough Toyotas, Nissans and even Mercedes to grace the capital's broad nim-tree-lined boulevards, and the soil and sea were rich enough to provide more than survival for most, as a visit to any of the town's many markets showed.

It was a pity that since then the security situation in the country had deteriorated so much. The press in the UK exaggerated the danger perhaps, but the violence had definitely assumed a more random nature. Travelling around the country had become risky. The checkpoints were manned by largely unpaid soldiers or police who were stoned half the time and routinely stole what they could, killing if they met resistance. Before the government began its campaign of vilification of foreigners, whites had been generally immune to the worst of these attacks; after that, they'd been seen as fair game. Now they were long gone, give or take the odd missionary and a few hardy correspondents. As long as Tiernan and his family stayed in Kindalu, there was little to worry about day to day. Bob had time on his hands, as any attempt to visit the Foreign Ministry yielded only a long wait in a wretched, un-air-conditioned hallway, and, if he was lucky, a brief, meaningless encounter with a junior official.

He remained cheerful all the same. However much of a

charade the election would be, it was causing excitement, and putting the place on the map internationally. And now he was in charge. He had been relieved to see the High Commissioner and his wife go. With so little civilised company left in Kindalu, Roger and Victoria had insisted that his staff and their wives dance constant social attendance on them, apparently for the sole purpose of listening politely to their unending stream of laments.

It was time to check out the incoming telegrams. In the absence of an expert to man the machinery, they had agreed with London that as many telegrams as possible should be sent *en clair*, to minimise the tedious business of manually decoding confidential missives using a one-time pad. Tiernan took a look through today's crop. There was the usual batch of routine stuff. And then one marked SECRET. It was a long time since they'd had received one of those. He began deciphering it, and gasped.

Had they taken leave of their senses? Did they not see how Nabote would use this? The idea that sending an aircraft carrier down here might help in any way was ridiculous. What was the point of having a mission in Kindalu if no one asked their opinion? Roger had been back in London for twenty-four hours now. Had he been consulted, or bypassed as well? What about Central African Department? Or Gordon-Booth? Had no one seen how this could backfire? Or was it more about keeping Parliament happy and bugger the impact on the ground?

At least they were right to instruct everyone, bar him, to get out. Alice, their three kids and the two other diplomats and their families. When he found out, Nabote would without question organise a demonstration outside the High Commission, and that could turn ugly. If the Presidential Guards were let off the leash, God knows what might happen. The instruction was for them to leave before the carrier turned up. At least with so few people visiting the country, and only privileged Numalans permitted to travel abroad, there should be no problem getting seats. Provided, of course, Numalan Airways could persuade one of their two poorly maintained Boeings to get off the ground. Would the government smell a rat and call him in to explain the departures? Might it be better to stagger their flights by even one day?

He'd better talk it through with Alice. She wouldn't be thrilled about leaving him behind. She would understand, though, that closing the High Commission would be a mistake. Apart from his family, the main things he would miss would be the bridge four and his regular tennis partner on the bumpy High Commission court. What about the Swiss Ambassador, his new neighbour directly opposite? He was the only other Western diplomat left in the place. Maybe he played tennis. If he drew a blank with him, perhaps he should try teaching one of the High Commission's dozen local employees.

*

Simon had a terrible headache. The Hercules transport aircraft had been airborne for five hours, and that was about five hours too long. Only the thought of what would happen next stopped him from willing the journey over. He wasn't sure whether he would be feeling better or worse if there had been time for a training jump.

The well-built instructor lumbered down the fuselage and gestured to Simon to take off his ear defenders. He had to yell to be heard.

'Okay, we're coming over the drop zone now. Remember, the parachute will open automatically. All you have to do is concentrate on bending your knees and keeping your legs together when you hit the water. *Tenacious* will surface soon after you splash.'

'Why can't it come up first?'

'Because you might hit her. Plus, they don't want to be on the

37

surface any longer than necessary. They're not keen to advertise their presence to any local fishing boats . . .' The instructor paused to listen to his headset. 'Okay, get your helmet on. Good. Now turn around so I can check your parachute again.'

The instructor patted him on the back and went over to open the starboard door, stepping back smartly to avoid being sucked out. The wind roar overwhelmed even the scream of the engines. Simon sat back down and gripped the edge of his seat.

The instructor gestured urgently, but his shout was borne away on the wind. What the hell was the matter with the boy? He had no choice but to make his way back to him, put his face two inches from Simon's and scream.

'What's the matter?'

Simon yelled back. 'I need the toilet.'

'Do it in the water. No one will know.'

Simon didn't budge. The instructor was getting frantic messages in his radio from the co-pilot. They were circling back; this had to be it. He grabbed hold of Simon's arm. In seconds they were at the open aperture. Simon stared in horror at the endless wrinkled blue ocean. Overcome by a new wave of panic, he turned and shouted.

'How are you sure that it's down there?'

'Intuition . . . Now one, two, three, go.' Simon felt a thump in the back and was gone.

He felt the parachute open and rip skywards, but any easing of his monumental fear was removed in a flash when he looked down and saw the ocean racing up fast. It wasn't looking wrinkled any more. Those were waves, real waves, bloody great waves.

He closed his eyes fully ten seconds before he smashed into the water. When he opened them, he was under, swallowing brine, unable to breathe, unable to see which way was up, struggling frantically for his life. Then the water looked brighter, and he was suddenly propelled, gasping and spluttering, into clean air.

He felt a presence behind, and a big wave crashed over him.

'Depth fifteen point five metres. Prepare to surface.'

'Prepare to surface, sir.'

Captain Owen Lewis let go the periscope. 'Recovery party stand by.'

'Recovery party standing by, sir.'

As Simon came up one more time, he saw no more than fifty yards away the bulbous, fearsome shape, nearly three hundred feet long, of a T-class nuclear-powered attack submarine breaching the surface. Moments later he could make out the shape of a diver emerging onto the deck and jumping in.

Surprisingly quickly, Simon had a lifeline wound round him, and he was towed back to the submarine, where he was dragged up onto the deck and in through the small door at the base of the conning tower. His attempts to climb down the vertical ladder ended on the first rung. His legs were too weak, his brain too scrambled for any coordination. He slid down out of control, landing heavily on an unfortunate rating standing below, and cannoned off onto the floor, where he lay panting like an exhausted bloodhound. Above him he heard a calm, reassuring Welsh voice.

'Mr Charters, I presume . . . Are you okay? We'll take you to sickbay and have you checked out.'

Simon tried to reply, but no words would come out. Big strong hands grabbed him under both armpits, and he was pulled up and carried down strange *Alice in Wonderland* passageways, past strange-looking people who looked at him curiously.

And then he was through another small door, and put down on some sort of bunk.

He felt his arm being shaken and opened an eye. That same lilting, boyo voice was speaking. It belonged to a kindly looking compact man of around thirty-five with reddish hair.

'Hello again. Let me introduce myself properly now. I'm Owen Lewis, the captain. Congratulations on your first jump. You'll soon get the hang of it . . .'

Simon felt sore everywhere. Maybe he'd forgotten about keeping his legs together or his knees bent, or something like that.

'I hope you had a good rest. We gave you a shot to help you sleep for a while. I'd like to have given you longer, but sadly we don't have that luxury. There are some clean clothes for you there.'

Simon was expecting some privacy, but the man stood right there while he got stiffly out of the narrow bunk and with difficulty pulled on the trousers.

'We picked you up a hundred miles out to sea, but now we're back on station, about ten miles off Kindalu . . . There's been a big increase in traffic, especially between the Koreans. From what we've picked up in English, there are a lot of references to the border with Zania . . .'

As they made their way down the passageways, Simon forgot to duck and clanged his head on a pipe. Owen smiled sympathetically.

'We all do that at first. Lucky you're not bald.'

Simon rubbed his forehead, struggling to stop tears welling up at the pain. God, that fucking hurt. And the idea that in any shape or form he was *lucky* was outrageous. Lewis didn't break stride.

'We have two intelligence operators who take turns to listen in. Like most of us on this ship, they work six-hour watches. However, sometimes when things get lively they do it in tandem. That's what they're doing right now, because we're trying to get back on top of what's happening after being off station for sixteen hours ... Ah, here we are, the WTO – wireless telegraphy office. It's where we do all our listening and sending.'

They came round a corner and saw two youthful men sitting side by side in what looked more like an extended cupboard. They wore headsets and delicate microphones. In front of them was a bank of dials and recorders. Both stood up as the captain approached them.

'Henley, McCauley, this is Simon Charters, who's going to help us find out exactly what's going on in Nabote's nasty little mind.'

4

When Nathan Nabote seized power, he swore never to forget the threat that armed forces can pose to a ruler. Although he had appointed his fellow conspirator, Laurence Mbekwe, as head of the army, he secretly resolved to weaken its power systematically. All these years later, Mbekwe was still in charge, but now the army was a ragtag outfit with antiquated equipment. Nabote had also let the country's fledgling air force wither altogether. He concentrated instead on building up his own Presidential Guard, staffed exclusively with members of the Ganda tribe, and, as soon as his son, Julius, was old enough, he put him in charge of it. The Guards were a perfect instrument of terror and enforcement.

Their power, though, grew so strong that he sensed the need for a counterbalance, and struck a pact with North Korea. In return for a regular supply of diamonds to augment their purchasing power in the blackest of markets and mining rights for certain exotic minerals, they offered a small militia of 'advisers' and access to serious hardware. It was a match made in heaven for all but Colonel Kim, the chief adviser, marooned in Kindalu for four years, denied any visit to his family in Pyongyang, and now nursing unconfidently the hope that the President's latest promise to let him leave would be honoured.

Nabote had not shown as much tenacity with his other big resolution. One of the objects of his greatest scorn had been the way his predecessor had spent so much of the country's modest income on lavish buildings, and he had publicly promised to stay true to his roots and live a simple soldier's life. Within two months, though, he moved into the main presidential palace. Ever since, it had grown in gaudy magnificence, with its eclectic mix of cultures – of cloisonné, shields, Louis XVI furniture, skins, damask and gold. Even this was nothing compared with his latest edifice, in the village of his birth, where a latter-day Versailles, complete with hall of mirrors, lay incongruously at the heart of a farm.

The President had only visited there for its grand opening. Cowed and grateful as the local people were, there was something which disturbed him. Fiercely superstitious, he had been horrified by his elderly *nganga*'s warning that chicken entrails had shown that he would die at the hands of someone who had known him in childhood. Nabote's vanity had required him to build this extravaganza, but his fear prevented him enjoying it.

In fact, the days when he liked to travel the country were gone. He felt happier and safer in Kindalu, and especially in his own palace, surrounded and comforted by his guard, his wives, his wider family and by the handful of ministers and advisers he, for a while, learned to trust. Some days he liked to eat simply, but other days there would be an impromptu banquet. Today was such a day.

He sat in the centre of a long gilded table, with all his guests on the same side, staring out at the mouldy magnificence of the empty ballroom. On his right side sat his tall, powerfully built son, dressed in the sharply pressed light blue uniform of the Presidential Guard, his shoulders heavy with braid, the round lenses of his Calvin Klein sunglasses reflecting the lights from the chandeliers.

On the President's other side was the compact tight figure of Colonel Kim. Kim, too, wore uniform, but his was a more sober affair. There was much more colour from the wives, daughters and other close relatives who made up most of the rest of the table. The only minister fortunate enough to be invited today had come in a black safari jacket, and had wondered whether he had got things badly wrong when he saw the President attired in a dark suit and brilliant white shirt.

The meal had passed almost in silence. Nabote could at times be garrulous, but if his mood was withdrawn, even the extrovert Julius had learnt to rein back his conversation.

Only when the chicken had been cleared away did Nabote become animated.

'Time for dessert.' He clapped his hands.

For a few seconds nothing happened. From a side door guards entered, dragging two victims. Nabote's eyes gleamed.

The two men were thrown to the ground. The clothes of both were torn, their hair matted with sweat, dust and blood. One was young – not more than twenty-five – and had a nasty open wound on his left cheek. The other looked so bowed he could have been sixty.

A servant had appeared behind Nabote bearing a small silver tray. On it was a small portable tape recorder. Without looking, Nabote snapped his finger and the dutiful servant pressed a button on the machine. A tinny recording began to play.

'A spokesman in Brussels for the European Union said that, following the refusal of the Numalan government to accept international observers, they feared that the opposition leader, Michael Endebbe, was being prevented from campaigning freely, and that the presidential election would be rigged.'

Nabote snapped his fingers again and the servant stopped the machine. Nabote looked into the eyes of the younger man.

'Whose voice is that?'

The young man hung his head. The guard standing behind him skilfully flicked a horsehair whip across his scarred calves.

'Mine.'

Nabote nodded. 'So you believe the election will be rigged?'

'No, Excellency. We were only reporting what was being said. It wasn't . . .'

There was fire in Nabote's eyes now. 'So you spread evil, malicious lies, knowing how much pain they would cause to the people of this country?'

'That was not our intention.'

'I know exactly what your intention was. Your intention was to cause unrest, to destroy my reputation, to overthrow me.'

'No, no.'

Nabote glared until the young man looked away. The President allowed his eyes to swing languidly to the right until they alighted on the older man, who needed a swipe from a guard to the back of the head to make him look up.

'Was the decision to broadcast this yours or his?'

The old man stole a sideways glance at his colleague, but kept silent.

'Who decided it?'

Two guards set on the old man with sticks. He tried feebly to parry the blows. Nabote's voice became almost gentle.

'Please. Tell me, who was it?'

'It was him.' He hung his head.

'Take him to the lemon bower.'

There were few in Kindalu who had not heard of the lemon bower, a quiet, pretty corner of the palace garden, from which no one but gardeners and guards ever returned. It was the guards' favourite spot for extra-judicial killings, where they were allowed to practise and extend their range of means of inflicting pain before the anti-climax of death.

As the younger man was forced to his feet and wrenched towards the door, he began a pitiful caterwauling. For one moment, before she checked it, a shadow of pity passed across the face of Nabote's youngest daughter. After the door banged shut, Nabote waited patiently until there was absolute silence, then returned to the crumpled shape of the older man. A guard looked for guidance as to whether to

45

whip him, but left him alone when he heard the measured tones.

'You are the manager of the radio station. Do you believe the station behaved responsibly?'

The older man looked up and shook his head.

'So why did you not prevent it?'

'It was my day off.'

The voice hardened again. 'And you think you will evade responsibility in that way? If I take a day of rest, do you think what my government does is not my affair?'

'No.'

'So you assume responsibility for that foolish young man's actions?'

His hesitation was countered with the crack of a whip like a gun going off.

'Yes.'

'Then maybe you should join your colleague in the lemon bower.' Nabote turned to his left. 'What do you think, Colonel Kim?'

Kim returned the President's look deferentially, managing to avoid sending a clear signal either way.

'Or should we pardon him?' Still Kim said nothing. Nabote looked back at the man.

'If I pardon you, will you solemnly swear that in future all – all – your broadcasts will be fair and reasonable?'

'I swear it. I will check every word myself. I will never take another day off.'

Nabote sighed as if bored and waved his right hand. 'Let him go.'

The man struggled to his feet, bowed with pathetic gratitude and hobbled out. When he had gone Nabote took a sip of sweet coffee and leant a degree or two nearer Kim. 'I find these moments of theatre distasteful and tedious. However, it is my experience that they are sometimes unavoidable.'

He put the dainty cup down and stood. 'I wish to speak privately with Colonel Kim and the Commander-in-Chief of the Guards.' The others wasted no time in filing out. The President led Kim and Julius towards a group of deeply upholstered and monogrammed chairs, positioned to take advantage of his favourite view towards the fountains.

'Is everything ready for Operation March?'

Kim nodded. 'The mining of the border area with Zania will soon be complete. Julius and I will go in person to inspect it.'

'Good. Julius, you know what to do with Mbekwe?'

'It is all planned. At dawn on the day after the election, the purge of the moderates will begin, starting with General Mbekwe himself. We will confine all ranks to barracks while we seize control of their armoury, and execute Lobu officers and men. When this is done, we will order all the remains of the army to help carry out the operation.'

'How long will everything take?'

'One month at most. Those in the Talu area will be quickest, of course, since they are near the border. For those in the rest of the country, it will take longer. We have only fifty or sixty trucks to transport the old and the children. Others will have to walk, perhaps fifteen miles a day.'

Nabote's face twitched. 'That is too long. We must give the so-called international community no time to react. If the Lobus think help is coming they will be encouraged to resist. We do not want a bloodbath on our soil. This should be an orderly repatriation. The key is to control the foreign media. It will be easier now that there are so few accredited foreign press here. We should arrange a special extended visit for the press corps to the north of the country, so that they do not witness the evacuation from Kindalu. When news finally breaks, we should arrange for some Lobu spokesmen to say something positive. It should be presented as a voluntary migration back to their ancestral homeland.'

Julius nodded gravely. 'It will be done.'

'Kim, in case things do not go to plan, our deterrents are ready?'

'Yes, Excellency. Some of my men are already stationed at the airport. Their SA-7s should prevent any enemy aircraft landing. And our attack boats have now been equipped with the Silkworm anti-ship missiles.'

'Will we have a test firing?'

'I do not recommend it. It would be detected by American satellites. We hope that so far they are unaware that we possess them. The missiles are at all times kept under covers.'

'Good. I will authorise the next consignment of diamonds to be sent to your government. In fact, I am so pleased with your performance, Colonel Kim, that I have a small present for you.' Nabote reached into his pocket and pulled out a small calfskin pouch.

Kim pulled out a gold tiepin with an extraordinary glittering stone in its centre. Kim bowed. 'I am very grateful, Mr President, but I cannot accept it.'

'Why? Are you afraid I will tell your government? You have my word that I will not.'

'I do not doubt it, Excellency. However, I have strict instructions.'

'I admire your obedience.' Nabote smiled and put the tiepin back in the pouch. He knew that Kim was wary about being vulnerable to blackmail. He had promised to let him return to North Korea as soon as Operation March was successfully completed. He had not decided whether he would let him leave or request a further extension of his posting from Pyongyang. He moved briskly on to other business.

'The checkpoints are monitoring Endebbe's whereabouts?'

Julius nodded.

'Where is he campaigning now?'

'In the south.'

'Are you stepping up the disruption as I ordered?'

'Endebbe will soon find people less keen to attend his meetings.'

'Excellent.'

The boy had been playing with the stick for over an hour, drawing patterns in the dirt as he sat in the broad shade of a baobab tree. Proud as he was of being charged with so responsible a task, he was bored. And thirsty. He glanced towards the centre of the village and the large hut where it was all happening, and began to wonder whether he could go to the well for a drink. He would only be away from his post for one minute. No, better not. He picked up his stick again and tried to draw a picture of the mud-caked 4X4 parked next to the hut.

Inside, Michael Endebbe's speech was reaching its climax. His face could be impassive at rest, but when he was fired with passion, his handsome features combined with extravagant hand gestures and sudden body movements, generating an intensity that gripped the audience. The whole village was in there, from breastfeeding mothers to toothless elders. They all sat on the hard clay floor. Endebbe looked around the room and took a deep breath. In English his voice sounded tenor, but somehow when he spoke Mendé it deepened to a richer baritone.

'Our country has been brought to its knees by Nabote's greed and brutality. He is holding this election not because he wants to, but because he *has* to. Internationally he is discredited, an embarrassment to other African leaders. In the African Union, he is snubbed. Numala used to be held up as an example of success. Now we are only an example of how bad things can get.'

He stopped to look into the eyes of those in the front.

'I know what you think, I can see into your hearts. You are asking, will Nabote let this election be fair, will he give Michael Endebbe a chance to win? And I answer you with honesty. No, he will not. So why, then, does it matter? It matters because it is the only means of resistance we have. If we do not vote, he will say that the people care nothing for the vote, that they do not want the vote, should not have the vote . . .'

The boy threw down the stick and skipped to the well, humming to himself as he went. He hoped the meeting would not go on too long. He worked the rusty lever gently, trying to make sure that no one inside heard its squeak and found him there. He drank deeply, wiped his mouth with the back of his hand and danced back towards his post.

As he was about to sit down again, he saw in the distance a cloud of dust and then through the heat haze the shape of khaki trucks. He ran pell-mell back to the big hut and dived in the door. He could hardly get the words out, but the urgency of his pointing hand stopped Michael Endebbe in mid-sentence. The headman jumped to his feet and beseeched Endebbe. 'Go, *go*.'

Endebbe and his aide dashed out of the hut and towards the 4X4. Their photographer, who was standing at the back of the hut, had beaten them to it, and the engine was already running. As the other two jumped in, he banged it into gear and the car screeched off. From the back seat, Endebbe turned and watched the first of the column of khaki trucks entering the far end of the village. He put out a hand.

'Stop.'

The photographer ignored him. They were less than two hundred yards away and in mortal danger if the guards opened fire.

'*Stop*.' The photographer hit the brakes and looked round accusingly. The aide looked equally horrified.

'Michael, we must get away while we can.'

'They saw us go and they are not following. We must watch what happens. Have your camera ready.'

Cursing, the photographer switched places with the young aide and rummaged in his bag to unearth a battered 500mm lens. He rotated it until the bayonet mounting clicked into place on the old Nikon body. He turned the knurled ring on the lens until it slipped into focus. Now he could see better than the naked eye.

'Only women and girls are coming out. The men and boys

must still be inside. Some of the women are trying to get back in, but the guards are beating them away . . .' He clicked the shutter button, wound the film on and took some more shots.

'What's happening now?'

'The guards are pouring something from cans onto the walls and roof of the hut.'

Endebbe closed his eyes.

'They're setting fire to it.'

The wails of the women carried to them on the wind. Soon a plume of smoke began rising from the roof of the hut and flames appeared, glowing brilliantly even in the sharp sunlight. The photographer broke down and let go of the camera.

Endebbe berated him. 'Do not stop. *Take pictures. Take many pictures.*'

Though the tears made it hard to see through the viewfinder, the photographer did as he was bidden. When the roll was finished, he reached for another camera body, changed the lens over and focused again. This time he could see the guards leading three young women roughly towards one of the other huts. He clicked the shutter as he saw an older woman – a mother, no doubt – get shot through the chest for trying to stop one of the girls being taken. One phrase from the photographer was enough to confirm what Endebbe had known would happen next. He put his hand on the shoulder of his aide.

'Let us go. There is nothing more for us to do here.'

When they had driven some way, Endebbe spoke quietly to his aide. 'If he is now willing to go this far, it cannot be long before he moves against the Lobus. We must go to the eastern border to see if what we heard can be true.'

The aide shook his head. 'The two of us will go.'

Endebbe stared bleakly at the landscape. 'I must see it with my own eyes.'

'Michael, we simply cannot risk you. For the country's sake, you must do as we ask.'

5

No moonlight broke through to the cold waters forty-three miles off the north-west of Morocco. Inside the seamen's mess, the mood was black too. No one had come to terms with the shock of the captain's broadcast the day before.

In the first forty-eight hours since *Indomitable* left Portsmouth, everything had gone roughly to plan. There were a lot of tests to do on the new gear, and the heavy winter seas in the Bay of Biscay had been as good a place as any to conduct them. There had been a few snags, of course, especially with the firefighting exercise. The simulated blaze in lower deck had taken too long to put out, and there had been an uncomfortable number of 'casualties'. The debrief hadn't been fun, but they'd learned the lessons. They all knew that fire practices were vital. For a warship at sea there was no emergency number to call, no red engine to come, siren blaring, to their rescue. They were their own fire service, and given the amount of fuel, aircraft and munitions they carried, the odds were high that a fire would be more than a flaming chip pan. Overall, though, things were in good shape. They were all on their mettle for Omega, well prepared to play their part, and gratified that, unlike the real thing, exercises tended to end on schedule, leaving them to make an orderly return in good time for Christmas.

And then came the broadcast. The way the captain had handled it had astonished them. For anyone who had served with or under him, Christopher Cameron was as much an enigma as an inspiration. He undeniably had an extraordinary memory for names, faces and personal circumstances, and possessed that knack of making anyone he talked with feel they were the centre of his universe for those few seconds. And yet, they all privately admitted, they found it next to impossible to work out what he was really thinking. But no one who had listened in to the broadcast was left in any doubt that the captain was every bit as pissed off as they were. It wasn't anything he had said. It was more what he hadn't. The word was that this couldn't have been accidental: he must've wanted them to know.

Billy Ward clinked his can of lager with his pals and charges, Phil McManus and Charlie Slim. For both of them it would be their first time across the equator, and neither was sure they would enjoy the traditional rite of passage of being plastered with green gunk and ducked in a tank, to the vast amusement of all the onlookers. For the likes of Ulster Phil, at nineteen, and Liverpool Charlie, a ripe old twenty-two, Leading Hand Billy was a mixture of grizzled drinking buddy, minder and paterfamilias. The thirty-seven-year-old Billy was as much a mystery to himself as anyone else. Why did he still enjoy sharing a couple of claustrophobic three-tier bunks with five spotty lads half his age? Why, whenever the chance of promotion to petty officer and on to warrant officer came along, was there always some scab-fisted incident in some bar ashore which got in the way? Was he unsure that he could hack it higher up? Or did he simply love being a dad to them all, and secretly dread the day – not far off now – when one way or another his world must finally change? In the meantime there was no one on board *Indomitable* who wanted that day to come quickly. He might be one hell of a handful in a bar in Lisbon, Valletta or Caracas, but on board Billy was bloody good at what he did, both with the junior ratings and at his post in the MCO.

Phil cracked another joke and they banged cans again, as Trish Moore and a couple of her mates came in to join them. Charlie reached for the drawer where they kept their stock of beers and slid one each in front of Pauline, Carol and Trish. Trish shook her head and pushed it back.

'Not for me.'

'You still on the wagon?'

Trish nodded. Phil smiled. 'Three days at sea and she ain't had a drink. That must've been some bender.'

'I don't want to think about it.'

Billy butted in. 'So, how you girls feeling about Christmas off Africa?'

Pauline pulled a face. 'Christmas in whites instead of white Christmas, eh? . . . You really think we won't be back?'

Billy nodded. 'Same thing happened to me in *Illustrious*. Almost home, we was. We could see England. Then they tell us we're off to Sierra Leone. Tell the truth, none of us knew where it was. I thought it was down near the Falklands. Some other lads thought it was in the Philippines. Anyway, that put paid to our Christmas.'

Trish changed her mind and had a swig of Carol's beer. 'What did you boys make of the broadcast?'

Charlie shook his head. 'Incredible. Sailing without escorts. Specially since we'll be in the tropics.'

Pauline frowned. 'What's that got to do with it?'

'Billy was telling us. They get such bad storms down there, half the time you can't launch aircraft.'

Phil joined in. 'I bet the captain gave Fleet one hell of a bollocking.'

Trish smiled. 'Pity he was on the secure line. I'd've give anything to listen in . . . D'you think there's any real danger, then, Billy?'

'Nah. We'll just wander around for days on end sunning ourselves. But imagine if we had to fight. We'd be sitting fucking ducks.'

Charlie looked puzzled. 'How else do ducks fuck?'

Christopher Cameron had chosen the words in his broadcast with care. On most occasions, whatever he thought of his orders, he never let any hint of his own thoughts seep through. This time his instinct was different. The best hope of salvaging morale was to let slip the impression that his feelings about the change of plan were pretty much like theirs. They would feel they were in it together, united in disappointment and adversity.

His style of leadership had always been a strange brew of the conventional and the unusual. That wouldn't have surprised anyone who had known him a long time. Throughout his early years in the navy, his superiors had been exasperated by his mix of exceptional promise and unsettling independence of mind. The change had come when one unusually perceptive, quietly spoken captain took him to the side of his destroyer, indicated with a flick of his head *Ark Royal* sailing in formation with them, and asked whether in old age he might regret spurning the chance to command such a ship.

For the first time Cameron realised how badly he wanted it. He buckled down, playing things by the book, masking impatience with staff posts, biting his tongue when dealing with civil servants and the politicians he loathed, doing his level best to stop the world seeing more than rare glimpses of that streak which he alone knew still lurked dangerously only just beneath the surface.

He wouldn't have made it without the help of his hero, Horatio Nelson. Like half the navy, he worshipped the man for his naval genius, his astonishingly modern thinking and his courage. In Cameron's case, it went back even farther. At his second school in England, the only teacher to catch his imagination was old Mr Mitchell, all scruffy stains, chalk dust and dandruff, but consumed with a fiery passion for history, and possessed of the talent for bringing figures from the past to holographic life. At fifteen, Cameron had listened, rapt, to tales of Nelson, outgunned and ordered to retreat by his admiral, putting his telescope to his blind eye, declaring that he saw nothing, and carrying on the desperate fight against the Danes. Or at Trafalgar, where he remained stubbornly on the quarterdeck clad in plumage that identified him so easily, offering a target that the French marksmen in the rigging could scarcely miss, perhaps choosing the moment for the glorious death that would make him immortal.

It was Nelson who had inspired him to join the navy, but applying the lessons of the great master was getting so much harder. However much he admired Nelson's breathtaking daring at the Battle of the Nile, where he chanced his ships in the shallows and caught the French on the wrong side, or his cunning at Trafalgar, hiding over the horizon until the French and Spanish thought it safe to come out, Cameron would never have a chance to emulate him. The era when the navy might seek out and engage an enemy fleet was over. Even Nelson's immense personal bravery would have had few outlets today. Cameron prized physical courage above everything, and was fascinated by the man's literal fearlessness. His own sole chance to match this had come and gone in the Falklands: during his attack run he had felt terror, and afterwards had felt a piercing sense of shame.

And yet there *were* lessons that could be applied. Nelson was pressed into constant service as his patron saint of indiscretion. Wherever he went, as well as his talismanic Crunchie bar wrapper, Cameron carried facsimiles of Nelson's more extraordinary letters. Importuning the Admiralty, Prime Ministers, royals. Complaining about outrages to his dignity or lack of advancement, indeed about anything that offended the acute sensibilities of a rampant ego. The man had got away with his first major act of insubordination, at the Battle of Cape St Vincent, only because they had won. After that he had become a law unto himself, proceeding to irritate and offend so many superior officers and politicians that, had it not been for war with Napoleon, when the imperative for survival overwhelmed pettier considerations, this squeakiest of wheels would never have been oiled and he would have sunk into the silt of history. He was a Churchill of the sea.

Whenever Cameron felt his fuse burning short, roused by impossible rules of engagement, or driven to distraction by the moral bankruptcy of politicians, he forced himself, before responding, to read at least one Nelson epistle. It was his way of counting to ten. It didn't always stop him going his own way. But it did make him consider carefully whether it was worth the fallout.

He felt that Horatio watched over and helped him, and had critically come to his rescue yet again when he got the infuriating signal about sailing to Africa without escorts.

The second Harrier screamed alongside, slowed to its hover, parallel to the flight deck, and gently nudged sideways until it could safely touch down. That was it for the night-flying exercise. It had gone well. Cameron exchanged a few quiet words with Wings and Hitchens, picked up his mug and sipped the coffee. Tara came into the bridge carrying a piece of paper.

'Another signal from Fleet, sir. The Lynx helos with Sea Skua missiles you asked for are on their way. They'll land on from Gibraltar tomorrow.'

Cameron took another sip. 'I suppose we should be grateful for small mercies. We'll have to land a couple of Merlin or Sea Kings.'

'One more thing, sir. The journalist who was going to cover the exercise . . .'

'Oh, yes. Thank God we don't have to worry about him now.'

'That's not yet clear, I'm afraid. The MoD spoke to the *Post*'s editor to see if he'd prefer to wait for the next exercise or send somebody anyway. It seems he opted for the latter course.'

'That's daft. Omega was one thing. What do they hope to gain having a journalist watch us do nothing?'

'It seems they were afraid that withdrawing the invitation altogether would be counter-productive. And the Foreign Office press office got on to them too, supporting the idea enthusiastically.'

'How would he get here, anyway?'

'The idea is to fly him in on one of the Lynx.'

Cameron nodded and bade them goodnight. Tara watched him go. She had never met the captain before she was posted to *Indomitable*, although his reputation had preceded him. One year on, she was still unsure what to make of this man. As a commanding officer, there was no doubt he was in the top flight. Experienced navy people always reckoned that they could tell the quality of a captain within seconds of stepping on his ship: it wasn't only the appearance of the ship itself, you could see it in the eyes of every member of the crew. Tara had never known a ship hum like this one. He took endless pains getting things right. Discipline was an example. Crews always watched with eagle eyes when punishment was meted out: they didn't enjoy seeing serious wrongdoers get off too lightly, yet if they felt someone was treated too harshly for a minor misdemeanour, a collective resentment would fester. Cameron had the knack of fitting the punishment precisely to the crime.

She had never known a captain who inspired such ferocious loyalty. All around she could see people falling under his spell. Robert Young, all puppyish exuberance, so obviously in thrall to him. Even bluff, hardbitten, seen-it-all Wings struggled to conceal the opinion that he walked on water. How did Cameron do it? Why had the navy promoted him so fast in spite of a blemished career, and a private life that was, in her view, disreputable? Tara was set on being the first woman to command a carrier, and there had to be things she could learn from him.

So what were the elements in the alchemy of his charisma? His hawk brow, strong jaw and powerful shoulders? The way he kept his cool even during flaps? That caged energy, the faint scent of danger he exuded? She felt like an apprentice conjuror, observing at close quarters a master magician, yet utterly unable to discern how the tricks worked. She was in danger of becoming obsessed by it, and would never admit to herself – let alone anyone else – that the captain danced through her dreams far more frequently than Richard, her attentive architect boyfriend back home in Winchester.

She looked up as Tom Hitchens came into the bridge carrying a mug of cocoa. She had served twice before with Tom and all of his anecdotes and jokes had become familiar friends. With his slight build, soft features and hint of a paunch, he didn't exactly cut the figure of a military man. But there was no one on board she trusted more, whose reaction was so comfortingly dependable, to whom she would turn so readily if she had a problem. Tom knew what was right, what worked and was ultimately a safer pair of hands than the captain. He was a beacon of common sense and decency in a complex and fast-changing world.

In the quiet confines of his sea cabin, Cameron put the coffee cup down and closed his eyes. It had been a lousy couple of days. Missing Omega was a bitter blow. For months he had hated the prospect of leaving *Indomitable*. The possibility remained that he might go to sea again as an admiral, but the odds were against it. In any case, this was the last ship he would command. He had loved his time at sea; every ship he had served in was engraved in his memory. Most of the action he had seen had involved fisheries protection, drug-busting and humanitarian assistance. Even when the navy was involved in warfare, it often involved chauffeuring marines or being a floating airfield, so exercises like Omega, with live missile firings, amphibious landings, all manner of anti-submarine operations and endless aircraft sorties gave as close a feel for the real thing as they could expect. Cameron derived immense satisfaction from tuning his team like a Stradivarius, and had been confident that they would out-perform the Americans. And now, instead of ending his command with a bang, it was to be this African whimper.

Having been given a carrier command at an unusually young age, he was on course for the very top jobs. There was no reason why he shouldn't aim for Commander-in-Chief Fleet, First Sea Lord or even Chief of the Defence Staff. A few years ago, this would have held little appeal. Now he saw it differently. He loved the navy with a passion. It was his family, his club, his identity. He had been in it for close on two-thirds of his life. If he couldn't command a ship, what better ambition to have than to run the whole thing? And yet right now, all he felt was deflated.

Perhaps it was the problem with Charlotte that was sap-ping his spirit. He had tried phoning and emailing many more times. It looked like she had definitely left him. Though she'd always denied it, he'd wondered before if she'd go back to her husband. In fact, if Tim had never found out about the affair, Charlotte would never have abandoned him. With less than convincing evidence to go on, Tim had probably chal-lenged her more out of curiosity than real suspicion. But then he had seen the lie in her eyes, or so she had thought, and she'd blurted the whole thing out and fled.

When she'd rung him on her mobile a mile from his flat, Cameron's reaction had been a mixture of shock, exhilaration and fear. He imagined how it would feel being confronted by an angry, wronged husband with every shred of right on his side. This anxiety vanished with the thrill of her arrival, when he took her face in his hands, kissed her fiercely, carried the one sad little bag in from her car and made passionate love to her right there in the hall.

The fallout was harder to cope with. Two of her three teenage children didn't speak to Charlotte for a year, and the youngest girl of nine, understanding so little, just desper-ately wanted everyone to be best friends again. Someone tipped off the papers. If there had been no election looming, if it hadn't been for Tim's speeches about family values or if Charlotte hadn't been so exceptionally photogenic, the affair wouldn't have merited more than a couple of half-columns on an inside page. But they got a lead in the *News of the World*, which brought cruel mockery for the children at school, outcast status for the shell-shocked Charlotte, hundreds of knowing smirks for Tim in the Commons and as many Emma Hamilton jibes for Cameron.

Ten years ago, the affair might have fatally harmed his career too. But with the change in public morality – whatever feelings his superiors might have privately harboured – it was no longer so catastrophic. All the same, it was lucky for him that the story died down fairly fast. There had been considerable lack of humour in the First Sea Lord's office about how the press had lampooned the navy, and if it had gone on, patience might have run out.

For the two of them, the only solace was that they were in love. The rest they tried to put out of their minds by travelling. Whenever his work allowed, they went away – to Granada, Ravello, Dublin, Salzburg. But when they got back, the tide of Charlotte's guilt and pain swept back in. His absences at sea made it worse. It was not just the loss of her children: she also missed the closeness of her now cool, uncomprehending parents, and sometimes even the steadfast, if undeclared, affection of her plodding husband.

Slowly though, scabs formed on the family's wounds. Charlotte and Tim contrived to talk to each other about practical matters. For both it was excruciating, with Tim thin-lipped, painfully to the point, and Charlotte drowning in embarrassment, trying to sound natural, unsure whether to ask how he was. With practice they developed a degree of civility, prompting the two older children to call an uneasy truce and agree to see their mother again, though they dodged her embraces and kept their distance from the new man in her life. Cameron had no family to disapprove, only his few close friends who were used to his ways, and who considered Charlotte a charming improvement on most of her predecessors.

As Charlotte's family adapted to a new reality, the surging voltage in their own relationship settled to a steadier current. They got used to each other's ways, and bickered over mundane things. Perhaps Charlotte changed too. Some of her sparkle and vigour seemed to fade. The subject of marriage began to come up regularly even before her decree absolute came through. Cameron didn't see the point, since Charlotte didn't want any more children. Tying the knot might reassure her in the short term, but, having had her excitement, what Charlotte craved was to be made whole again, and he didn't believe he could do that. Should he nonetheless have taken the plunge, if only to secure her for longer? His instincts screamed against it, as they had always done before. Many of his previous women had tried to persuade him to have therapy to uncover why he found it so hard to commit. Was it that he wouldn't compromise, or was there some deeper problem?

*

However unhappy Grace had been leaving London, she had to admit that, after two tedious days hanging around in Gibraltar, things were beginning to look up. Her pulse surprised her by rising noticeably when the car dropped her off at the base and the good-looking navigator helped her into the orange suit and led her across the tarmac to the whirling Lynx helicopter. If she hadn't still felt so guilty about pinching Jason's story, she would have wanted to call him right there so he could share the moment.

She'd got over her temper with him when he called her and grovelled, though she'd been damned if she'd be the one to phone first. He was even quite sweet about it and wished her a good time, only tempering his comments with another dire warning about the Casanova captain. Jason could be tricky, but he was okay, basically. Her friends mainly liked him. He could be devastatingly witty when he was in the mood. If his impulsiveness sometimes caused problems, it was only the flip side of a spontaneous nature. In fact, he'd proposed on their first proper date, and though she'd laughed in his face, he'd kept the pressure up until she agreed. He was, it had to be admitted, remarkably good looking, with fine, almost feminine features reminiscent of many film stars, enhanced with designer stubble and gelled black curly hair.

She was only twenty-eight when she said yes, and getting married hadn't seemed a priority. Three years on, it was time to commit or go their own ways. It was true that more doubts had set in as she understood his nature better. It wasn't so much his flashes of temper, which she could handle, or his flirtatiousness, which she was willing to tolerate as long as he didn't actually screw around. Her concerns ran deeper than these surface things. Much as she applauded his drive and ambition, she worried about how he cut moral corners. On the other hand, she knew Jason had his issues with her too, and there were times when she probably wasn't easy to be around. They had both dwelt on the matter too long, which was why they had finally set a date.

Right now she had more immediate things to worry about. The editor had given her a big chance, and she had to make sure she did a good job. She wished she knew more about Africa generally. Some of her dad's relatives in Ghana had invited her and her brother to visit, but there were lots of other places higher up her list of dream trips, and she wasn't into the roots thing. All the same, it would be odd getting so close to Africa without actually going there.

She was torn from her thoughts when the navigator turned and jabbed a gloved finger towards the front screen. Grace felt a rush of adrenalin as she spotted the tiny grey shape ten miles ahead.

When word came of the approach of the two Lynx helicopters, Robert Young and Tara Wynn made their way from the Ops Room to the small compartment next to the flight deck. Tara turned to Robert.

'Did you get the final confirmation of his name?'

Robert shook his head. 'No, but we were told it would probably be their deputy defence correspondent, Jason Carvill.'

They watched through the open door as one of the aircraft handlers helped a slight figure in the regulation orange waterproof overall and flying helmet step down onto the deck. The figure walked the few yards, stepped into the compartment and the helmet came off. Robert couldn't stop a vast grin forming. He whispered to Tara.

'Doesn't look like a Jason to me.'

The petty officer helped remove the clinging rubberised suit. Grace stepped towards Robert and Tara.

'Surprised?'

Robert did his best to stop smiling. 'Absolutely not. Welcome to *Indomitable*. This is Tara Wynn, the Operations Officer. I'm Robert Young, Weapons Electrical Commander. We're both going to look after you.'

Grace smiled and put out her hand. 'Grace Parsons.'

Robert shook Grace's hand warmly. Grace sensed that the woman's handshake was less friendly. Whatever. With one hand Tara indicated the way.

'I'll take you to your cabin. Don't worry about your bag. Please follow me.'

They started walking. Tara kept up a commentary as she went.

'There are eleven levels on the ship five beneath the flight deck and five above. Watch out for the ladders. They're very steep. We go down them facing out like a staircase, but we recommend visitors do it the other way round, like you would with a domestic ladder.'

Grace tried the first one. This woman wasn't kidding.

'Robert will give you a proper tour of the ship tomorrow, but I'll point out a few things as we go . . . This is the MCO – the main communications office. From here we control all incoming and outgoing comms, including telephone, video-phone and everyone's email. This is Leading Seaman Ward and Seaman Moore.'

Billy and Trish smiled welcomingly and carried on with their work. Tara was already leading her down the next passageway, and into a vast room in semi-darkness, lit by the green, yellow and red glow from the banks of huge screens.

'This is the Ops Room, the nerve centre of the ship. Over there are our sonars, and these men are the warfare officers who control our defensive systems. At sea level, radar only sees to the horizon, but when we hook up with the radar on our helos – sorry, jargon already – helicopters, we can extend its range to up to two hundred miles. Many of the people in the Ops Room are from our warfare department, and they're experts in anti-air, surface, underwater or electronic warfare. The man nearest to you is the PWO – the Principal Warfare Officer. The female rating sitting just beyond him controls our Goalkeeper guns, our last line of defence against incoming missiles . . . Don't worry about memorising this now – you'll get a full briefing tomorrow.'

Tara swept on, taking in the sickbay, the photographers' office . . . As they approached the cabin set aside for her, Colin Dewar was coming down the passage.

'Hi, Tara.'

'This is the OCRM Captain Colin Dewar – Officer Commanding Royal Marines . . . This is Grace Parsons.'

'How d'you do?'

'We have around fifty marines aboard. They were supposed to be pushed to the limit in our exercise, but now they're just having a cruise.'

Dewar smiled warmly. 'That's right. Sunning ourselves on the flight deck, we are . . . See you both in the wardroom later.'

Tara opened the cabin door. Grace's bag had already arrived.

'Better service than Heathrow.'

Tara nodded curtly and completed a circuit of the tiny room, demonstrating the retaining rail and safety belt in the bunk and the little basin.

'Not exactly the Hilton, I'm afraid. We've wired this cabin up so you can send your emails direct. They still pass through the MCO, of course, but it'll save you some hassle . . . Right, it's seventeen thirty. I suggest you unpack and relax for a while. I have some things to take care of, so why don't I collect you in forty-five minutes, and take you to the wardroom? You can meet the other HoDs – Heads of Department – and some of the other officers.'

'I hope I'll get to meet some ordinary people too.'

'Officers *are* ordinary people. However, if you mean petty officers and junior ratings, yes, of course. Indeed, since you met Ward and Moore, I'll ask them to show you around their mess decks tomorrow . . . As for tonight, the Captain's invited you to dinner in his harbour cabin.'

Grace was still off balance from her gaffe, and stumbled right into another. 'What, just me? In his *cabin*?'

Tara's fingers curled slightly. 'Yes. Do you have a problem with that?'

'No, no. Of course not.'

'Good. Then I'll see you again at eighteen fifteen.'

Grace hesitated. What if Jason was right about this man? More than one of the celebrities she'd met had come on strong and, ever since, she'd avoided doing interviews in their suites. She looked at Tara, trying to weigh up whether she could confide in her.

'Listen, this is probably a dumb thing to ask, but I don't know the first thing about the navy. People on board aren't allowed to – you know – get personal, are they?'

'What? You mean have sex? Anyone stupid enough to even *think* about it would land in serious trouble.'

And she turned on her heels and marched off.

6

Once at sea, a captain rarely uses his harbour cabin for anything other than entertaining guests. With its polished mahogany table, silver-plated cutlery, fine glassware and china, it suits the purpose admirably. The young lieutenant who had collected Grace from her cabin showed her in, was thanked by the captain, and withdrew.

As they shook hands, Cameron smiled inwardly. Robert Young had told him that she was attractive, which was certainly true, but had let him experience the rest of the surprise for himself. The captain asked her to sit down, and offered her a drink. Grace was curious but wary. Assuming the press clippings didn't lie – and usually they exaggerated rather than invented the facts – this man had two and half strikes against him as child-abandoner, home-breaker and, probably, womaniser. As they exchanged introductory remarks, she examined him to see where his alleged attractiveness might lie. He was not conventionally good-looking. It was a strong face, but a little craggy, and, apart from his striking blue eyes, there wasn't that much to get excited about. She noticed his nose was slightly crooked, and there were a few flecks of grey in his curly brown hair. Grace had never understood the appeal of older men, and she wasn't even sure he would appealed to her if he'd been fifteen years younger.

As they finished their drinks, the steward brought in the first course. She reached down to her handbag and pulled out a micro-recorder.

'Mind if I switch this on? Saves me having to take notes while I eat.'

'Suit yourself.'

For a few seconds they ate in silence.

'All right if I ask a few questions?'

'Sure.'

'You'll have to forgive my total ignorance of the navy. I was only sent at the last minute.'

'So I gather. We'd been told to expect someone called Carvill.'

'Yes, he's our deputy defence correspondent, and, as it happens, my fiancé. He's very disappointed, but I hope he'll get another chance. I'm a feature writer. The editor sent me because I once interviewed Michael Endebbe, the Numalan Opposition leader. '

Cameron nodded.

'Yes, he was impressive . . . So, how long have you been captain?'

'Of *Indomitable*? Eighteen months. I hand over to my successor at the end of this mission.'

'And then?'

'I'll be commanding a desk.'

'Doesn't sound like you're looking forward to it.'

Cameron shrugged.

'You must have had a fascinating life.'

'I've no complaints.'

'Your accent. I can't place it.'

'I was born in Australia.'

'Why the *Royal* Navy, then?'

'Long story.'

The steward came back, cleared away the plates, recharged the wine glasses and brought their main courses. Grace was beginning to twitch with discomfort. She moved her hand towards the tape recorder.

'This was a mistake, wasn't it?'

'Makes no difference to me.'

'I'm sorry . . . Okay, tonight is totally off the record.' She pressed the button to switch it off. There was no shift in his body language. 'You don't trust me, do you? Or do you just hate all journalists?'

'How could anyone hate them?'

Grace acknowledged the sarcasm with a grimace, but before she could say any more, he had moved on.

'Tell me more about Endebbe.'

'He was charismatic, articulate, well educated – he spent a year at Harvard. Not obviously corrupt.'

'He hasn't had the chance yet, has he?'

'That's a fair point. For the moment, he's being pretty brave. He must be putting his life on the line.'

Cameron nodded in appreciation. 'What do you know about Nabote?'

'Not much. I talked about him with Endebbe and I mugged up on the history a bit. He was born in a village in the north and got some elementary education from Scottish nuns. He was in the army for nearly twenty years, never getting beyond the rank of lieutenant. When the old President was abroad on some trip, he and a bunch of other officers seized power, and he's ruled with an iron fist ever since. It seems he has an ability to divide and rule which would have impressed Stalin or Mao. Some of his ministers have been very smart, but ultimately he doesn't trust anyone except his family. He's marginalised the army by under-equipping and underpaying them, and built up his own Presidential Guard, who are formidable and totally loyal to him, and are commanded by his own son, Julius. He's a real piece of work, that one. Spoilt, vicious, clever. He was slung out of Columbia University for repeated sexual harassment, and only escaped a rape charge in France by claiming diplomatic immunity.'

'How many of these guards are there?'

'Seven or eight hundred.'

'And the regular army?'

'Around three or four thousand, but who knows what their fighting ability is. Why are you asking?'

'Just curiosity. Our plans changed too late for me to get much of a briefing.'

'But we *are* just going to patrol off the coast, aren't we? We won't be in any danger.'

'I certainly hope not. We're sailing without escorts – the ships that form our defensive shield. All we have is the Royal Fleet Auxiliary *Fort George*, which keeps us fuelled, victualled and supplied with ammunition.'

'But surely the Numalans don't have anything for you to worry about? Bombers, or whatever?'

Cameron shook his head. 'As far as we know, they have no serviceable military aircraft at all. But we believe that they recently acquired fast attack boats mounted with Chinese Silkworm missiles.'

'What are those?'

'I don't suppose you know much about the Falklands War?'

'Sorry – I was only just out of nappies.'

'Down there the Argentinians had French Exocets – anti-ship missiles which destroyed some British ships and came uncomfortably close to winning the war for them. If they'd had any more than half a dozen, they probably *would* have won. Silkworms are a modern Chinese equivalent, only three times bigger.'

'Could they sink a ship this size?'

'Probably not with a single hit, unless they got very lucky. But with two – yes, they could take us out.'

'No one told me that we could be at risk.'

'It's too late now, I'm afraid. We've just gone out of helo range of Gibraltar . . . Tell you what, before we get off Numala, we'll put you in a lifeboat and tow you. If we get hit, remember to cut the rope before we go down.'

Grace laughed. All the same, she was mad at her editor for not levelling with her.

'So who decided this? About the escorts.'

Cameron smiled enigmatically. Grace gestured with her right hand towards the tape recorder.

'This is off the record, remember?'

Cameron looked her in the eye and remained silent. Grace had no choice but to try deduction. 'Okay, if it's *that* unusual, I doubt it was a navy decision.'

She pressed on. 'I suppose it could have been a civil servant. But most likely not in the Ministry of Defence, since I imagine they would rely on the experts.'

'Not necessarily.'

'No, but probably. And I doubt that the civil servants in any other ministry would have the authority. That only leaves politicians. Nigel Walker, the Defence Secretary? But I don't see what's in it for him . . . Hang on, Dawnay took all that flak in Parliament over this. It was him, wasn't it?'

'I'm saying nothing.'

'Don't worry. Your secret is safe with me.'

'It's not my secret.'

'Mine, then. I'll still keep it . . . Have you ever run across him? Patrick Dawnay.'

'Mmmm.' The cheeseboard had arrived. Grace shook her head and Cameron helped himself to a wedge of Stilton.

'And?'

He thought for a moment, wondering whether to be drawn. Perhaps there was no harm. 'It wasn't the happiest encounter. I was commanding a frigate, HMS *Chatsworth*, on a goodwill visit to Copenhagen. Dawnay was a back-bencher then, and on some Select Committee junket fact-finding on Danish bacon, or whatever. We invited them all to a party on board I was hosting for local dignitaries. When they turned up, they were all fairly well oiled. Dawnay was as drunk as a lord, and abusive with it. Within five minutes he'd insulted three prominent Danes. I sent two of my officers to suggest discreetly that he might like to rest up a bit in a cabin. He refused, so I had no alternative.'

Grace laughed out loud. 'You threw the future Foreign Secretary off your ship? Nice career move.'

Cameron smiled. 'You could say that. He made rather a

fuss at the time, I recall, both with the Ambassador in Copenhagen and the MoD. Fortunately they backed me up.'

'And now he's sent you to Numala.'

'I didn't say any such thing.'

'But he does know that *Indomitable* is heading that way.'

'That is for sure.'

'And does he know who's in command?'

'I very much doubt that he bothers with such low-level details.'

After they drained their coffee, Cameron stood up.

'I believe your editor has agreed to an embargo until our deployment is officially announced.' Grace nodded. 'Then you might as well have some fun. If you can bear an early start, we're launching some Harriers at seven. Now, let me arrange for an escort to take you back to your cabin.'

'It won't be necessary. I made a point of remembering the way.'

'Good night, then. Sleep well.'

Grace thanked him and left. Back in her cabin, brushing her teeth, she reflected that it hadn't been the ordeal she had feared. Not at all, in fact. Once he'd warmed up, he'd almost been good company.

*

There was no rain, but darting flashes lit up the sky to the west. Whenever the lightning stopped long enough, even the sliver of crescent moon faintly lit up the terrain.

They had waited in Talu until nightfall, and then driven a hazardous cross-country route to avoid the checkpoints on the road towards the border. By ten they had begun climbing, and by eleven they were over the ridge and descending towards the river that marked the border and the vast swampy plains beyond. They drove on down as far as they dared, then cut the engine and eased the car the last few hundred yards down and pushed it off what passed for a track.

Both men slumped down by the tyres, their chests heaving. They stayed there for a while, to make absolutely sure no one had detected their arrival.

The aide twisted his wrist this way and that, trying to make out the time, then tapped the photographer, who reached back into the 4X4 and pulled out a camera body already complete with his long lens. He stuffed a spare roll of ultra-fast film in the chest pocket of his tattered denim jacket and nodded his readiness. They got to their feet and, began their crouching approach towards the slight, distant glow. As they got closer, they fell to their knees and crawled. The aide gestured, hoping that they were close enough. The photographer took one quick look, shook his head, and pointed to another large outcrop, forty yards nearer.

Kim and Julius stepped out of the tent with the young Korean officer. Julius was smoking a joint. The officer pointed towards the long line stretching away as far as the eye could see, where, under nets and using only low lights, men were digging into the dirt and others were cradling discus-shaped objects and gingerly lowering them into the ground along the riverbank. The young officer spoke in halting English.

'By the day after tomorrow, we will have laid mines all along our side of the border with Zania. Five hundred and twenty-three kilometres in total. Of course, we work only at night, so the Zanians or satellites do not see what we do.'

Kim took a close look at some of the workers as they stepped along. 'How long will it take to assemble the bridge?'

'Ten, twelve hours. It will be a floating structure.'

The aide watched with growing alarm. The three men had veered away from the lights and were now strolling in their direction. The photographer had changed rolls and was snapping again, but the aide held his hand out to stop him, terrified that the click of the shutter would give them away. He looked back behind him, trying to calculate whether they should sneak away now or stay still and hope that they would not be noticed. With trembling fingers, he reached down to his belt and slowly pulled out a pistol.

The distant lightning crackle had ceased and now the voices carried clear through the cool night air. Julius stopped and took a long puff.

'How many can we force across in an hour?'

The young officer had done his sums. 'Depends on their age and condition. Maximum thirty thousand. When the last ones are through, we will remove the bridge and lay mines across the gap. There will be no way for them to get back.'

Kim nodded and turned to Julius. 'Then they will no longer be your problem.'

Julius laughed. 'In those swamps, within two weeks most of them won't be anyone's problem.'

The three began walking again.

If they didn't move now, they'd be right on top of them. The aide and the photographer began crawling backwards, wriggling like snakes, desperate to make no sound. At last they reached the safety of another rock, but the photographer's nervous movement knocked the lens against it.

Kim stopped in his tracks. 'What was that?'

At first there was silence, then a sudden scurrying noise and they saw something moving quickly up the hill. The young officer instinctively began to move forward, but both he and Colonel Kim had left their side arms in the tent. Julius threw the joint down, and yelled at the young officer to get out the way, as he pulled his Magnum from its holster and loosed off three shots.

The figures were still scrambling on up. Soon the night would swallow their shadows. Julius fired another round.

Kim's fury got the better of him. 'Give me that.' He stuck out his hand.

Julius's eyes flashed. Angrily he swung the gun out of reach, and aimed one more time.

'They're getting away.'

Julius grudgingly handed it over and Kim took careful aim. Even in daylight it would have been a tricky shot. He was lucky that in their panic they were climbing in a straight line. He squeezed the trigger.

As he heard the zing of the fifth bullet, the aide ducked again, then looked over his shoulder as he heard the yell. He ran back the few paces to where his friend had crashed down. The strap had been shot right through as the bullet rammed into his right shoulder blade, and the camera had skidded to a dust-covered halt three yards below. The aide looked back down towards the pursuers and tried to tug at the photographer's left arm. He cried out in pain.

'Go, *go.*'

'I can't leave you here.'

'Take the film. My top pocket.'

The aide stuck his hand in and grabbed it.

'Shoot me.'

'*What?*'

'Do it now. *Now.*'

Kim had sent the officer back to fetch help while he and Julius scrambled forward. They had seen one man fall, but could not see what had happened to the other. Then a shot rang out above them and instinctively they threw themselves to the ground. As Kim dragged himself back to his feet, he saw a glimpse of movement up ahead and heard the sound of a car door clanging shut, an engine starting and the echo as it roared off up towards the ridge.

Kim and Julius climbed fast till they got to where the man had fallen. The young officer was arriving with three other soldiers in a jeep and in its headlights they could all see that the man's face was half shot away. Julius looked down.

'Pity you killed him.'

Kim used his foot to turn the man's body over. There were two separate wounds. 'I didn't.'

Julius stepped over to where the camera lay, pulled the back open, and smiled broadly as he yanked the film out.

Kim barked in Korean to a soldier, who rummaged through the dead man's pockets. Kim looked up the hill and issued another order. The soldiers jumped back into the jeep, and soon its rear lights were bouncing drunkenly against the night sky. Kim and Julius were left alone. The anxiety in Kim's voice was clear.

'He may have heard something, and he could have other rolls of film. If we do not catch him, your father will not forgive us.'

'If we do not catch him, it would be better not to burden my father with the whole truth.'

7

Grace had sent several emails to Jason, but she was careful not to say she was enjoying herself. Her first night had been sleepless, not on account of any discomfort – there was so little sense of motion, you could forget you were in a ship altogether – but from the tension of the unfamiliar faint claustrophobia in the bunk. After that, she had slept like a baby. Robert Young had bubbled with enthusiasm as her tour guide on the first full day. After watching the Harrier launches, he had taken her just about everywhere, providing explanations about how everything worked. Oddly, the thing that had surprised her most was the many TV sets round the ship showing normal satellite news. On the third day she had particularly enjoyed the precision of 'rasing' – replenishing at sea – when the *Fort George*, as big as the carrier itself, came alongside and the two ships cavorted like synchronised swimmers while thousands of tons of fuel were pumped across the gap, and a helicopter buzzed endlessly to and fro picking up supplies of food, drink and munitions.

As the days passed, she felt she was on the way to becoming friends with Robert and Colin. Robert had warm, kind eyes, and she liked the loving way he talked about his wife and kids. It had taken her a while to detect the dry wit in Colin's much rarer utterances. He reminded her of that expression about speaking quietly and carrying a big stick. If she ever needed a bodyguard, he would be perfect: gentle when not roused, but clearly capable of making any assailants who messed with him regret it for a very long time.

Tonight the two had kept her company in the wardroom

late into the evening. Wings had come over and joined them for a drink, adding a touch of avuncular bonhomie before going off to make sure the pilots wouldn't be nursing hang-overs when they came in range of Numala the next morning. Tara Wynn was a different kettle of fish. Whenever their paths crossed, she seemed to be preoccupied with something or other. They had somehow got off on the wrong foot and Tara evidently wasn't interested in trying again. What wor-ried Grace more was that the Commander, Tom Hitchens, also seemed slightly cool. Had Tara set him against her? She looked around the emptying wardroom to see if she could try to be friendly to him. He was nowhere to be seen.

In fact Tom was in the captain's sea cabin. Although they'd gone through everything in the planning meeting at five, Cameron had wanted to run through it one more time. The plan was to sail right up to the twelve-mile limit as soon as they arrived, and to send some helos aloft to make sure they were noticed. Hitchens sipped from his mug.

'What if the Numalans don't react at all?'

'I think that's unlikely. If they don't see us, they'll hear all about it when Dawnay makes his statement to the Commons. I'd be very surprised if our friend Nabote doesn't respond.'

Hitchens nodded. 'I dare say you're right, sir. The Foreign Secretary's statement triggers the end of the embargo for our own little newshound as well.'

'Mmmm. God knows what she's making of it all.'

'Word is, most of the younger officers fancy her something rotten.' Tom took another sip and looked closely at the Captain. Cameron pulled a face.

'Frankly, Tom, I find the concept of an attractive journalist an oxymoron. Like a charming crocodile.'

Tom grinned. 'Tara's worried about security. She suggested that we draw up some sort of guidelines on which parts of the ship Grace should be free to visit unescorted.'

Cameron scratched his head. 'I can't see it working. We can hardly confine her to her cabin or the wardroom most of

79

the time, and I'm damned if I'll tie up someone full time chaperoning her. As long as she understands she can't attend our confidential briefings or see signals going in and out of the MCO, I think we should let her go where she wants. Hopefully from first thing tomorrow she'll be much more interested in what's going in Kindalu than anything that happens in *Indomitable*.'

*

It was a game the children played for hours every day. They all had improvised their own versions of surfboards, using anything that would float. The bigger boys fought their way out beyond the front line of breakers and played a game of chicken, seeing how much they could be engulfed on the incoming wave without losing the grip of their precious device. The younger ones had their own tamer version, running at full pelt along the sand just as the ripples were sucked back by the jealous sea, throwing their boards down and diving full-length onto them, gliding fast through the shallows, as if they were flying across ice. The youngest of all – no more than five – was made by his brothers to sit on the sand watching.

He had been sitting there grumpily for half an hour when something in the distance caught his eye. He watched, entranced, for a few seconds, then stood up and pointed at it. His twelve-year-old brother saw this, looked round, and yelled to his pals. They all knew what helicopters were, even if they had never seen one before.

Suddenly there came a noise so loud it overpowered the crash of the surf. The boys looked down towards the river mouth where three boats screamed out, bouncing as their bows hit the rollers. It was only when the children followed the direction the boats were taking that they saw, right on the horizon, a very unfamiliar silhouette.

*

Cameron and Hitchens were at their posts in the Ops Room, intently watching large screens. A radar operator called out.

'Three craft approaching. Range thirteen miles.'

Cameron gave rapid-fire orders to turn the ship away and to scramble two Harriers, before telling Hitchens that he was going up to the bridge.

'Right, sir.'

Up there, Grace, standing next to Robert Young, was fascinated by the calm with which the young female rating was steering the ship smoothly to its evasive course. Cameron emerged from his personal lift and walked past them both to Flyco.

'Are they both airborne, Wings?'

'Yes, sir. Demon Two launched thirty seconds ago.'

The fighter controller picked up the radio handset.

'OK, Demon One?'

Grace had quietly made her way to Flyco and heard the crackle of the pilot's voice on the radio.

'Holding hands.' The two aircraft had established visual contact with each other and were ready to be on their way. Grace could see in the far distance that the pair had already swooped into formation.

'Roger, Demon One.'

Grace stepped closer to Cameron and whispered.

'What happens now?'

'Hopefully those boats will turn away.'

'And if they don't?'

'Then we'll launch your lifeboat pretty damn quick. Silkworms travel at nearly Mach one. From where the boats are now, the missiles could be on us in sixty seconds. That doesn't give much time to react.'

From a loudspeaker there came a voice from the Ops room. 'Contacts maintaining course, range nine miles.'

Cameron turned to Wings. 'How long to intercept?'

'Twenty seconds, sir.'

The operator's voice came again. 'Maintaining course. Range eight point five miles.'

Grace was wondering where to throw herself if the missile was launched.

The crackle from the Harrier came again. 'Craft altering course, over.'

'Roger, Demon One.'

There was a little less tension in the operator's voice too. 'Contacts changing course. Now heading due east.'

Cameron nodded. 'Thanks, Wings . . .' He smiled at Grace. 'Looks like you can breathe again.'

Grace swallowed. 'That was . . . exciting. Were you concerned?'

Wings smiled and shook his head. 'They'd be mad to attack us outside their waters. They must know that HMG would have to respond with massive force. That was only to show us they're awake.'

*

Patrick Dawnay returned to his office. It had gone well. His press office had inspired a story in the *Mail* indicating that something in Numala was afoot, which in turn had prompted Radio 4's *Today* programme to get him that morning. He had been careful not to give much away, suspecting, probably rightly, that the back-bench MPs who made such a song and dance on the subject would go on the warpath if their dignity was sullied by the first announcement being made other than in Parliament. However, the trailer had ensured maximum attention for his statement.

In the House, he had delivered the text in statesmanlike tones, and the reaction from both sides had been good. The Prime Minister had nodded in the right places, which was one in the eye for the Chancellor. All the indications were that tomorrow's press would be favourable, and he'd been invited on *Newsnight* for that evening. When he'd briefed the French and German Foreign Ministers, they had been gratified by his assurance that there would be no military intervention. The US Ambassador, called in that morning, had been cooler, but for once the Americans were less important. Overall, though it was too early to tell, it looked like the verdict would be that his action was a judicious balance between brave and foolhardy.

Much would depend on how Nabote reacted. Some sort of ritual condemnation of the action had been foreseen and discounted. What happened after that was the key. Dawnay believed that personally he was in a win–win position. In his experience, intelligence reports were usually exaggerated; that was the natural tendency of intelligence agencies, since dramatic stories bolstered their importance. In this case, the satellite pictures had defied convincing analysis. The other material picked up by the navy and MI6 was perhaps more persuasive, but it was patchy and, according to all his advisers, didn't amount to much. The chances were that Nabote never intended to do more to the Lobus than pinch a few farms. If this was right, it meant that even if the Numalans ignored the carrier altogether and did whatever they would have done anyway, the Foreign Office could claim credit for stopping worse happening. If on the other hand the situation deteriorated, Dawnay would look prescient for spotting the risk.

He could convert what had been an irritant into a significant boost for him, both internationally and domestically. Not many months ago all the pundits had considered the Chancellor a shoe-in if the Prime Minister were to stand down. However the combination of a deteriorating economic outlook and the Chancellor's lacklustre performance at the party conference had helped hugely. The bastard might still be in front, but he had clipped a couple of fences and his lead was diminishing.

*

Nathan Nabote was furious. Kim had gone pale and his voice was close to a tremble. Julius stood next to Kim, knowing, as he had done since early childhood, that there were times when obsequious silence was the only way out.

'This photographer cannot have been alone. If I find you have lied to me, you will be shot. This is your last chance to tell the truth. Kim, was he alone?'

'Yes, Excellency.'

Nabote circled round and looked into Julius's eyes. 'You?'

'He was alone, Excellency, I swear it.'

'The man should never have been allowed to get within a mile of there. Why was it not guarded properly? Kim, you have failed me.'

Kim hung his head. 'Mr President, I offer my most humble apologies. As soon as I realised the threat, I immediately ordered a guard to be placed night and day. It will not happen again.'

The subservience appeased Nabote. 'It is good that you discovered him. This was very dangerous. Do you know who he is?'

Julius would have preferred to stay silent until he was certain the storm had blown over, but Nabote prodded him.

'His face was blown away and he had no identification. He must have been one of Endebbe's.'

Nabote nodded. 'Endebbe has been making much mischief in the provinces. Maybe we should encourage him to come back to Kindalu where we can watch him more easily. Julius, I want you to send some of your men to his wife tonight. They should not wear uniform.'

Julius bowed. 'I will take care of it personally.'

'Now let us return to the British impudence. Are my ministers waiting?'

'They are gathered outside, ready to support whatever action you propose.'

'Colonel Kim, you say that their warship did not enter our waters. But surely their planes came into our airspace?'

'It is possible, Excellency.'

'And this is all because I refused the European election observers?' He laughed dismissively. 'The British are not our masters now. Do they think a gunboat will make me bow to them?' He strode to his desk and picked up the fax of the Foreign Secretary's statement, scanning it for the phrase he wanted '"President Nabote must understand that the presidential election process now lacks any credibility, and if he violates the human rights of any of his people, he will be held to account."' He smiled. 'How entertaining. *Held to account*? By the *British*?'

Julius thought he'd caught the mood and went on the offensive. 'We should strike against them immediately. Our gunboats should attack the carrier without delay.'

Nabote stepped past them and over to the French window. Finally he turned round.

'Attacking would play into their hands. It would give them a perfect excuse to send a task force to invade. No, there are better moves I can make. The British and Americans have portrayed me as a despot. Even some African leaders have, to their undying shame, been seduced by this propaganda. But no African statesman would allow imperialists to dictate to them and their peoples. This may be the opportunity I have waited for.'

He went behind his desk, picked up a pen and wrote something down.

'Julius, I want some spontaneous anti-British demonstrations in the streets and outside the British High Commission. Summon their chargé d'affaires to the Foreign Ministry to explain their conduct. Make sure he is jostled and jeered on the journey, and that the CNN people are tipped off where best to film. And I wish you to have a word with the head of our broadcasting service. Tell him to urge the people to give me a landslide victory to show the British what we think of them. I will telephone the leaders of Nigeria, South Africa and Ghana to ask for their public support. I will make Patrick Dawnay regret taking me on.'

He dismissed Kim and Julius with a gesture. As Julius reached the door, Nabote called after him.

'Do not forget about Endebbe.'

8

The storm was almost overhead, the thunder hard on the heels of the lightning. Rain drummed on the tin roofs that capped most of the little houses in the quiet district a mile south of the centre of Kindalu. There had been a power cut again, and except when there were flashes overhead, the whole area was swathed in blackness.

Theresa Endebbe always slept lightly, from years of listening out for cries from her children. Their first born, Vincent, had been a healthy child, but there had been many times when they had both wondered how long they would have their daughter Sasha. She was five now, small and weak for her age, but she'd come through so much that it was clear she was a battler.

Theresa had gone to bed early, as she always did when Michael was away. After saying prayers with the children, kneeling together by their bedsides, she'd cleared up the supper plates and fallen asleep by nine. When the sound of the cars woke her, she looked at the luminous hands of the clock. Eleven forty.

She got out of bed and pulled the curtain back an inch. She saw three men get out of the first car, more from the second, and felt a chill. Were they coming for Michael? Would they not know he was away? She reached to the bedside for the mobile phone Michael had given her and jabbed in his number, as she heard the footsteps of the men running through the rain to the porch. Answer, *answer*.

The first knock was polite. *Answer, Michael, please answer.*

The second knock was impatient. *Oh, God be my help.*

Answer me, Michael. Through the gap in the curtain she saw the shape of a man at the bedroom window. She stumbled though to the hallway and stood there trembling as the flimsy door begin to shake with the thumping. She pressed redial. *Answer, Lord, make him answer.*

At last her prayer was answered. Michael's voice was sleepy. He was staying with friends in Talu after another exhausting day. The panic in Theresa's voice snapped his bleariness away and he told her to get furniture against the door. The only light was the faint green glow from the phone. She shoved forward the chair in the hallway and then tried to pull the mahogany table from the kitchen. It was heavy, so heavy.

'Michael, it's no good. What do I do, what do I do? Oh, Jesus, tell me what to do.'

Michael must have already known in his heart that there was nothing anyone could do to stop what was going to happen.

As a lightning flash lit up the sky, for a terrifying moment she saw the silhouette of nails beginning to come free from the door-frame. The children, the children. She dropped the phone and, running her hands against both walls, found her way to their room and shook their sleeping shapes.

'Quick!' Vincent muttered some complaint, till the hammering noise got through to his senses. Sasha, was too deeply asleep. Theresa picked her up in her arms. Where could she go, though? There was no way out the back, and if they tried to escape through the window the men would catch them. The only hope was the cupboard.

She got herself and the two little ones inside it seconds before the door crashed down, crushing the flimsy chair. In the cupboard, Theresa hugged her children close and silently mouthed a prayer. Through the crack under the door she could see rapid movements of torchlight and hear the low voices as the men went by. She tried to force herself to breathe more quietly.

Julius walked into the bedroom and put his hand on the bedsheet. It was warm. He lifted the sheet to his face and took a deep draught of the scent of a woman. She was here. One of his men came in carrying the mobile phone he had found on the kitchen floor. As Julius took it, even over the noise of the rain he heard a faint sound coming from it. He held it to his ear and listened, an evil smile forming on his face.

'Is that Michael Endebbe?'

There was silence for a second, then a voice said, *'Who is that?'*

'I hear your wife has breasts like ripe mangoes . . . Why don't you listen while we play hide and seek with her? . . . Theresa, *The-re-sa* . . .'

A shout came from the hall, where one of his men had pulled open the cupboard door. Julius strode out there and grinned at the three faces, one asleep, the other two staring pathetically up at him. He raised the phone back up.

'Guess what? We've found her. Time for another game. I'm going to need both of my hands for this one, but I'll have someone hold it up so you can listen.'

Julius tossed the phone to one of the men and crooked a finger at Theresa. 'Come on, little woman. Time for you to come out and play.'

Theresa shrank back, holding the children tighter to her, mumbling a prayer.

'Come out.' The voice was harder now. When she didn't move, Julius reached in, wrenched the boy away from her and threw him across the floor. Theresa instinctively stretched out a hand towards the child. One of the men grabbed the hand and yanked her out and up on her feet. Still holding the girl, she tried to push towards her boy. Julius blocked her way. He slapped her hard across the cheek.

She staggered and fell back, still clinging to Sasha. Vincent was back on his feet now, fiercely determined to protect his mama. He ran at Julius's back and began kicking his calves with all his strength. Julius turned furiously, caught the lad by the arm, and swung him in a fast arc, smashing his head with full force into the wall. The boy fell lifeless to the ground.

'Oh Jesus, Lord.' Theresa tried to run to the tiny, prone figure, but two men caught her and ripped the little girl away. They pinioned Theresa's arms and held her upright in front of Julius. Through short, snatched breaths, she incantated. 'Jesus, Mary, Joseph, Jesus, Mary, Joseph.'

Julius gestured to the man with the cellphone, making him hold it near her mouth so Endebbe might hear her terror. Then he waved him away again and put his face close to Theresa's and told her to shut up.

She wasn't listening, couldn't hear, already half crazy with grief and fear. 'Jesus, Mary, Joseph.'

He slapped her hard again, silencing her for a while. He put his right hand very carefully on her chemise and tenderly felt the shape of each breast. Then he put his hand to the neck and ripped the cloth down.

He clicked his fingers. 'Light.'

Parting the hanging shreds so the torch could better illuminate the breasts, he slowly lowered his mouth and bit one of her nipples so hard she yelped.

'Knife.'

A vicious blade glinted in the torchlight. He ran it across her breasts, suddenly moved it downwards and with a fast stroke cut through the elastic of her pants. They fell gently to the floor. He put his hand roughly down and felt her crotch. With a smile, he turned to one of the men.

'You brought the dice?'

The man laughed. He had it ready in his hand.

'Then do it.'

One by one, the men squatted and started tossing it across the floor. Julius clicked his fingers and got the phone.

'Want to know what my men are doing now? Rolling dice to decide which of them goes first. After me, naturally.'

90

'Jesus, Mary, Joseph.'

Unhurriedly, Julius began unbuckling his belt.

'Christ, protect me. Oh Lord God, my saviour . . .'

After Julius was through, he lit up a joint while he watched the others. When the last man finished and was standing over her, zipping up his black jeans, Julius pushed him aside and held his hand out for the knife. He rolled her limp body over and carved a neat N on each breast. By then she was past feeling the pain.

*

The eavesdroppers in *Tenacious* were working through the night. Simon was finally settling to his task. He'd been so terrified by the thought of being cooped up in a cigar tube under the waves. It made him feel better that to make use of their main antennae they had to stay at periscope depth: *Tenacious* could also pick up some signals using the long wire it trailed, but only if they were very low-frequency. So he'd made the best of it, kept the complaints to a minimum, and got on with the job. He'd been helped in part by Martin, the XO, who learned of his sweet tooth and discreetly arranged for him to be given a generous supply of chocolate bars and biscuits. Most of the crew, including his two fellow listeners, worked in six-hour shifts, one on, one off, hot-bunking, reading, playing computer games or working out in the cramped exercise area when they weren't sleeping. As the only linguist, Simon sometimes had to stay at his post for up to ten hours, which was exhausting.

The other thing about submarines that bothered him was the nuclear reactor. His mother had always been an organic sort of person, and regarded nuclear power stations as accidents waiting to happen. Three Mile Island and Chernobyl had gratified her enormously. Some of this phobia had been transmitted to her son, and sitting at work within thirty feet of a nuclear device felt like being trapped in an X-ray machine. He had been unsure about going on the full Cook's tour of the ship, and had been strangely let down by the tiny size of the device. Moreover, he'd been astonished to find out that all this funny box did was generate steam. He was, though, fascinated to hear that this little box of tricks meant that the submarine could stay submerged for fully three months, and that it was shortage of food, rather than power, which would curtail its deep patrol. He was relieved to discover that *Tenacious* carried no Trident nuclear weapons – that being a task for the even larger *Vanguard* class, known as 'bombers' in the trade. However, he took a close look at the Spearfish torpedoes, nearly twenty-five feet long in their racks, and imagined the havoc they could unleash.

The thing that surprised Simon most was how civil everyone was. At school, the rugger-buggers had bullied him mercilessly, and compulsory excursions to sports fields or gyms had been a weekly humiliation. He had of course given the widest of berths to the army cadet training corps. His few friends at school or later at college were invariably geeky outcasts like him, and it had never crossed his mind that anyone of a sporty disposition would give him the time of day. Yet here he was, entombed with a hundred men, all clearly macho and athletic, and all being very pleasant to him.

Although Simon had been initially indifferent to the news that *Indomitable* would be arriving, he found himself infected by the excitement among the rest of the crew. Now that the ship had got here, the buzz had increased even more. Owen Lewis came to the WTO for a chat and admitted how glad he was that his old friend Christopher Cameron was overhead.

No one could be in any doubt of the political importance of what their antennae were picking up. They had not succeeded so far in obtaining any intercepts of Nabote's own conversations, but there was enough second-hand comment to illustrate the scale of the diplomatic offensive which the Numalans were launching, especially at the African Union in

Addis Ababa. Simon had recorded telling conversations between someone who was evidently commanding the fast attack boats and a Colonel Kim, reputedly the top Korean adviser to Nabote. He had heard Kim issue clear orders not to repeat the approach to the carrier. Lewis gave him a pat on the back for that one, and made very sure it was relayed double quick to *Indomitable*, as well as London.

*

As Michael Endebbe drove on through the night, still over three hundred miles from Kindalu, Theresa, half insane with grief and pain, had dragged herself to comfort her silent, traumatised daughter and begin her long vigil over the body of her son. She stammered out some kind of prayer, to what end she knew not. Even once the black cars had roared off, the neighbours all stayed resolutely inside their own houses, too scared to risk coming to see what had happened. It took over half an hour before the first friends, sent there by Michael, stepped over the smashed remains of the front door and gasped at the sight that confronted them.

No more than fourteen miles away, Grace, Wings and Robert were taking a nightcap. Young had pulled out a photo from his hip pocket. Grace examined it and smiled.

'So how old are these monsters?'

'Three and five.'

Wings took a careful look at Grace.

'How old are you?' The question took her breath away. In her world no man would ever have asked something so bluntly, but there was nothing for it but to answer.

'Thirty-one.'

'Isn't it time you sprouted kids yourself?' Grace wondered how long he could keep this up. If he wasn't so obviously without side, she might have considered getting annoyed. 'How long have you been engaged?'

'About three years.'

'Three *years*? Bloody hell. When Millie collared me, I only hung on for three months. What are you waiting for?'

'Oh, there's been a lot going on. Neither of us was in a hurry.'

'Is he a . . . ?'

She was becoming so used to Wings' bluntness, she didn't wait for him to finish.

'No, he's white, as it happens.'

Wings grinned. 'Actually I was going to ask if he was another journalist. I'm not *that* tactless, you know.'

Grace smiled. 'Sorry. Yes, he works on the same paper. By the way, don't feel you have to pussyfoot round me on the black thing. I'm as relaxed about my colour as you are about yours.'

Robert was still inclined to take it easy, but Wings took her at her word. 'Isn't it, you know different, being with a black and a white?'

'Not that I've ever noticed, and I've tried a Chinese too. You get smart ones and thick ones, kind ones and mean ones, and – if I can venture a guess at what you'll ask next, Wings – no, blacks don't all have humdingers.'

'What about your family, though? Aren't they disappointed you're not marrying a black guy?'

Grace shrugged. 'Sort of. My mum's Canadian and she just wants me to be happy. My dad's of Ghanaian stock, but born in the UK. He wants to see me with someone who's getting on. I suppose an ambitious guy from Ghana would've been his ideal, but he'd rather I was with a hard-working white than a lazy African, and either would be better in his eyes than me marrying, say, a Jamaican.'

Even Robert looked surprised. Grace carried on. 'Don't believe that blacks only ever dislike whites. We can hate other blacks much more. West Africans think Caribbeans are all gun-toting druggies, and Caribbeans think Nigerians are all con men.'

Wings took a sip of whisky. He'd liked the look of Grace

94

from the off, and now he was warming to her more. 'So your parents approve of your feller, then?'

'Jason? Oh sure, they like him. He's charming when they're around, and he *will* get on, believe me.'

'So why aren't you wearing a ring?'

'Oh, that's nothing. I . . . was just afraid I'd damage it on this trip.'

'He's keeping in touch, is he, while you're with us?'

'Oh, yeah. In fact he sent me an email two hours ago. He was trying to be helpful, saying I should have been more critical of what you lot are doing. Said the mood was shifting in London.'

Robert nodded. 'I'm not surprised. I caught the CNN bulletin on my way here. They weren't too positive either.'

*

The midnight oil was being burned in the Foreign Office. Things were no longer looking so good. Dawnay had handled *Newsnight* poorly. With the Prime Minister about to depart on a long tour of Asia, the last thing Number Ten wanted was an African hitch, and Adair had to assure them that everything was under control.

That was looking slightly doubtful. Soon after the Commons statement was delivered, heads of UK missions to all major sub-Saharan African countries had been instructed to brief their host governments and to seek support. Toby Gordon-Booth had been confident that most of the key capitals – especially Lagos, Pretoria and Accra – would side with Britain. However, the early reports were decidedly mixed. The Nigerians had been opaque and, more worryingly, the South Africans had expressed serious concerns about what signal this sent.

In the course of the day, CNN and BBC World had hardened their tone. The images of Bob Tiernan being jostled as he left the Foreign Ministry were alarming. Worst of all, the first editions of the broadsheets were far more negative than had seemed likely only hours earlier. Even the *Post* had balanced a supportive report from the carrier with a far less helpful editorial.

Toby Gordon-Booth wasn't seriously concerned yet. When something unexpected occurred, it was often a while before the press got their eye in and settled their line. Until then, their opinions tended to bob around wildly. Hopefully things would go better in the next days. If not, there might be something to really worry about.

*

Alone in his cabin, Cameron lay on his bed. He too had watched CNN, as many of the ship's company would have done. They'd already been disappointed about missing Omega and were fretting that they had been sent on a wild-goose chase that might deprive them of Christmas with their loved ones. He knew from experience that if the media became openly critical, it would have a doubly negative impact on ship's morale. They would not only question the value of what they were doing: they would know that their relatives and friends would see the same news and, instead of feeling proud of them, would feel confused and upset. It would be a big task for him to stop things getting too bad.

The more he reflected on this mission, the more unhappy it made him. In pure naval terms, sending them down here without escorts had bordered on dereliction. Nonetheless, if there was at least a political imperative, he might have agreed reluctantly that it was legitimate. If it turned out that Dawnay had got the politics wrong too, it would confirm what Cameron had deduced from his previous encounter – that the man was an arrogant, blundering fool.

9

The shadows of the kapok branches played on the white-washed facade of the pretty little Catholic church set high on one of the hills overlooking Kindalu. A small group of people stood in one corner of the graveyard, listening to the tall, slim priest in the long white vestment. As he spoke, he bent down, picked up a handful of reddish earth and threw it down into the open grave. One by one the mourners did the same and joined in one last prayer. Then each came up and exchanged quiet words with the couple standing nearest to the grave before taking their leave. The priest was the last to go.

Left alone, they stood silently for a while before Michael took Theresa's hand. It felt lifeless in his. Her eyes were still closed. He looked at her bruises and cuts and, once again, felt the swelling of anger and guilt. She opened her eyes.

'Theresa, as long as I live, I will never forgive myself for letting this happen.'

Since he returned, he had said a hundred times that he should never have left her and the children unprotected.

'Nothing can be worth this. I have come to the conclusion that I must withdraw from the election immediately.'

Theresa stared past him. 'You must do God's will.'

'God would not wish me to risk my family's safety.'

'God asks sacrifices of us all.'

'My mind is made up. I will tell the party tonight.'

'You must do God's will.'

'I don't know what God's will is any more. I only know what my conscience is saying.'

'Does your conscience not say that if you withdraw, you will betray Vincent and everyone else who has died?'

'I cannot campaign from home, and if I leave they could come again.'

'Then let them. They have taken everything already.'

'No, they have not killed you or Sasha.'

Her voice sounded bleaker than ever. 'For myself I care nothing. We can send Sasha to your sister.'

'Theresa, nothing will make me repeat this mistake. If I am to carry on, you must go away, out of Numala.'

'It is impossible. They will stop me at the checkpoints. It will make matters worse.'

'I will think of a way.'

He took her in his arms. Over her head he saw on the horizon the ship that Nabote was making such a fuss about.

*

Just after midnight, the phone rang. Jason had been deeply asleep and it took him time to come to and put out a flailing hand to pick up the receiver.

'Jason?'

'Who is this? Oh, sorry, yeah, hi, John. What is it?'

'Have you been in touch with Grace in the last twenty-four hours?'

'Only by email. Why?'

'It's looking more and more like Dawnay's got this one badly wrong. The Africans are up in arms. There's talk of the African Union issuing some sort of resolution against us. All the other papers are going for the jugular . . . I'm worried that Grace isn't picking up the vibe. I've had to edit her second piece pretty heavily. Frankly, compared with what everyone else is saying it still sounds too jingoistic. Our brave lads doing a great job in difficult circumstances, etc. I wonder if you wouldn't mind helping me.'

Jason shifted on to one elbow and switched the light on. 'Course. Happy to.'

'If I say anything directly, it could demotivate her. But if you were to give her a gentle hint, just a tiny touch on the tiller, know what I mean?'

'No problem.' Jason sank back in the pillow.

'Thanks. I mean *gentle*.'

'You got it.'

'Okay. Sorry to bother you so late.'

Jason put the phone down and reached to switch off the light.

'Who was it?'

'The editor.'

'What did he want?'

'Nothing. Go back to sleep.' A few seconds later under his breath he muttered to himself, 'I knew she wasn't up to it.'

*

The two men struggled to pull the boat through the soft sand. The moon had grown fatter and was casting a dangerously bright light. They heaved again until the first little waves lapped the bows. Then from the dunes a crouched, slender woman appeared, followed by seven or eight children. The woman was carrying a child in her arms, and had a canvas bag over her shoulder. The children were hoisted into the boat, the bag stowed and one of the men embraced the mother and child together, before taking a pouch from inside his shirt and whispering.

'There's a sign in the boat. If they send an aircraft to investigate, hold it up clearly. If you reach the ship, give this to the captain.'

She nodded, took it, and stepped into the boat. He joined in one last grunting shove, and the other man jumped aboard as soon as it floated, lifting the oars and dipping them into the seething foam. Only when he had fought his way through fifty yards of breakers did he take the risk of dropping the little outboard into the water and pulling on the rope to start it.

The man who had remained on the shore retreated back to the dunes. He surveyed the scene carefully and crept away. If he had stayed any longer he might have noticed a flicker of movement further down the beach. It would have been too far to hear one guard tell another to run back and radio in what they'd seen out at sea.

Doubtful as he was that there was any real danger from the Numalans, Cameron had taken no chances. He knew that, except in a dead calm, small craft could get very close before being detected by radar, and he had ordered the posting of lookouts round the clock.

He was on the bridge when he got the word that the lookout on the quarterdeck had spotted something approaching them at a range of one to two miles. He picked up the microphone and spoke to him direct.

'Can you estimate its speed?'

The voice came back. 'No sign of a bow wave, sir, so it's probably travelling quite slowly.'

Cameron turned back. 'Officer of the watch, turn the ship away and keep this contact at no less than one mile. Put a couple more engines on in case we need more speed . . . I'm going down to the Ops Room.'

When he got there, Tom and Tara were already gathered behind a radar operator looking over his shoulder at the screen. A tiny trace was now visible. The operator realised that the captain had joined the group.

'Looks like a very small craft, sir. Certainly not an attack boat.'

Tara Wynn looked at Cameron. 'Could be a suicide bomber.'

Cameron paused for a second and reached for a micro-phone. 'Flyco, launch both alert Sea Kings.'

He sat down at his post as they all waited for the helos to intercept.

There was quite a swell. Some of the children were crying. Theresa tried to comfort them as best she could without let-ting go of Sasha. She and the boatman had seen the lights of the helicopters coming towards them.

Nearer and nearer the helicopters came, their noise grow-ing deafening, until they were clattering overhead, their rotors whipping the water into a frenzy. Theresa could hardly look up, the searchlights were so blinding. She remembered the sign and reached down for it.

Back in the Ops Room, they listened to the pilots' reports.

'This is Kestrel Two? Over.'

Cameron had taken direct charge. 'What do you have, Kestrel Two? Over.'

'As far as I can see, there's only one man and one woman. The rest are kids. The woman is holding a sign saying "PLEASE HELP US". Doesn't look like they have any weapons. Over.'

None of this was reducing Tara's concerns. 'It could be a trick, sir. Since the boat hasn't turned away, according to the book –'

Cameron quietly cut her off. 'I know what the book says, Tara, but I don't think this is a threat.'

Tara glanced across at Tom Hitchens. Tom stepped nearer to the Captain.

'Sir, I agree that it's unlikely to be a threat. It's far more likely that they're asylum seekers. But do we really want them on board? If we take this lot, God knows how many other locals may do the same. Think of the complications.'

Cameron thought for a moment. 'I'm sure you're right, and I'll probably regret it, but they've taken one hell of a chance coming out here, and I'd hate to think what will happen to them if they get caught on the way back.' He reached again for the microphone. 'Can you winch them in, Kestrel Two?'

'Roger. We'll try. Out.'

The boatman held his craft as steady as he could, and helped get the terrified mites into the harnesses. The two helicopters shared the task. It took a good fifteen minutes before Theresa went swinging aloft too. The winchman came back down for the boatman, but he shook his head, waved goodbye, and swung the tiller round. Before the second helicopter was gone, the little boat was already making its way back towards the coast.

The helicopters touched down, and the charges were taken inside, where blankets had been piled up in expectation. As Theresa came inside, clutching Sasha, Robert Young made a point of going up to her, smiling reassuringly, trying not to stare at the bruising on her face. Grace had come down too and stood behind him, watching the woman as she opened her bag and took out the pouch. She looked at the braid on Robert's shoulders.

'Are you the captain?'

'No, but if that's for him, I can deliver it.'

Theresa pulled it back sharply. Robert tried hard not to show any reaction.

'We need to know who you are and why you are here.'

'I will tell only the captain.'

Grace touched his arm. 'Robert, can I make a suggestion? She may need time to recover. If you can get someone to look

102

after the other kids, why don't you let me take her and the child to my cabin?'

The return journey had been easier and the boatman was close to the coast. He zigzagged a little, checking the beach for any movement. He knew he wouldn't be able to get the boat over the dunes single-handed, but if he could drag it clear of the water, he would get help in the morning.

He revved it up a little to give more momentum, and as it veered into the shore, he cut the engine, deftly pulled the outboard up, hopped over the edge and put his back into pulling it up.

The guards watched until he had berthed it firmly on the sand before stepping forward to surround him, their automatic rifles trained on his chest.

They waited expectantly in the small briefing room beyond the Ops Room, Cameron, Hitchens, Wynn, Young and Wings. Grace came in, carrying the pouch. She sat down and looked straight at Cameron.

'You may have more than you bargained for. The woman is Theresa Endebbe . . . Yes, the Opposition leader's wife. Two days ago, when her husband was away from Kindalu campaigning, some of Nabote's men paid her a visit. She thinks his son was the ringleader. They murdered her seven-year-old son in front of her and her daughter – the one she won't let go of – and gang-raped her. They carved Nabote's initials on her breasts.'

Wings shuddered. 'Jesus.'

'Her husband reckoned that the only safe thing was to get them out to this ship.'

Tom nodded. 'So who are the other children?'

103

'They've all been orphaned by Nabote.'

Wynn crossed her arms and looked at Cameron. 'Sir, this is a real hot potato.'

For a second Grace glared at Tara.

'There's more.' She handed the pouch to Cameron. 'This is for you. It contains some photographs. Some are shots of Presidential Guards behaving not very nicely in a village; others are of activity at the eastern border. There's also a letter to you from her husband. She told me the gist. Apparently he believes that after the election Nabote won't just be stealing assets from the Lobus, he may round up the whole tribe and march them out of the country. He's mining the border to stop them coming back.'

'Operation March.' Almost as soon as he'd said it, Robert bit his tongue. Wynn and Hitchens glared at him. Grace noticed the reaction.

'What did you say, Robert?'

'Oh, nothing.'

Cameron intervened. 'Grace, none of this is for publication, right?'

Before Grace could argue, he went on.

'That letter was personal. In any case, anything you wrote in your paper – even the fact that she's here – would obviously put Michael Endebbe in grave jeopardy.'

Grace pulled a disappointed face. She was under severe pressure. Jason had sent her another shitty email, saying the editor thought she was fucking up big time. For the first time since she'd stepped on *Indomitable*, she had a good angle. And now this man was taking it away from her. To make it worse, he was probably right.

'It sounds like I don't have much choice.'

Cameron was still recalibrating the extent to which the arrival of Endebbe's wife had changed the situation. Whether they liked it or not, Grace now possessed a key piece of intelligence. He'd watched her face when Robert made his faux pas, and was pretty sure she'd twigged that this wasn't the first they'd heard of Nabote's plans. Up to a point they could try to pressurise her not to use it. However, it might be smarter to try to get her onside. Trusting journalists was deeply against his religion, but exceptional circumstances sometimes called for unusual measures.

'Tom, can you please pass the map of the region? It's right behind you . . .' They spread it out. He pored over it for a while then looked up at Grace.

'I'm going to tell you something in confidence, and I expect you to respect it.'

He looked penetratingly at her. Tara looked appalled. Grace nodded, and Cameron continued.

'That phrase Robert let slip – Operation March – is something our intelligence people have picked up. They also identified some strange goings-on along the eastern border, but had no idea what it was about. They wondered if Nabote was planning on invading Zania, but that made no sense unless he was desperate to distract attention from his domestic difficulties. Even by African standards, Zania is poor and has damn-all strategic or economic value.'

He gestured to the map. 'See here. The border with Zania is tiny – not much more than three hundred miles. As you can see, Zania's shaped like a dagger. It gradually widens as you go east, and that's where its main land mass, its capital, and the great bulk of its population are. One of the reasons is that the land near its western border is virtually uninhabitable. It's all swamp badlands. It's too wet for trees to grow, there's not much to eat and it's infested with tsetse flies. If a large group was abandoned there without food, shelter and medicine, only the fittest would survive more than two weeks. There would be little Zania could do about it – even if their government wanted to. Any international relief operation would take too long to mount, especially if Numala was trying to suppress news of what was happening. The net result is that Nabote wouldn't have to murder a single Lobu – this would be nature's own holocaust.'

105

There was silence. Cameron looked at the photos and passed them around, then read the letter. He handed it to Tom, who took in the contents and nodded.

'What do you think, sir?'

'For now all we can do is to get this lot digitised and sent off to London and *Tenacious*.'

Young picked up the letter and photos and put them carefully back in the pouch. The others had already stood up and he joined them filing out. Cameron called after Grace and asked her to stay. She sat back down. He waited carefully until the door was closed behind the others.

'First, thank you for the way you handled that.'

'That's okay.'

'I have a favour to ask of you. The ship's company have been pretty down in the dumps. They were diverted away at the last minute from something they'd been looking forward to, and had worked hard to prepare for. Since we've been stuck here, apart from one brief flurry of excitement with the attack boats, we've been literally drifting with the currents. Now they've watched day after day of television news saying it's a balls up, that we're wasting our time. They know nothing about African politics, and they don't see what the situation has to do with them anyway. What they *do* know is it's the thirteenth of December, Christmas is coming and there's little sign that they'll get home in time. Now, in addition to everything else, they're going to have to play nursemaid to a bunch of kids.'

Nothing he'd said had come as a surprise to Grace. She'd picked up some of the grumbles, especially in the petty officers' and seamen's messes.

'I think it would be better if they knew who our guests are, what happened to them and why they are here. I plan to make a broadcast to the whole ship tomorrow morning. It would help if Mrs Endebbe was prepared to say a few words herself. It seems that she's responded well to you, and you're probably more likely to get her to agree than any of us . . . If

106

she does, since you're the only skilled writer on board, perhaps you'd be willing to help her prepare a short statement.'

Grace thought about it for a second. 'Okay. But I think she's in too much of a state tonight. I'll have a word with her first thing, see what she says.'

'If she's not up to reading it herself, would you do it on her behalf?'

She nodded.

'Thank you. I appreciate it.'

Grace got up and left him. She was still resentful about losing her story, but the chat at the end had gone some way towards restoring her spirits. At least doing something would be better than just hanging around for something to happen that she *could* write about. The way he'd taken her into his confidence warmed her, made her feel part of the team. For the first time she could understand why they all hung on his words.

She got little sleep that night. Whenever she drifted off, she was jolted awake by Sasha's crying. Theresa hummed gently to try to soothe the poor child and uttered snatches of prayers. Once Grace was woken by a terrible scream. She shot upright, banging her head on the bunk above. But it was only Theresa in her dreams. The piercing sound had roused the child, though. She began crying, woke her mother and the cycle of lament started again.

10

Breakfasts were good in *Tenacious*. Simon had shovelled a second sausage into his mouth. Chewing contentedly, he watched as Owen Lewis came in, helped himself to a more modest breakfast and sat at the next seat. Lewis emptied a small glass of orange juice and turned to him.

'What did you make of the signal from *Indomitable*?'

Simon bit off a corner of toast. 'Heavy duty stuff, eh? Fits with the satellite pictures.'

'And the mention you picked up before of "Long March".'

Simon emptied the remains of the sugar bowl into his coffee. 'On the other hand, it could just be Endebbe shit-stirring. He knows that with all the rigging, he's going to lose the election. He must be aware that, as things stand today, sending *Indomitable* down here has backfired horrif-ically. If he could give us a reason to intervene now – before the election – who knows what might happen? Nabote could be forced out, and Endebbe would be wait-ing in the wings with his message of "No more Mr Bad Guy".'

'So you think he concocted the whole thing?'

Simon stirred his coffee and reflected. 'If he did, he's one bad sonofabitch. If his wife was caught with those materials, I hate to think what would have happened to her.'

'Mmmm.'

'And even if she didn't get captured or drowned getting out to the ship, she'd have to be a consummate actress to play the part of the brutalised, traumatised victim, never once letting the mask slip. I can't see many women volunteering to have their tits carved just for cover. Not to mention the risk that her five-year-old spills the beans. Remember what W. C. Fields said about acting with children or animals.'

One of the other operators came in. 'Sorry to interrupt, sir. Can Simon come right away? We've just picked up another burst of Korean.'

Lewis was curious enough to follow them back to their station and wait till Simon listened twice to the tape. He pulled the headset down to his neck.

'They've caught and tortured the boatman. He's told them who he took out to *Indomitable*.'

'What about the letter and the pictures?'

'All he knew was that Endebbe gave his wife something for the captain. Sounds like the brown stuff's hitting the air conditioning in Kindalu big time.'

'We'd better tell Fleet and Cameron.'

*

Tom Hitchens was still slightly cool with Grace, but it was usually easier if Tara wasn't around. At last Grace had found an opportunity for a one-to-one with him over lunch. It was unfortunate timing that, just as he was approaching the punchline of some tired old joke, Robert Young bounded up.

'Scuse me, sir.'

Tom had no choice but to break off.

'Grace, can you spare a moment?'

'Can't it wait?'

'No, come quick. There's something I want you to see.'

Grace smiled apologetically to Hitchens and followed Robert at a trot.

'Where are we going?'

'You'll see.'

It was Billy Ward's mess deck. Grace gasped as they entered. In the confined space Billy, Charlie and Phil had rigged up a puppet show. All the children were sitting on the floor, spellbound. Grace noticed that even Sasha was coming out of her shell enough to smile shyly.

Robert, unnoticed by the kids, gave a thumbs-up to Billy. Grace beamed too. Billy nodded as quietly they slipped back out. Back in the passageway, Robert stopped for a word.

'Your broadcast did the trick, Grace. And the experts in *Tenacious* say that Endebbe's line seems to mesh with what they've picked up . . . There's one bit of less good news, I'm afraid. Nabote knows that Endebbe's wife is on board.'

'How?'

'They captured the boatman and "persuaded" him to tell them. Nabote's gone public with it.'

'Does that mean I can write about it?'

'Not about the boatman, because we got that . . . discreetly. But about the fact that she's here, yes, no problem. Tara wasn't too sure about it, but the captain overruled her. You might want to check with Theresa first.'

'I'll ask her now.'

'Why not invite her to dinner in the wardroom tonight? The captain's coming.'

*

It was a particularly happy evening. CNN had picked up the comment on Numalan Radio about Theresa. Although they were doubtful of Endebbe's motives for sending her to the ship, at least it looked to the world that *Indomitable* was doing something. Morale was now soaring, and no one was whingeing about Christmas. Theresa was sitting with Young, Dewar and Wings, and together they had coaxed a few words and even one half smile from her. Even Tara and Tom came and joined the group for coffee. Grace found herself alone at the end of the table with Cameron. She smiled at him.

'Can I make a confession?'

'Shall I call the padre?'

Grace smiled again. 'Before I came here, I checked the press files on you.'

'And?'

'You have a son who got into trouble with the police and blamed it on you.'

'Is this an interview?'

'Off the record. *Really.*'

Cameron decided to trust her a little. The way Grace had handled Theresa's arrival had made him warm to her. She'd shown more decency than he'd expected from a journalist.

'In my early twenties I got someone pregnant. I have no idea to this day whether it really was mine. It wasn't exactly a long-term relationship – more like a three-night stand. I agreed to pay all the child's costs, but when I refused to marry the girl, she denied me all access. I don't imagine I'd have enjoyed the version she told the boy. When I tried writing to him, I never got a reply. I found out later that he'd been in trouble with the police from the age of thirteen. The first I heard about it was when the press doorstepped me. He'd been busted for pushing drugs in Miami. His lawyer went for the broken-home sympathy vote, and didn't let the truth get in the way of good advocacy. You've read it. You know what they said about me.'

'Do you blame him?'

'Good God, no. I can understand why he's mad at me.'

'Would you want to see him?'

'I don't think he would have the slightest interest, and probably the moment's passed for me too.'

'Why wouldn't you marry her?'

'We hardly knew each other. An unplanned pregnancy with a virtual stranger strikes me as a pretty dumb reason to get hitched.'

'Did that make you more cautious about relationships?'

'It certainly did. Junior navy officers aren't paid a fortune. I wasn't sure I could finance another mistake.'

111

'I can imagine . . . D'you mind if I ask another question?'

'More scandals?'

'Yup. The papers made a big fuss when you ran off with the wife of some Tory MP. How do you plead to this one?'

'Guilty as hell.'

'Are you still with her?'

'Charlotte? I wish I knew. I think she's left me.'

'Same reason?'

'Pretty much . . . Maybe swearing to love, honour and obey the navy was as much of a vow as I could handle.'

'The navy lark seems to have gone better, apart from one minor court martial.'

Cameron laughed. 'I feel like I'm on *This is Your Life*. When do I get to hear the dirt on you, eh?'

Grace smiled and ignored him. 'I've left the best bit till last. You got a medal for something in the Falklands, right? What did you do?'

'I misheard an order.'

Grace watched, waiting to see if he would launch into the story. It seemed he wasn't planning to, so she let it pass.

'So, what happens next? Here, I mean.'

'I suppose it depends how Nabote's efforts with the African Union and the Commonwealth work out. There's no doubt that Theresa coming here has upped the ante. As you saw on TV, Nabote is claiming that we actively colluded with the Opposition in spiriting her out here. But I hope that any fallout will be outweighed by the importance of the additional intelligence we've picked up. That might be enough to convince the US and the Europeans. At a minimum the Foreign Secretary should warn Nabote publicly not to move against the Lobus. Better still, an international force could be stationed in the border area rapidly to inspect what he's done there and pre-empt his next step.'

'So you're optimistic?'

'Christ knows what goes on in the heads of politicians, but having taken a fair bit of flak for sending us down here, the government would be mad to pass up the chance to show that they were right in the first place.'

'So it looks like Christmas afloat? I hope you've got some turkey in those big fridges.'

*

Jason was knackered. He'd had a couple of heavy nights. So he left his mates in the bar in Clerkenwell, grabbed a cab and was back home in Hoxton by quarter to eleven. He got a Grolsch from the fridge, sprawled on the sofa and flicked over the satellite channels.

A story was breaking. After a late-night session in Addis Ababa, the African Union had issued a resolution condemning the UK. The TV station had got experts from the UK, America and other countries lining up to put the boot in to the British government. They were showing a clip of Patrick Dawnay having eggs thrown at him when he'd emerged earlier in the evening from a Council of Ministers meeting in Brussels. A consensus was forming that there must be more to this Theresa Endebbe tale than met the eye. It didn't help that no one seemed to be able to say whether she was seeking asylum in the UK and, if not, when and under what circumstances she would go back to Kindalu. The item ended with reporters in Tokyo saying that the Prime Minister had just stepped off his plane at the start of his Asian tour and had been forced to dodge a barrage of questions about Numala.

Jason had a swig from the bottle and grinned. What a fuck up. And what a wasted opportunity. He hoped the editor realised what *he* would have made of this story, given the chance. Grace was fine at features, where you did your homework well in advance, met the subject, who invariably was promoting a film, a book or a restaurant and had every reason to want to be helpful. If you liked them, you wrote a positive piece. If you thought they were tossers, you knifed them, unless they knew the editor, of course. It was simple stuff. There was no need whatever for true journalist's instincts, catching the mood of the moment, setting an agenda rather than reacting to it.

There had been many acid mutterings about Grace's performance at the morning meetings, and plenty of people had stopped by his desk to chat about it. However much he stood up for her, it was clear they all thought she'd blown a huge opportunity. If the government were forced to pull the carrier out, Dawnay would have egg on his face as well as his suit, and Grace's last chance would have gone.

If the editor was sufficiently pissed off, he might even lever her out. Not right away, of course, but after a decent interval. He supposed she would get another job on some paper eventually. Not on any of the broadsheets, though, after a fiasco like this. What would that mean for the two of them? He would have to do some hard thinking about the future. Their wedding day was getting close. If Grace's career was going to stall, how would she handle it as he forged ahead? Would she want to quit work altogether, or would she be content languishing where she was? And how much strain would her growing frustration put on the relationship?

Looking back, they'd both been impetuous, getting engaged so soon. Around that time, several of his mates had signed up their life partners, and he hadn't wanted to feel left out. In fact, he'd trumped the whole bunch. Having a black fiancée – specially one looking like Grace – had been exceptionally cool. As for himself, he'd always honestly felt that the race point didn't matter. Of course, you couldn't rule out the possibility that as the years went by they would find there were bigger cultural differences than they'd imagined. If so, what would that mean for their children? Would it be fair to them? It was the sort of thing you had to think through properly, out of fairness to all concerned.

The eleven o'clock bulletin was coming on. Time to see what Sky were saying about it . . . Shit, who the hell was that?

He went over to the entryphone, pressed a button and

listened. He had a very big rule about uninvited guests. This one would get one hell of a bollocking, time like this.

*

Theresa and Sasha had been moved to a cabin of their own, which meant that Grace could really zonk, and when she finally awoke it was well past nine. As she expected, they'd pretty much finished serving breakfast in the wardroom, but a kindly steward got her some coffee, toast and marmalade.

Ten minutes later she was on her way to the bridge. She stretched as she came in and smiled happily. 'Morning, everyone.'

No one replied. Cameron stared straight ahead. Wynn and Hitchens were discussing a signal. Only Robert turned and greeted her, in all but a whisper.

'What's the matter? . . . Hey, why are we sailing so fast? . . . Where's the coast?'

Robert could hardly look her in the eye. 'We're sixty miles from Kindalu. We got new orders three hours ago.'

'To do what?'

'To sail back to Portsmouth.'

'What the *hell* do you mean?'

When Robert hesitated, Tara willingly stepped into the breach.

'The African Union has issued a resolution condemning the UK. The presidents of six African countries have said that Britain should be kicked out of the Commonwealth. France and Germany have distanced themselves publicly. Parliament is up in arms. Number Ten's terrified that the rumpus will ruin the PM's Asian tour. In short, the Foreign Secretary's gamble has gone wrong and he's cutting his losses.'

'What about Endebbe's letter?'

Robert explained. 'The Foreign Office say it's conjecture. Nothing they can act on.'

115

'Bollocks . . . So that's it? No intervention. No pressure on Nabote. If he wants to massacre the Lobus, he can do it with impunity?'

Robert stepped closer, trying to show sympathy, but Grace was in no mood for that.

'How Nabote must be crowing. He huffs and puffs and the brave little British sailors all scurry away.'

Wynn looked daggers at her. Hitchens, too, looked affronted. Grace didn't care. Nothing was going to stop her.

'You're all as bad as politicians. Is a million deaths only a statistic to you? You know, for five minutes I believed you were real people, who actually cared about doing the right thing, rather than worrying about your own careers. What a fool I was . . .'

Robert tried once again. 'Grace, all we can do is put our point of view. The captain tried hard, believe me. In the end we have no choice but to follow orders.'

Grace was having none of it. 'The captain doesn't mind mishearing orders when it suits him. I bet it'd be different if a million whites were about to be killed . . . But in those circumstances, he might have a better chance of another medal.'

There was a sharp intake of breath from Tara. Robert looked horrified, Hitchens very angry. If they thought Grace was abashed, they were wrong.

'You know what I think about you lot?'

Cameron turned towards her.

'What?'

She stared right back at him. 'There isn't one of you worthy of the uniform you're wearing.'

Above the distant thrum of the machine, you could have heard a pin drop. They all turned to Cameron for a lead. He looked right at Grace.

'Is Mrs Endebbe awake? I should go and tell her.'

'Don't bother. I'll do your dirty work.'

'No, thank you.'

He brushed past her and left.

Theresa sat silently. Sasha was on her lap, playing with a tiny wooden doll. Cameron tried to explain what had happened. He did not add that he had challenged the orders three times before they were confirmed. Nor that he tried strenuously to persuade them to let him send a clandestine marine mission into the hinterland to corroborate the evidence of the border mining.

Yet again he expressed profound regret. She didn't reply. Sasha wriggled out from her mother's grasp and ran the few paces towards Cameron, holding the doll out for inspection. Before he could take it, Theresa lunged forward and snatched the child back. Cameron stood up.

'I'm very sorry.'

'If you didn't mean to help, you should not have come and given us hope . . . I will ask God to forgive you.'

He nodded, stood up and left. A lieutenant stepped out of his way, surprised that the captain didn't acknowledge his presence.

11

Bob Tiernan was under pressure. After he'd left the Foreign Ministry three days before, he'd told his driver to take him home, suspecting that the crowd outside the High Commission could only have grown more hostile. However, his house a mile away had turned out to be little better. There were two Presidential Guards holding at bay a gang of thirty or forty youths chanting and throwing stones. The driver stopped fifty yards away and, at Tiernan's order, reversed and got the hell out the moment they saw the mob running down the street towards them.

Bob assumed that it was the guards who had recruited the yobs. After all, he and Alice didn't live anywhere half as fancy as the Fairfaxes' official residence. Why should the youths of Kindalu suddenly be so aware of the domestic whereabouts of a relatively junior diplomat? With nowhere else to go, they headed back to the High Commission. Bob could see that his driver was close to panic and had to force him to slow down as they approached the wrought-iron gates. All they needed now was to mow down a local teenager. He noticed the film crew and the relaxed look on the face of the guards as the missiles rained down on the roof of the Jaguar. Perhaps it would've been better if he'd driven his own Landie instead of using Roger's official car. It would certainly need a respray. As soon as he made it inside, he told the driver to clear off home and not come back till the fuss had died down. He had planned to do the same with the other local employees, but he found that they'd beaten him to it.

Since then he'd lived on coffee, bottled water and a generous supply of digestive biscuits. If things went on like this, he'd just have to run the gauntlet and go in search of food. At least it was good for him in one sense: he'd developed a bit of a beer belly and had been meaning for ages to give up smoking. It was a pity there was nowhere comfortable to sleep. He tried Roger's high-backed chair, tried his own shorter version, tried the floor, and never got more than the odd hour. He was unshaven, exhausted, increasingly malodorous, yet not too downcast. His hunch was that this was all government-inspired posturing; they would gain nothing by harming him. Apprehensive as he was, he was enjoying being in a real diplomatic storm, and nothing would have persuaded him to swap with Roger Fairfax, twiddling his thumbs in damp Dulwich.

Keeping in touch was another thing. As long as the power was working, either from the dodgy mains or their diesel generator, the satellite dish on the roof should keep the telegrams coming. However, email depended on the landlines working. It was a relief that the mobile network, set up three years before by a Spanish company, usually held up robustly, if only because so many top Numalans depended on it, and made sure that their best engineers kept it going. Since his confinement had started, Bob had relied on his little Nokia.

The only thing the building lacked was a normal radio. If he was going to listen to what promised to be an important broadcast, he would have to go out and sit in the Jaguar and take the jeers in good part as he drove it round to the back of the building.

Nathan Nabote basked in the riotous applause of his most rabid supporters. He had played for formidable odds and won. When the carrier sat there, visible from every hill in

119

Kindalu, it had not only been an insult to Numala, but a challenge to him personally. His informants had told him that it was giving hope and confidence to those who opposed him. If it had remained there much longer, it could have set off a serious wave of unrest which might have snowballed. The Europeans might have felt emboldened to force-search the border area. Although he had a cover story prepared, it was hard to explain convincingly the need for the area to be mined. It would have been another hammer blow to his reputation in Africa. The Americans, who had up to now shown little interest, might have felt the need to support a move against Numala in the Security Council. If it got raised there, his country could muster perilously few friends. The momentum to unseat him would have gathered both internationally and at home until it became unstoppable.

Although he had shared this with no one, bar the Governor of the Bank of Numala, he had long been preparing for the risk of trouble. He had villas in Switzerland, Cap Ferrat and Corfu. His bank accounts in Liechtenstein, the Cook Islands and Turks and Caicos were stuffed fat to ensure a lavish exile for him and his family. However, that was only a backup. He regarded himself as President for life, and, if he was ever to hand over the reins while he drew breath, it should be to Julius and nobody else. And Julius was still a hothead, and far from ready.

Now he had turned the prospect of defeat into glorious victory. The Opposition had been cowed when they heard that the carrier had gone. Endebbe was now in hiding, his credibility in smithereens. Nabote hoped that, wherever he was, that hated man was listening to the broadcast of this rally. It would be a perfect way for him to learn what else fate had in store for him.

Resplendent in a gold and red gown and hat, holding the ceremonial spear of a Ganda chieftain, he held up a hand to silence the crowd. Nabote waited patiently in front of the bank of microphones for the cacophony to die down.

'This is a great day for Numala, for Africa, a great day for every one of you, man or woman, girl or boy. The British thought they could send a gunboat called *Indomitable* and subjugate us as they did in days of Empire. They thought they could make us their slaves again. But did we let them?'

A shout went up from the crowd. Nabote smiled and cupped his ear.

'I cannot hear you.'

The roar of 'No' was louder.

'Now say it so loud they can hear it in the British Parliament.'

This time it was thunderous. They began a chant of 'No! No! No!', waving their arms above their heads and dancing to the rhythm of it.

He held his hand up again.

'It was not the British who were *indomitable*. Their sailors are now running away like frightened rabbits. What was *indomitable* was the Numalan people.'

Six miles due west of Kindalu, *Tenacious* cruised gently beneath the surface, its antennae a few feet above the water. Owen Lewis, Simon Charters and several officers were gathered listening to the broadcast.

'Through fearless strength and courage, the Numalan people defeated the would-be imperialists and drove them away . . .' The crackle of more cheers. 'I would like to say that every Numalan rejoiced at this. Sadly I cannot make such a statement. To his undying shame, one base villain welcomed the British here, invited them to stay longer, wanted them to come in and crush us. He did not have the courage to go to them himself, so he sent a woman . . .' There were sounds of mocking derision in the crowd. 'Yes, it is true. Even now, as this ship scuttles home, his wife remains on board . . . But it was not only his wife this coward sent to the carrier. He gave

121

her Numalan state documents to sell to the British for thirty pieces of silver . . .'

Nabote gave them time to work themselves up into more of a fury before continuing.

'Is it not unbelievable . . .'

The priest had withdrawn and left them to listen alone. The aide sat with his ear pressed to the transistor radio. Michael Endebbe was only inches away.

'I repeat, is it not unbelievable that any Numalan should commit such a heinous crime? . . . But when the man in question aspires to be president of the very country he has betrayed, it is *obscene*. It is the highest form of treason imaginable . . . What do you think? Should this man answer for his crimes?'

They were baying for it.

'Are you sure?'

'Yes, yes, *yes!*'

'Very well, I will obey your command. A warrant will be issued today for his arrest. However, we will show the world – yes, even the perfidious British – that we Numalans are respecters of democracy. It will be the people who will be Endebbe's true judge. Neither the courts nor I will prevent him from contesting the election on Thursday. If he wins, I will accept this. However, I have full confidence that the Numalan people will never vote for a traitor. And if he loses, as surely he will, he will face the full force of the law.'

The jubilation was lost in a storm of noisy distortion. The aide turned the volume down.

'What will you do?'

'I will give myself up.'

'Michael, you *cannot*.'

Endebbe sounded strangely calm. 'Wherever I go, sooner or later, they will find me. I do not want Nabote to have the satisfaction of saying I ran away.'

'You know he will kill you.'

'I have known that for a long time.'

'I will come with you.'

'No . . . That will accomplish nothing. You have no wife, but you have a sister and brothers. Make sure they are safe.'

*

Cameron was alone in his cabin. His supper had come and gone, untouched. He could not get rid of this uncomfortable feeling, and couldn't get Grace's words out of his head. Was she wrong when she said it would be different if it were a million whites? And her comment about them being unworthy of the uniform? Why did this woman have the power to trouble him so much? Was it just because her remark had inevitably triggered in him the question of how Nelson would have reacted if someone had declared him unfit to wear his uniform? Immoderately, of course. But, apart from in his colourful personal life, would Nelson ever have conducted himself in a way that this would have been conceivable? He reached into a drawer and pulled out the portfolio. In one of the letters there was a passage he wanted to find.

There was a knock at the door.

'Hello, Tom, what is it?'

'Sorry to bother you, sir. Thought you'd like to see this signal.'

'More news from Kindalu?'

Hitchens nodded. 'They've decided to name yesterday a national holiday in perpetuity. December the fifteenth will be known as *Indomitable Day*.'

'Great.'

'There's more news, I'm afraid. Endebbe's been captured and tried.'

Cameron put his hand to his forehead.

'You don't have to tell me the verdict. What's the sentence?'

'Death.'

123

'What happened to Nabote's promise to let him fight the election?'

'He didn't mention the small print. He's now saying that Endebbe can campaign from his prison cell. After he loses, he will be executed immediately.'

'Does his wife know?'

'I ran across Grace on my way here. She offered to break the news herself. I told her I'd have to check with you first, but she gave me rather short shrift. I didn't think there was much I could do to stop her. Hope you don't mind, sir.'

Cameron took a deep breath. 'No, it's probably for the best.'

Tara Wynn appeared behind them at the open door. 'Sir, CNN have announced that Endebbe will be publicly executed.'

Hitchens waved the signal from *Tenacious*. Cameron nodded. 'We know.'

Billy and Trish had exchanged some banter while tapping away at their consoles. Phil, Charlie and Carol joined in too. It had been joyless. They would be home by Christmas, no doubt about it, but there would be no tinsel on the tree.

Charlie noticed that the door to the MCO was being pushed slightly ajar, and stood up to investigate. When he pulled it open, one eight-year-old, who'd been pushing hard against it, almost fell over. Behind him was a whole host of kids, and bringing up the rear, a harassed-looking young female rating. They all charged past Charlie and over to where Billy sat. Sasha was in the vanguard of the little mob. She called out.

'Billy, Billy.'

Billy looked down and reached to pick her up.

'How the 'ell did you get 'ere?'

The rating looked abashed. 'Sorry, Billy. She wouldn't take no for an answer. I'm looking after her since her mum . . .'

Billy nodded and smiled at Sasha. 'What d'you want, eh?'

From her pocket, Sasha pulled out her doll and pointed at the other children.

'What? You want me to make toys for all them too?'

Sasha nodded.

'Okay, okay, I'll make 'em tonight . . .'

Sasha threw herself forward and gave Billy a big kiss.

'Now you better let me get on with my job.'

The rating shepherded the giggling group together and ushered them out the door. Sasha gave Billy a final wave. Billy waved back, muttering under his breath to Trish.

'Breaks your fuckin' 'eart, don't it?'

Cameron and Grace were standing opposite each other in a passageway. Young was with them, keeping tactfully quiet. From time to time, sailors passed by, trying not to catch their eyes. After a long silence, Cameron spoke up.

'How is she?'

'What do you expect?' None of the fire had gone from Grace's voice. 'She wants you to get her back there.'

'That's mad. She'd be accused of treason and killed too. Even if we thought it right, we're two days' sailing away from there, and well out of helo range.'

'Then turn back south . . .'

Grace didn't expect him to reply, and he didn't.

'You're not going to do anything to help, so let's not waste any more time talking . . . By the way, I sent you a copy of the piece I filed. My editor was complaining that I was too uncritical of you guys. I don't think he'll do that this time.'

Young watched as she walked off and looked back at the captain.

'Sir, I don't want to overstep the mark here, but you ought to know that feelings are running high among the ship's company.'

'You think I don't know?'

'Some of the officers feel so strongly that they're wondering if it's worth trying again to persuade London . . . I've discussed it with the other HoDs.'

Cameron's eyes narrowed a fraction. 'You have?'

'Yes, sir.'

'Then you'd better get them together.'

They gathered. This time, more than ever, they found Cameron's expression hard to read. Would he be sympathetic or tear a strip a foot wide off them? Hitchens, in particular, was feeling twitchy. If this was a thoroughly bad idea, he was the one who should have stamped on it. When Young had proposed it, that had been his first instinct, but Robert's passion had overwhelmed his defences. Tara Wynn wasn't much happier. Until she'd heard that Tom was part of this, she had sucked through her teeth. Now as she sensed his anxiety, she felt very ill at ease. Even Wings picked up the mood. Though his gut feeling was clear enough, he was less than sure how well he could articulate his views if challenged.

Hitchens defaulted to Robert to put the case. Even to Robert's own ears, his arguments sounded less convincing than earlier. When his voice died away, Cameron nodded slowly and looked round the room, carefully surveying their faces.

'So you all think I should make a personal appeal direct to the CDS? May I ask, who here thinks it would make the slightest difference?'

His voice was arid with scepticism. There was no answer, so he prompted one.

'Tom?'

Hitchens shifted uncomfortably. He didn't want to drop Robert in it.

'Frankly, no, sir, but I see no harm in trying.'

Cameron's gaze switched to Young.

'Sir, you're the nearest they have to a man on the ground. We should definitely try it.'

'Tara?'

Wynn took her time to answer. She was trying to imply that she was less than fully committed, without too obviously distancing herself.

'In principle, I'm in favour. Provided we can be confident that it won't reflect poorly on you, sir.'

Cameron smiled inwardly at that one. 'You, Wings?'

'You never know, sir. Now that the death sentence has been passed, they could be wavering in London. It's your call, of course, but I'd be inclined to give it a go, even if it's a one per cent chance.'

Cameron looked back at Wings. 'Want to know what I think? I think it's a nil per cent chance . . .' He looked around all the faces again. 'However, if you're unanimous that I should give it a go, that's what I'll do. As you all know, this is sensationally irregular, going over the heads of Commander-in-Chief Fleet and the First Sea Lord. I have no idea whatsoever if the CDS will take the call . . . All I can do is try. Tom, would you ask Ward to try to get through on the video link?'

12

It took Billy Ward an hour to set up the call. When Cameron came down to the briefing room so he could take it alone, Billy was making a last-minute adjustment.

'We've finally tracked him down, sir. He's currently with the Foreign Secretary. They're asking whether you mind if we patch the call through there.'

Cameron raised his eyebrows. That was the last thing he'd expected, and he wasn't sure he was happy about it. However, he was in no position to refuse. He nodded and Ward pressed another button. Soon a jerky picture appeared on the TV screen. Billy gestured the captain to sit, and checked that the tiny set-top camera was adjusted correctly.

'Okay, sir. I'll leave you to it. I'll be right outside if you need me.'

The incoming call from *Indomitable* had caused much surprise in Whitehall, where they were in damage-limitation mode. The Foreign Office had all but admitted publicly that it had been a fiasco. Patrick Dawnay was fighting to avoid being shunted into any sort of formal apology, either to Parliament or, even worse, to Nabote. The closest he had got was to send their chargé d'affaires in Kindalu round to the Foreign Ministry to hand over a note indicating that Britain had no plans for any other naval vessels to visit the region for the foreseeable future. Toby Gordon-Booth had calculated that this private assurance might encourage Nabote to tone down his public pronouncements.

The MoD was aggrieved at having been bounced into a no-win mission. In an era when the navy was keen to look relevant and purposeful, the last thing they needed was an episode like this. They were all unhappy that the Defence Secretary had neither challenged the original premise, nor was in the trenches with them now as the Foreign Office sought to deflect the blame for a botched job, claiming that it was Cameron's decision to take Mrs Endebbe on board that had doomed the initiative.

The CDS's dialogue with the Foreign Secretary was plumbing new depths when the message came through that Cameron wanted to speak urgently with him. It was the Private Secretary's idea that they should take the call together. Perhaps handling the matter jointly, rather than antagonistically, might help mend relations. Video-conferencing gear had been installed in the Foreign Secretary's office two years before, and one of the Assistant Private Secretaries had become a dab hand at making it work. The two main men took up position opposite the camera, leaving Toby Gordon-Booth, Crispin Adair and the other officials sitting in the background. The CDS recognised the image flickering through.

'That's him now . . . Good afternoon, Captain Cameron. In view of the political importance of this matter, we decided to take your call together.'

A voice penetrated the static. 'That's quite all right, sir.'

The Foreign Secretary was already looking impatient. The man's face brought back unpleasant memories.

'We understand you have something important to say to us.'

There was another satellite delay. Dawnay was just about to repeat himself when Cameron's voice came on.

'We in *Indomitable* feel that the situation has changed fundamentally since we were ordered away from Numala. It is not only the death sentence on Endebbe. We've seen the intelligence which *Tenacious* has picked up today about a plan to purge the army of Lobus. That would be a natural step before seeking to expel the whole tribe. I am increasingly convinced that the views expressed in Endebbe's letter to me are correct and what Nabote is planning is genocide. If we turn a blind eye, we will have the Lobus' blood on our hands.'

Dawnay leaned forward.

'Captain Cameron, we have shared all the intelligence with our allies. Their assessment is essentially the same as ours – that there is no clear proof of any such intentions, and that we cannot act without it.'

'With respect, Secretary of State, by the time you have clear proof, it will be too late.'

Dawnay looked crossly sideways at the CDS and back at the camera.

'May we get to the point? Do you have any new information?'

'No.'

'Then we should leave it there. This situation is more complex than you appear to realise. After Iraq, we cannot afford another damaging split with our European allies. They will not support an international operation, and unilateral action by Britain is out of the question. There are also other factors which you are not privy to. However, we appreciate your concern and are grateful for your contribution. You have your orders.'

There was a delay, longer than before.

'I'm sorry, I didn't hear that.'

The Foreign Secretary cleared his throat and spoke louder. 'I said, you have your orders.'

They waited for his response.

'Sorry, I'm losing sound altogether now.'

The Assistant Private Secretary turned a knob on the microphone panel. Cameron's voice was still coming through loud and clear.

'If I lose the connection, I presume you'll want me to use my discretion.'

Dawnay was colouring fast. 'No, Cameron, you will do exactly as I . . .'

The picture faded into a snowstorm. Dawnay cursed. Crispin Adair spoke quietly to the assistant.

'Try to get back to him.'

It took time. Some of the officials stayed in their seats. The Foreign Secretary used the time to call his wife. The CDS stroked his chin pensively. A phone rang and the young assistant picked it up, had a brief conversation and turned to the room in general.

'They can't seem to get through on any line.'

Dawnay told him to keep trying and got on with another call. Thirty minutes passed. He glanced up from his desk at the CDS, a superior smile on his face.

'It's really time you bought them better equipment. Can't think what all that defence vote goes on.'

Sir Alan looked back, his expression giving no hint of being offended or amused.

'Let's hope that's the problem.'

Toby Gordon-Booth, who had chuckled at Dawnay's jibe, looked bemused.

'What *are* you on about?'

'Like all our warships, *Indomitable* has multiple communications systems. It would be surprising if this were a technical fault.'

Gordon-Booth snorted derisively. 'What else could it be, for God's sake?'

Sir Alan looked past him at the Private Secretary. 'Is there somewhere I can make a call?'

Adair found him a room nearby. He rang the First Sea Lord and the Director of Naval Operations and asked them to join him right away. The lines to Fleet headquarters in Northwood were soon humming. However, when the CDS finally returned to the Foreign Secretary's office, he brought no good tidings.

'We're doing all we can to make contact. The Commander-in-Chief Fleet has sent a personal signal to Cameron demanding an explanation. We know that *Indomitable*'s receiving; we checked with the satellite ground station and the satcom handshake is still there.'

Dawnay looked unimpressed. 'I don't get it. Surely you don't think that the captain of a Royal Navy ship is refusing to follow orders?'

Sir Alan hesitated. 'I still regard it as unlikely. However, if we don't hear from him soon, I may be forced to change that view.'

'You have too much faith in equipment. A pound to a penny, this is just a technical balls-up. Why on earth would Cameron do such a thing? Unless of course he's gone right off his rocker.'

The CDS shrugged. 'I have no idea.'

They called an awkward truce and the room fell into uncomfortable silence. It took the better part of half an hour before a call came through for the CDS. His own voice fell to a hush as relayed the message.

'*Indomitable* is still not responding. Fleet have reluctantly concluded that they must assume it is a deliberate act.'

For once Crispin Adair looked rattled. Gordon-Booth's face was a picture of utter bafflement. Only the Foreign Secretary articulated it.

'*Fuck.*'

For the first time fear showed on his face. He rounded on the CDS. 'What is the procedure to restore proper command?'

'No navy captain has ever done such a thing. There *is* no procedure.'

'*What?* This is *outrageous.*'

'If it's a personal protest or if Cameron is clearly acting irrationally, his second in command, Commander Hitchens, should take over and quickly re-establish contact. It goes without saying that if that's not the case, and other officers support Cameron in this, the implications will be very much graver.'

Sir Alan paused and scanned the faces. 'The navy needs officers who are intelligent and resourceful, and we place

132

them in situations which every year become more complex and faster moving. Modern communications have seduced us into believing that we can fine-tune reactions in far-off places, as if we had a ten-thousand-mile long screwdriver. However, we have been increasingly aware that one day someone on the spot might decide that he is better placed to judge than we are back here.'

Dawnay's anger was mastering his fear. 'I want that carrier back under control immediately.'

'I share the sentiment, Foreign Secretary, and I have discussed this with the First Sea Lord. If *Indomitable* was surrounded by her escorts, it would be relatively easy. However, in their absence . . .'

'*Tenacious* is down there, isn't it?'

'We can hardly torpedo her.'

Gordon-Booth was anxious to sound helpful. 'Surely it wouldn't take long to fly special forces down there.'

'Probably not. But remember that special forces work best like April Fool pranks – when no one's expecting them. Cameron is a very able officer and it's the first thing he'll anticipate. Don't forget that the SBS are drawn from the Royal Marines. Cameron has fifty marines of his own. Plus, think of the defensive position. That carrier is sailing through high seas at anything up to thirty knots and her flight deck is fifty feet above the water. Not the easiest target, I can tell you.'

The Foreign Secretary was beside himself. 'So, what the hell *can* you do?'

'We could order RFA *Fort George* to detach. If Cameron does not succeed in countermanding the order, that would cut them to around four days of aviation fuel, assuming a normal level of operations. And we can certainly have *Tenacious* shadowing her within twenty-four hours.'

Dawnay was far from satisfied. '*And?*'

'We could send a task force of surface ships with enough marines on board to take *Indomitable* through sheer weight of numbers, hopefully bloodlessly.'

'How long would that take?'

'If *Indomitable* maintains her present northward course, two or three days. If she turns south, as I expect, more like four . . . The Numalan election takes place in three days. Nabote plans to kill Endebbe that same day. I'd wager a year's pay that Cameron intends to get back there by then.'

As the full horror began to dawn, some of the fight drained out of the Foreign Secretary. 'What will he do when he gets there?'

'I don't think he'll deliver a diplomatic note.'

Adair and Gordon-Booth looked at Dawnay. It seemed to spur him to some sort of action. All was not lost yet. If this was a crisis, staying in charge was important.

'Very well. If we don't hear from *Indomitable* within the hour, I expect you to come up with a plan for immediate action . . .' He turned to Adair. 'I'd better wake up the Prime Minister, wherever he is.'

'Seoul.'

'Okay. We need to convene a COBRA Committee meeting. In the circumstances, I propose to chair it myself. I'll clear that with the PM too.' The acronym originated in Cabinet Office Briefing Room A. It is the top-level group for handling defence and foreign affairs crises.

Adair was considering other angles. 'We'll have to think about the press.'

'I want a total media blackout.'

'Don't forget, the *Post* has a reporter on board.'

'Then we must invoke whatever powers we need to stop them using this information. We *must* keep the lid on this until we resolve it.'

'What about our allies?'

Toby Gordon-Booth took up the charge. 'We should try to keep this under wraps as long as possible. The potential for embarrassment is extreme.'

To the surprise of them all, the Assistant Private Secretary tentatively raised a forearm. 'If we've got to try to guess what

Cameron might do, mightn't it be worth getting a psychologist in?'

Dawnay nodded. 'I suppose it would help to know what sort of madman we're dealing with.'

*

Cameron stood at the side of the flight deck, staring through the safety netting down at the ocean. He had been there twenty minutes, Nelson's words ringing in his head.

Robert Young had been looking everywhere for him. He emerged from the door opposite and, leaning against the stiff breeze, fought his way across. He had to shout to be heard.

'What happened, sir?'

'Are the others in the briefing room?'

'Yes.'

'Tell them I'll be in right away.'

Young did as he was told. Cameron gave it another five minutes before he joined the anxious group. Hitchens led off.

'How did it go, sir?'

'I spoke directly with the Foreign Secretary. He said the evidence was too weak for them to take any action.'

There was a silence, broken by Wynn.

'So that's it?' She had expected more of a tussle.

Wings looked deflated. 'Pity. Still, it was worth a try.'

Young nodded in sad agreement. 'Yes. Thank you, sir.'

'He told me we had our orders . . .' The way he left the phrase hanging suggested to Tom that there was more.

'And?'

'I told him I was losing sound contact.'

'What?'

'And that if we couldn't restore it, I'd act at my own discretion.'

Wynn was confused. 'Sir, are you saying we have a comms problem?'

Cameron shook his head.

'I don't understand, sir. You can't mean you've . . .'

'That's right, Tara, I've implied that I won't follow orders.'

There was a deathly silence. Robert's mouth fell open. The others' expressions were a mix of consternation and blank astonishment. Tom spoke up first.

'Captain, you can't mean this.'

Wynn implored him. 'Please go and call London right away, sir. If you haven't actually *said* it, you can pretend it was a genuine fault. Ward will support you.'

Cameron sighed and leaned back. 'I thought you all cared about Endebbe and the Lobus. A million lives, remember?'

'We never meant anything like this. Your career will be finished. You'll be jailed.'

'I think you're right there, Tara . . . Unfortunately, simply heading home is no longer a viable option for me. I couldn't live with my conscience if I did.'

Tara was far from persuaded, and her shock was quickly giving way to outrage. 'Surely you're not expecting any of *us* to go along with this? Tom, tell him.'

'Absolutely.'

Cameron shrugged. 'Well, I can't do much alone. There are five of us here. I'll take one vote. If the majority is against me, I'll hand the ship over to Commander Hitchens and say no more.'

Tom looked as if his world was falling in.

'Sir, this is the last thing I can imagine saying to anyone, least of all you. No one could fail to understand and respect your concern for the Lobus and Michael Endebbe, but what you are doing is profoundly wrong. I must make totally clear that I want no part of this. There are many times in a serviceman's life when he has to follow orders that he disagrees with. It goes with the territory. You can't pick and choose, or we'd have anarchy.'

The captain turned to Tara.

'The Commander's said all that needs to be said.'

'That makes it two against. Robert?'

'Of course I agree with the Commander, generally speaking. But surely the history of the last hundred years shows there are exceptional circumstances when "just following orders" isn't good enough, that sometimes you have to follow your conscience.'

Wynn glared at Robert. Hitchens stared coldly through him. Cameron nodded slowly.

'Including me, that makes it two all. Wings, looks like you've got the casting vote.'

Wings put his fingers behind the back of his head and scratched his scalp.

'I don't know how to say this. Speaking frankly, sir, if you'd told me in advance what you were planning, I'd've told you not to be such a stupid prat . . .'

Wynn relaxed in her chair a little as Wings carried on.

'You all know me, I'm not the exactly the studious sort. But if I remember my history halfway right, there was some battle where Nelson called the commanders he fought with his "Band of Brothers".'

Robert nodded appreciatively. 'The Nile.'

'I don't care which it was . . . all I know is that's how I feel about us lot . . . Plus, I've grown rather fond of Theresa and Sasha. The net result is, whether I like it or not, sir, I have no choice but to back you up . . . I dread to think what Millie'll do to me when she finds out.'

There was a powerful silence as they all tried to digest it. Tom stood up slowly.

'If that counts as a decision, I have to tell you, Captain, that as second in command, I regard it as my duty to do everything in my power to return this ship to proper authority. If, God forbid, you're not prepared to cooperate in this, I cannot answer for the consequences.'

Shaking his head with bitter reproach, Tom left the room. Tara was plainly fighting back tears. She tried to say something else, but the right words wouldn't come and she rushed out.

That left the three of them. Wings spoke up.

'So what's the masterplan now? It won't take those two long to go to the MCO and try to raise Fleet.'

'I told Ward not to let anyone transmit or respond to any form of comms until I gave the order.'

Young looked pale. 'What are we going to do, sir? *Is* there a plan?'

'Only sort of. The first thing I must do is address the ship's company.'

'*What?* Everyone?'

'You know what ships are like. Word will get round in ten minutes. This isn't something I can do over the tannoy. Wings, can you please give the order to clear lower deck? I want every man and woman who isn't on watch there. Aircrew, marines, everyone. Robert, I don't want a journalist seeing or hearing any of this. I know she won't be thrilled, but I want Grace confined to her cabin until we sort this all out.'

They all looked up as the door flew open. Tara was standing in front of them, pointing a pistol. Behind her stood Colin Dewar and four marines.

Cameron looked more curious than concerned. Tara's voice was trembling.

'Captain, we're relieving you of your command. You two as well.'

Dewar stepped forward. 'Hang on, Tara.' Wynn had told him there was trouble. She hadn't said what it was.

'I'm acting with the express authority of Commander Hitchens, who is now in charge of this ship. He is at this moment communicating with Fleet.'

Colin didn't know what to do, and his marines were looking equally baffled. All he could do was look at Cameron for some sort of steer.

'Sir, is this true?'

'It's true that for the time being I have decided to use my own discretion rather than follow orders. Commanders Butler and Young support me. Hitchens and Wynn are against. I'll tell you why . . .'

'No.' Tara was terrified of losing control. 'Captain Dewar, please arrest these three gentlemen.'

'Sorry, Tara, I don't think I can do that. Not without understanding better what's going on.'

'Then call the MCO. Speak with the Commander. He'll tell you.' She kept her gun trained on them.

Dewar was at a total loss. Cameron gestured towards a phone. 'Colin, why not do as Tara says?'

Dewar dialled. They all watched as he listened, the amazement spreading on his face. He put the phone down and turned back to Cameron.

'That was Leading Seaman Ward. He said the Commander arrived with two junior officers and insisted on calling Fleet. Seems that when Ward disagreed there was a slight fisticuffs. The Commander's being attended to in sick bay. Under guard, apparently.'

Wynn looked horrified, but she wasn't giving up. She knew her duty. Her instinct told her she couldn't depend on the marines.

'Captain, as the Commander said, it is our duty to restore proper authority by whatever means necessary. That includes force. Unless you surrender now and give your word that you remain in your harbour cabin for the remainder of this mission, I will have no alternative but to use this weapon.'

She stepped a pace forward.

'Okay, Tara.'

'You surrender?'

Cameron smiled gently. 'No. I mean that I understand that you have no choice. Wings, Robert, after I'm gone, I'll leave it to you whether you choose to carry on.'

Robert was having none of this. 'I can tell you the answer

right now, sir. Tara, if you plan to kill the captain, you better do the same to me.'

Wings moved towards her. 'Me too.'

The tears were coming back. 'I mean it.'

From behind her, Colin was creeping up. Young was also trying to calculate how close he'd have to get to knock the gun out of her hand. Cameron saw this and with a flash of his eyes vetoed the moves. There was too big a risk of it going off. It was Wings who ran out of patience first.

'Don't be so bloody silly. With Tom out of action, you're buggered. You're not going to kill anybody.'

They saw her finger move, and, with deafening noise, the screen of a TV behind them exploded. Wings staggered backwards.

Now that she'd fired once, Cameron knew the situation was much more dangerous. Wynn looked shot away emotionally. She might do anything. He slowly stood up, ignoring her command to stay seated.

'This is between Tara and me. Everyone else out.'

Dewar and his boys had turned and left. Wings and Young brushed past her. The door banged shut and she was left facing him.

'Right, Tara, if you're going to do it, *do* it.'

'You're bluffing.'

'Then get on with it . . . While you make your mind up, I'm having a coffee.'

'Don't you *dare* . . .'

He shrugged, picked up an empty mug and pressed the plunger on the dispenser to fill it.

'You . . .' She advanced to within one foot of him, boiling with rage.

The black coffee was very hot too. It flew from the mug right across her right hand. She yelped as the gun dropped from it.

Cameron picked it up before she could recover and walked past her and out. Dewar was waiting outside.

'Confine her in her cabin, Colin.'

'Yes, sir.'

Wings had taken a couple of the marines with him to the sickbay to check that all was okay with Hitchens. He was told by the medic that Tom had suffered some cuts, bruises and a black eye. Wings relieved the two ratings from the MCO and asked the marines to escort the Commander to his cabin. He then got on with clearing lower deck. Robert chose the tougher assignment of dealing with Grace and he took a marine corporal to be on the safe side. Robert guessed correctly that Grace would be with Theresa. He knocked on the door and opened it.

'Excuse me, Theresa . . . Grace, can I have a word in private?'

Grace looked unimpressed, but stepped into the passageway. She took in the corporal's presence without comment.

'What is it?'

'I don't know the best way to say this. The captain would appreciate it if you went to your cabin.'

Grace crossed her arms. 'My compliments to the captain and tell him to piss off. I'll go where I please.'

'Sorry, Grace. I don't have time to debate it.'

She looked again at the corporal. 'You're not confining me there, are you?'

'It's only for a while. Sorry, I have to go now . . . Corporal.'

Young dashed off.

'Come along, please, miss.'

'*Don't* you "miss" me.'

Her footsteps resounded louder than his as they made the short journey. She opened the cabin door and slammed it shut with a clang. Marching over to the small desk, she threw open the lid of her laptop, drummed her fingers impatiently while Word loaded, and licked her lips.

'*Right.*'

13

It was an eerily dramatic backdrop. The Harriers could look quite small when lined up on the expanse of the flight deck. In the confined, dark space of the hangar, they looked massive. The Sea Kings and Lynx were behemoths too, but the aircraft which looked most frightening of all were the gigantic, insectlike Merlins. From the gloom they radiated menace.

Apart from those on watch, the ship's company were all there, eleven hundred men and women arrayed in well-ordered ranks. Cameron had given orders that no one should wear caps. He planned to stand on a box and wanted to make sure he could see everyone's eyes. As the captain strode in, the air crackled with anticipation. Word had already raced round the ship that something momentous was happening. As he hopped lightly up on the packing case, Cameron doubted that even the wildest rumour would match the reality.

'Thank you for coming. I'm going to try to keep this simple and short. Less than an hour ago I spoke to the Foreign Secretary. I told him what many of you know. The only man in Numala who has offered any opposition to the dictatorship of President Nabote will be executed in three days, as soon as the election is over. This is not an election as you and I understand it. Nabote is deeply unpopular, and if the votes were freely counted, it's unlikely he would win. But the votes won't be counted properly, so the conclusion is foregone.'

He paused to allow time for them to digest it.

'When he has "won", not only will he murder Michael Endebbe, whose wife and child are our guests, he may try to eradicate the entire Lobu population of Numala. That is around one million people. Imagine Old Trafford, Villa Park or Stamford Bridge stadium filled fifteen times over – that is how many could lose their lives. Men and women, the old and the young, children just like the ones we see running round this ship. It will be ethnic cleansing as bad as anything in the Balkans or Rwanda.'

He looked round, fishing for their reaction. So far he was picking up little.

'You may fairly ask what this has to do with British interests. Well, the Foreign Secretary thinks not very much, and even if it might have, he believes simple sailors like us can't be expected to see the bigger picture ... Well, imagine one week from now. A Lobu child is dying in the arms of his starving mother. Please ask yourself, what does the bigger picture mean to them? ... You could also ask what this has to do with the Royal Navy. Isn't this the responsibility of the international community? And of course you'd be right. But where are the international cavalry? And what if they don't come thundering over the hill? For sadly it's clear that they won't ... It boils down to this. The only thing that stands between Nabote and this heinous act is *Indomitable*. If we do nothing, the fate of Michael Endebbe and the Lobu people is sealed. I have tried to persuade our political masters, but I have failed and they have confirmed the order to leave the Lobus to their fate.'

He paused once again. The key moment was coming. He scanned the rows and deliberately caught many eyes.

'I have decided that I cannot do that. I am therefore now acting in direct contravention of Whitehall's orders.'

In the tall space the intakes of breath were amplified. There was much furtive exchanging of looks.

'You may imagine that this is a decision I reached only after careful and painful deliberation. In common with many men and women in the Royal Navy, my hero is Nelson. Last night I reminded myself of a letter he once wrote to a senior officer . . . "I am fully aware of the act I have committed. I am prepared for any fate which may await my disobedience. I have done what I thought right".'

He left a moment for the resonance of the great man's words to sink in.

'However, it is one thing for me to listen to my conscience and another to be able to do something about it. That can only be possible if enough of you see it the same way. If you do go with me, I must warn you that you choose a hard path. Apart from the normal risks of military action, our own government may use force against us. Even if we survive both, you will have to face the consequences back home. I have already resigned myself to the fact that I will be court-martialled and imprisoned for a long period before being discharged with disgrace. I hope that others will be treated more leniently, but I cannot guarantee it. The consequences for your future career and your family could be calamitous. You must think about that very carefully.'

It was time now for full disclosure, with all the attendant dangers.

'I will not conceal from you that two of our most senior officers, the Commander and Lieutenant Commander Wynn, are strongly opposed to this. They are now under guard in their cabins. When this meeting is over I intend to ask them to transfer over to *Fort George*, which I know will be ordered to leave us. We have just enough fuel and provisions for what we need to do and I will not seek to prevent her from going. Any man or woman who does not want to follow me should also leave aboard her. Then it will be clear to everyone back home that you bear no responsibility for what the rest of us may do.'

One last pause. He tried to catch the eye of some of the true opinion-formers on the ship, to gauge how they were responding – the Yeoman, the Master at Arms, the Chief Stoker, the Chaplain, the Surgeon Commander, one of the popular chief petty officers. He wasn't sure if he had them.

'Please consider this very carefully. I would like to give you as much time to decide as you need. However, Michael Endebbe and the Lobus do not have time on their side, and I must ask you to make up your mind in just half an hour. Do any of you have questions?'

There was a silence as Cameron stepped down off the box, broken only by a few indecipherable mutterings.

In the sixth row, Phil McManus whispered to Charlie Slim. 'He can't expect us to decide just like that.'

Charlie nodded. 'Fuckin' right.'

Trish Moore, standing immediately in front, caught this exchange, turned and gave Phil the eye. 'Bollocks.'

Billy nodded vigorously. 'You thinkin' what I'm thinkin', Trish?'

'Go for it, Billy.'

Billy Ward stepped a few feet clear of his row and raised his hand. It took a second for anyone to notice it. Wings had to prompt Cameron, who nodded in his direction.

'Yes, Leading Seaman Ward.'

'Sir, some of us 'ave made up our minds already. Is it all right if we don't wait the thirty minutes?'

'Yes, of course. But anyone who wants the time should leave now.'

There was a move to go, an awkward shuffling. Fewer than fifteen people people walked out.

'Very well. Will anyone who is with me step forward a pace? Those who wish to transfer to *Fort George* should stay where they are.'

Billy and Trish were the first to step forward. They were followed by Trish's close friends. Many of the younger officers did the same. In spite of themselves, Phil and Charlie found themselves part of the surging tide. In the end no more than twenty men stood behind, and not a single woman.

Robert Young was ecstatic. Wings was shaking his head happily. Cameron held up his hand.

'Thank you all. Right, let's get back to our stations. Those transferring to *Fort George* should prepare to leave within the hour. As soon as that is complete I will turn this ship south.'

A fierce deep-throated cheer echoed round the hangar.

It took over an hour for a Sea King to complete the transfer of the twenty-six leavers. As a precaution Cameron had ordered that Hitchens and Wynn should go over last. He offered to shake their hands, but they refused and went on their way. The captain of *Fort George* sent a signal by flashing light offering fuel or any other supplies. Cameron declined. They had 'rased' only days before, and with minimal flying since, he had all he needed. He did not want to risk getting the man in trouble and was well aware that Hitchens and Wynn would file a full report on their return to England.

When the helicopter made its final return, *Fort George* began slowly to turn away. Its signal lights flashed again. The rating interpreted it for Cameron.

'It's personal for you from their captain again, sir. He says, "We are sad to leave you. Good luck."'

Cameron nodded to the seaman, waved to the bridge of *Fort George* and turned back. Two minutes later he was on his own bridge.

'Officer of the watch, turn her about. Shape course for Kindalu.'

Before the ship had completed its turn, he summoned the Group Warfare Office Communicator.

'We might as well keep them guessing for a while. Switch off all the equipment that automatically transmits our position, and send reports indicating that we are continuing on our northerly course.'

They had been sailing south for over half an hour when another thought crossed Cameron's mind.

'Robert, it occurs to me we should think about letting Grace out.'

Grace had put the three hours of incarceration to good use. What she had written was magisterial stuff. She reread the last paragraph, nodded with grim satisfaction and hit 'send'. Again. She heard her cabin door opening and turned to see Robert grinning broadly at her.

'This is not fucking funny. What have you done to my email?'

'Oh yeah, sorry about that. It's been blocked. Captain's orders.'

'I do *not* believe this . . . Tell me, am I free to leave here now?'

'Absolutely.'

She marched up to Young and eyeballed him. 'Right, where *is* he? Where's the captain?'

'Oh, on the bridge, I believe . . . Before you say anything to him, Grace, there's something I ought to tell you.'

'There's *nothing* I want to hear from you.'

'Suit yourself.' She had already brushed past him when he said it. A hint of a smile played on his lips as he followed at his own pace.

When she reached the bridge, Cameron was deep in conversation with Wings and Dewar.

'I want a word with you. *Now.*'

Without looking up, Cameron carried on making his point, tracing a line on a chart with one finger.

'Right there.'

Dewar and Wings nodded agreement. When Young

arrived he could see Grace was about to explode. Cameron looked up and smiled sweetly at her.

'Sorry, did you want something?'

'Yes, you bastard. I want to know why my email was switched off and when it'll be back on.'

'It won't.'

'What d'you mean?'

'I've sent a personal email to the next of kin of all the ship's company, telling them not to expect to hear anything for a few days. Although our systems will remain on, there will be no outward communications from the ship.'

'You've got to be joking. What about my reports?'

'You could try pigeon post.'

She stepped towards him. 'This is all because of my last piece, right? One bit of criticism and you start censoring . . . Well I tell you, the moment we get to Portsmouth, I'm going to get my editor to go straight to the Minister.'

From the other side of the bridge, Wings chipped in. 'You'll have to wait for that for a while, Grace. We're not going to Portsmouth yet.'

'So where the hell are we going?'

'Kindalu.'

Grace's angry expression turned to incomprehension. '*What?* What are you talking about? Did Whitehall change their mind?'

'Not altogether.' Wings was looking even more entertained.

'I don't get it. Who ordered you back?'

'No one did. We just thought it was a nice idea.'

'What *are* you talking about?' She looked right at Cameron. 'You *didn't* . . . ?'

Cameron caught her glance and turned away. When she looked around her, Wings' smile was broadening into an enormous grin. Involuntarily Grace found herself following suit.

'*Bloody hell.*'

Then the implications began to seep through.

'But . . . won't you get in trouble?'

The comical understatement was the trigger for full-scale laughter. It took a while for it to subside.

'So, what are you going to do? Rescue Endebbe?'

Robert nodded. 'We're going to give it a go.'

Grace clasped her hands together and brought them up to her mouth. She dashed over to Robert, wrapped her arms about his scarcely protesting frame and planted a big kiss on his cheek. Soon she had done the same to Wings and Dewar. Lastly she went to Cameron, who was staring out the front screen. Some instinct made her hold back from invading his airspace. She simply stood next to him until he turned towards her.

'Captain, I owe you an apology. I underestimated you. Hugely.'

Cameron nodded, but moved quickly on. 'We haven't had a chance to tell Mrs Endebbe. I thought maybe you'd like to do that. Don't get her hopes up too high. The odds are stacked against us. Our own side will do all they can to stop us. And if Nabote hears we're coming, he might kill Endebbe immediately. That's why I can't let you write anything, at least until we see whether Whitehall goes public.'

'I understand . . . Thank you, all of you.'

Cameron's eyes followed her as she went.

'Right, let's get on. As I was saying, by now they'll have sent *Tenacious* back to shadow us, and by the time she gets near they could have put special forces on her. Wings, we should keep Merlin aloft at all times to detect her. And Colin, we'll need your boys to mount a round-the-clock guard on the flight deck.'

'Of course, sir.'

'We need to think hard about what else they'll be planning.'

Robert nodded. 'What I'd give to be a fly on the wall back home!'

14

The Foreign Secretary had insisted on convening the COBRA Committee meeting in his office. It was against convention, but only the PM could overrule it and no one thought it worth bothering him in Beijing.

It was going to be a long night. The long-case clock said one twenty-five. The table was full to overflowing with officials from the Foreign Office, MoD, the Cabinet Office and the navy. Many had taken off their jackets and Patrick Dawnay had loosened his tie. He helped himself to one of the last of the sandwiches and yawned, glancing over his shoulder to the corner where a uniformed naval official was finishing off a phone call. He put the receiver down and resumed his position at the far end of the table.

'As we anticipated, Cameron has been trying to mislead us. Although the ship is continuing to send position reports indicating a steady course north-west, the INMARSAT signal shows that she's turned around and is heading south-east. The Americans have noticed the change in course and want to know what *Indomitable*'s up to. The French have picked it up too. For the time being we've stalled them. It won't be long before they detect our task force as well.'

Gordon-Booth had another concern. 'What about *Fort George*?'

'We've ordered her to remain at sea, to keep the crew and the men from *Indomitable* effectively in quarantine. They are all being denied personal communications.'

Dawnay ran his hand through his thinning hair. 'If our

allies don't leak this, when's the earliest Nabote might hear, CDS?'

'We calculate that at her present speed, *Indomitable* will approach Numala by late on Wednesday, the nineteenth.'

Gordon-Booth could hardly bear the thought. 'Just imagine the brouhaha when he finds out she's back.' Before the meeting, he had shared with the Foreign Secretary his exasperation at the MoD's feebleness in predicting what might happen. It showed in his tone of voice.

'Have you tried to assess Nabote's defensive strength?'

'We've done our best. The biggest single threat to *Indomitable* will be the North Korean "advisers" and all the equipment they've supplied. We estimate that there are between sixty and a hundred of them operating there, and they might well be pressed into the front line. As for the Presidential Guard, if they keep their discipline, local knowledge could make them formidable in urban exchanges. The army's harder to comment on. You've all seen the intelligence reports: they're poorly equipped, morale is at rock bottom, and their Commander-in-Chief, General Mbekwe, is believed to be very disaffected. There must be doubts about their loyalty and will to fight. Taken as a whole, though, the defences could be a tough nut to crack. Cameron has air power, of course, but very limited forces to deploy on the ground. Whatever his objectives, this will be no cakewalk.'

'We appreciate that you don't know what Cameron is planning, but as a naval man, surely you can hazard *some* guess of what his first move will be. When they get near Kindalu, will the ship just roll into view, like last time?'

'No, if I were him, I would adopt the poise position.'

Dawnay snapped irritably. 'What the hell's that?'

'It's what Nelson did before Trafalgar. You hang back just over the horizon until you're ready to strike. Without aircraft to extend it, Numalan radar range will be twenty miles maximum. Nabote may not know what's hit him.'

That remark did nothing to calm the Foreign Secretary. 'Have we alerted Tiernan yet?'

Gordon-Booth shook his head. 'No . . . We can't be sure enough about the security situation at the High Commission. Apparently the mob is still outside, despite the departure of our ship. If by any chance they broke in, they might find the telegram. And if we told him by phone, they might still . . . get it out of him. In this case, ignorance is probably bliss.'

'Very wise . . . Crispin, is the shrink here yet?' He looked at the Private Secretary.

'He's waiting outside.' Adair went to the door and ushered in a short, portly, bespectacled man carrying a slim file of papers. The most junior official ceded his place at the table. Dawnay did his best to summon a wry smile.

'Okay. Let's hear it. What sort of straitjacket should we be ordering?'

The psychologist opened his file and spread it in front of him.

'I've read through the papers. Some of you will know the main facts already. He spent his early years as an only child in a small town in Queensland. His mother abandoned his father and him when he was about twelve and a year later the father was killed in a road accident. Young Cameron was packed off to be cared for by his father's parents in England. He was expelled from his first school here, but eventually settled down, and went to Dartmouth at sixteen.'

The CDS reckoned he knew the history well and wanted to stop the man wasting too much time. 'He was a pilot initially, then took the exams to transfer to the mainstream navy.'

'That's right. He was decorated for his service in the Falklands, and later trained as an air warfare instructor, before going on to command a minesweeper, HMS *Quorn*, and a Type 23 frigate, *Chatsworth*. He served in the Plans Division in the MoD, and subsequently was posted as second in command of HMS *Ocean*. Immediately before his present post he was at the Royal College of Defence Studies followed by Principal Staff Officer to the previous CDS.'

Dawnay made a hurrying-up gesture. The psychologist didn't feel like being rushed.

'From all the reports, there seems to be a clear pattern. Wherever he goes, he is invariably regarded by his staff as an inspirational leader. His superiors, too, appreciate his abilities, but he makes them nervous. Let me read you a couple of extracts. The first comes from when he was the CO of 899 Naval Air Squadron. "He must learn to curb a tendency to follow his own judgement when he should take guidance from his superiors." And another – this one from Sir Alan's predecessor – "If I have a criticism, it is that on some occasions his interpretation of my wishes exceeds his brief. That the outcomes were generally successful is a tribute to his judgement, but he should be wary of acting like the Chief of the Defence Staff before he gets there himself.'

The CDS smiled as the psychologist carried on.

'Our man had a number of brushes with authority, and his career was in serious jeopardy when he was court-martialled over picking up boat people. According to regulations, he was not permitted to do that unless the boat was in grave and immediate danger because of high seas. He was accused of having invented a storm, or at least exaggerated its severity, in order to rescue them. There was another instance when he appears to have pursued drug runners into Venezuelan waters. Our Mountie got his man, but there was an unpleasant fuss about it.'

Dawnay let out a bored sigh, again with no discernible effect.

'Moving on to his private life, he's never married, but he has one estranged son who is in prison in America. You may recall the fuss when he got involved with the wife of an MP, Tim Creswell. As far as we know, he's still involved with her.'

'Do we know where he was expelled from and why?'

Gordon-Booth was particularly curious to know what school it was.

'Revesdale. A minor public school in Yorkshire.'

'Never heard of it.'

'No, it's not very well known. Without giving the game away, I spoke to the secretary there. Fortunately their records go back to the Seventies. The facts were disputed, but Cameron's version was that a prefect was bullying one of his pals. What's clear is that, despite the age difference, he gave the prefect a good hiding.'

Gordon-Booth looked appalled, the CDS faintly amused. Dawnay looked exasperated.

'Have you talked to the officers who left the ship?'

'On the satellite phone . . . They feel angry, betrayed. They always found him hard to read, but never thought he could do something like this. One of them – Lieutenant Commander Wynn – thought the journalist aboard, Grace Parsons, could've been a particularly bad influence.'

'Never mind about that. What's *your* verdict?'

'Christopher Cameron is intelligent, courageous, highly charismatic and a very powerful leader. He has a strong maverick streak, reacts instinctively against injustice and is a natural supporter of the underdog. Losing his parents and being uprooted at a difficult age may have left him with the permanent feeling of being an outsider, and paradoxically that may have been a prime motivation for him to join the navy. Something for him to belong to, a surrogate family.'

Gordon-Booth couldn't resist the jibe. 'Fine way he's thanked the family.'

The psychologist ignored him and carried on. 'His independent nature has been held in check by the sense of duty inculcated in him over the years, aided, no doubt, by a healthy dose of ambition. The staff reports suggest that he would have continued to have a glittering career. I can only guess at the emotional turmoil he must have gone through to throw it all away. Having done so, however, his relatively

barren private life means he won't be restrained by considerations about the impact on anyone close to him.'

He looked around the table.

'To sum up, Secretary of State, I believe you are dealing
with an idealist who, having crossed the Rubicon, has little
more to lose, and will now be guided by his own moral com-
pass, not anyone else's.'

'What are trying to tell me? I want practical advice from
you.'

'What I'm *trying* to tell you, is that I don't think *anything*
will persuade him to turn back now.'

'For Christ's sake, who put this moron in charge of an aircraft carrier?'

One of the naval officers looked up at the ceiling. The CDS
had the grace to look slightly embarrassed.

'I believe *I* did.'

*

The task force had been at sea for twenty-four hours and the
marines seemed to have spent most of it exercising. Nothing
but bloody sit-ups and press-ups. One of the lads asked the
sergeant if officers preferred balls-ups or fuck-ups, and was
rewarded with another hundred repetitions for the whole
filthy lot of them. As they laboured, they looked out over the
aft deck of the destroyer. Even to their seen-it-all eyes, four
warships sailing together was a fine sight.

One marine panted the words out to his equally shattered
mate.

'You found out what this is all about yet?'

His neighbour shook his head, the movement releasing
droplets of sweat from his chin. 'I asked the sergeant. He
don't know nothing neither.'

A voice came from the row behind. 'One of the stewards in
the wardroom over'eard an officer saying only the captain 'as
any idea. All the rest know is we're off to Africa.'

155

'Good. Should mean we miss Christmas. I was fuckin' dreadin' it.'

*

Simon's mind was not on the chocolate digestives. He was grazing on autopilot. He hadn't breathed a word to his two colleagues in the WTO, but he was certainly going to ask some questions the next time he got a chance. His chance wasn't long coming. He looked up and saw Owen Lewis and the XO come into the wardroom and settle down for a coffee. Owen saw Simon and smiled.

'You enjoying the break from the slog?'

Simon made sure no one else was within earshot. 'It's nice to have a break, sure. But to be honest I'm having trouble getting my head round this "exercise" lark.'

The XO flashed a glance at the captain. Ah-hah, thought, Simon, I *am* on to something. Owen did his best to look business as usual.

'We do things like this all the time, using other ships as quarry. It makes a change for the crew, after patrolling the same waters for weeks on end. Don't worry, though, we'll be back there soon enough.'

The captain watched carefully. He could see from Simon's eyes that he wasn't convinced. The lad might be a bit odd, but he was clever and he was used to evaluating data. Would a submarine doing vital intelligence work really leave its station at a critical moment to take part in an exercise? This was a hard one to call. His orders were clear – information on what had happened was to be limited to the XO, Ops Officer and Signals Officer. However, if Simon was close to working it out anyway, there were equal dangers in maintaining the line. Owen decided to risk it.

'As it happens, Simon, there's something the XO and I *did* want to discuss with you. Would you mind if we went to my cabin?'

Having been the editor's assistant for nigh on ten years, Karen Stelling knew the exact pace at which he wound himself up. Since she couldn't get through to Jason by email or phone, she'd better go and collar the boy before the boss blew his stack.

When she got there, Jason had his feet up on his desk and was laughing loudly into the phone. Karen's patience was quickly exhausted. Debbie tried to be chatty.

'Like my new bag? I got it last weekend in the Champs-Élysées.'

Karen looked through her.

Finally Jason ended the call and swung round. Karen wasn't exactly his favourite person on the paper, and he didn't care for the attitude she'd been showing him in recent days.

'Yes? What d'you want?'

'John wants to see you right away.'

'Okay.'

He pulled on his jacket and walked over. The editor came straight to the point.

'Have you heard from Grace in the last thirty-six hours?'

'Let me think. We're Tuesday, right? No, I haven't heard since Sunday. What's the big deal? We're winding the story down, aren't we?'

'She was due to send one more article on the reaction on board.'

'They may have stopped talking to her, after the way she slagged them off in that last piece. Does it matter? Surely this'll be stale news by the weekend.'

'Maybe, maybe not. I've had a couple of odd calls this morning. The first was from a deputy secretary in the MoD. He seemed very well briefed on what we agreed with the navy, that if Grace wrote anything which jeopardised security, we had undertaken not to use it.'

'And?'

'He asked us not to print *anything* we get from her until further notice.'

'What reasons did he give?'

'He said he couldn't go into it, but they expected to be able to lift the ban soon.'

'Soon? The carrier should be back in Portsmouth by Friday . . . What did you say?'

'I agreed. Frankly I didn't have very much choice. It wasn't worth falling out with the MoD over.'

'So that's it?'

'It *was*. But then I get another call, from our man in Manila. He says there's a rumour going round that the PM might cut his Asian tour short. His press people are denying it outright, so nobody's running it. But he says the rumour won't go away. If the two calls hadn't come one after the other, it would never have crossed my mind that there could be any connection. I still think it's unlikely. On the other hand, I can't think of any domestic problem that would warrant him coming home early, and Numala's been the only big international story this week.'

Jason couldn't see it either, but he kept quiet.

'I want you to do some sniffing about. Talk to your contact in the navy press office, anyone else you can think of. Try to pick up signs of what's going on with *Indomitable*. Is there some new crisis brewing elsewhere? Could it be the Middle East?'

'What about not upsetting the MoD?'

'This is different. We'll stick to the letter of the agreement and not use anything from Grace. Since we're not getting a dickie bird anyway, it's hardly a sacrifice. But as to what we can unearth elsewhere – that's open season.'

'Okay, I'll get on to it.'

As Jason got up to go, the editor pointed a finger at him. 'I don't want this story doing the rounds in the wine bars and it ending up in some other paper. I've mentioned it to Peter, Karen and you. Don't tell *anyone* else.'

Jason let the door swing closed. As he went by Karen's desk she looked sharply at him.

'Don't forget, "anyone" includes Debbie.'

*

Cameron completed yet another tour of the ship. Even in normal times, he took trouble to be visible. In these circumstances, his presence was vital. He was conscious that many of the men and women would be experiencing sharp mood swings, as the consequences of what they were doing sank in. Some might be regretting passing up the chance to cross to *Fort George*. Others could be questioning why regular rules and procedures needed still to apply. Almost all would be apprehensive about going into action. He needed to be right among them, sensing the mood, encouraging them with a friendly word here and a quiet smile there, and making sure they concentrated on getting on with business as usual. For morale as much as safety and efficiency, standards must not be allowed to slip one inch. It was a relief that, so far, the government had evidently managed to keep a lid on the story. If CNN or the BBC got hold of it, he would have to consider ordering the ship's TV sets to be switched off: the crew might take rants by MPs in their stride, but interviews with worried relatives could knock them badly off balance.

As soon as he entered the briefing room, the group got on with the planning. Grace had been invited because it seemed churlish to exclude her since Theresa, with her local knowledge, simply had to be there. A map of Kindalu was spread out in front of them and Theresa began pointing out key sites, including the parliament, the prison and the presidential palace.

'And this here is the town hall. That's the place where the ballot boxes will be taken to be counted. Officially, anyway.'

Young looked surprised. 'There's only one counting station for the whole country?'

'Only one for the west, where seventy per cent of the population lives. There will be one in Talu too, and some smaller ones in the north and south.'

'So how will they get all the boxes from the outlying districts to Kindalu so quickly?'

'Michael thinks they won't. They will disregard or destroy them.'

'Then why bother counting any ballots at all? Why not junk the lot?'

'Even Nabote needs to pretend there's a real vote. If people keep watch outside the town hall and nothing arrives, it will be too obvious.'

Colin Dewar wanted to move on to other matters. 'Theresa, the town hall – have you been inside it?'

'Many times.'

'Can you describe it?'

'It is from the colonial era. Behind the facade there is a small entrance hall with some offices leading off it. The main hall is large and tall . . .' She drew a large cube with her hands.

'What sort of ceiling does it have?'

'It is made of glass.'

'What? The whole ceiling?'

'Yes, many glass panels in an iron frame. The British built it that way so there could be light without electricity. When I first went there as a child, it was made of coloured glass, like a church. Now there are very few of those left – when they repair it, they use ordinary glass.'

'Will there be anyone there to count the votes?'

'Yes, the election officials.'

'And Presidential Guards?'

'Beyond doubt.'

Wings put his finger on another point on the map. 'This "NBC building" . . . Am I right that this is the state broadcaster?'

Theresa nodded. 'The Numalan Broadcasting Corporation.

You can see it from all over the city. It is on a hill and has a big mast on the top. I have never been there, so I have no idea what's inside.'

'Never mind.' He moved his finger again. 'And this is the national football stadium, where everything will, er, happen.'

'Grace has told me. That is where the election result will be announced, Nabote will make his speech of acceptance and my husband will be murdered.'

She had not given up hope, and was praying constantly with her rosary, asking God for His intercession, but promising to accept whatever outcome He in His goodness determined.

Cameron's tone was matter of fact. 'As Grace has told you, Theresa, the state radio is saying that the result will be announced there at twenty hundred hours – eight o'clock. There's no way we can rely on that timing. We need to know if there is a good vantage point on any of the hills round the city where someone with powerful binoculars could see what's happening on the pitch.'

Theresa looked carefully at the map. 'Perhaps from *here* . . . or *here*. But I am not sure. The stadium has no roof, but the side terraces are tall, and it is built on high ground. You may not be able to see.'

The captain exchanged worried looks with Wings and Dewar. Theresa had just blown a big hole in their plan.

'In that case, how hard would it be for us to infiltrate someone into the stadium itself? It would have to be one of our black marines, I imagine.'

'It will be difficult. The only foreigners who will be there will be diplomats. They will arrive by car, through the tunnel entrance. All those cars will have special blue diplomatic plates.'

'What about mingling with the rest of the crowd?'

'The Presidential Guards will be all over the place, at every entrance. You may think, Captain Cameron, that all blacks look alike, but to us we are as dissimilar as Mexicans and

161

Swedes are to you. Everyone going in will be checked – especially men.'

'Right . . . I don't immediately see a way out of this. Any brainwaves, Wings?'

It was Theresa who had the idea.

'A woman would have more chance. I will go willingly, if you have a way to get me there.'

Young looked horrified. 'You *can't*, Theresa. You would be recognised. And even if you managed to get in, you might have to witness the execution. You must understand, any operation we mount is a long shot.'

'Watching Michael being killed will be terrible. But it is better than letting him die with no friend there. Only supporters of Nabote will go to the stadium.'

Cameron cut across the debate. 'I'm not letting you do it, Theresa, and that's that. If they catch you, they'll kill you too. If only for little Sasha, I won't have that on my conscience.'

He looked at Robert. 'What about Valerie Winston?'

'The Goalkeeper controller? We'll need her badly if they fire Silkworms at us . . . And she's the only black woman we have.'

There was a silence. Grace noticed Theresa looking at her. Dewar and Wings were eyeing her too.

'No way. Absolutely no *way*.'

No one said anything. Grace went on. 'I completely agree that Theresa shouldn't go, but I have no experience, no training, I don't speak a word of Mendé, and even in English my accent is totally different. It would be hopeless. We'll have to think up some other way. Surely they'll broadcast it on state radio?'

Young shook his head. 'Even if they do, how can we be sure that they'll announce when Michael's brought into the stadium? It could be before they give the result or afterwards. We can't rely on it.'

'Then what about rescuing him from prison – hitting them when they're least expecting it?'

It fell to Wings to answer. 'We know where the prison is, Grace, and we *assume* that's where he's being held. Even if we're right, we have no idea where he is within the prison complex. The moment they realised what was happening, they'd kill him.'

Robert nodded in vigorous agreement. '*And* blame it on us . . . Our only chance is when he's out in the open, and then timing is everything.'

Grace folded her arms. 'I'm sorry, I'm a journalist. I'm not paid to put my life on the line.'

There was an uncomfortable silence.

'You can stop looking at me that way.'

Cameron turned away from her. 'Colin, it sounds like it's going to have to be the prison, after all.'

'Sir, apart from the very slim chance of success, we'd sustain very high casualties.'

Wings was unhappy, and his voice crackled with sarcasm. 'That's okay, Colin. Remember, we're paid to be killed.'

Grace tried another tack. 'Wings, has it ever occurred to you that, apart from what Theresa said about our looks, we walk differently, dress differently? I'd stick out like a sore thumb. Right, Theresa?'

Theresa nodded, but without enthusiasm. Robert scratched his chin.

'Surely we can fix one of those problems. Theresa, if you swapped clothes with Grace, and did her hair like yours . . . And you could teach her a few words of the lingo, so she could bluff.'

Grace was having none of this. 'Robert, will you shut up? I said *no.*'

Robert shut up. Not so Wings.

'Grace, what was it you said in your last article about the importance of moral principles? Or are principles only things you *write* about?'

Grace bit her lip. Colin went to say something, but Cameron intervened.

'Leave her. Grace is what she is.'

For a few seconds she was grateful to the captain for taking her side. Then as the words burned in, she felt the stinging shame.

'Captain, are you telling me *honestly* that if I don't go, you can't rescue him?'

'No, I'm not. But our chances, which are ridiculously low anyway, become infinitesimal.'

'I can't believe you're even saying this. Do you have any idea what will happen to me if I'm caught?'

No one answered.

'Okay, okay, I'll think about it.'

Robert reached out and touched her shoulder. 'Well done, Grace.'

'I said *think*.' She got up and left. Cameron watched her go with a half smile. He waited for the door to close, and leant conspiratorially towards Theresa.

'As soon as Grace has finished her thinking, can you start getting her ready? We don't have a lot of time. We'll need to land her under cover of darkness tonight.'

15

Toby Gordon-Booth strode into the private office, nodded to one of the girls, and headed straight for Crispin Adair's desk.

'What's this about the National Security Advisor?'

'She tried to get through to the Foreign Secretary and wasn't too thrilled to be stalled. We've heard that the White House has been on to the PM direct. He's held the line for now, but he's cut his trip to Jakarta to one day, and he'll be back first thing tomorrow. According to the Number Ten press office, the *Post* plans to run a story saying there's a connection. We don't know what they've got yet, but somehow or other they may have pieced it together.'

'That's most unfortunate.'

'You *could* say that. Meantime, my man – ' Adair gestured with a tiny movement of his brow towards Dawnay's office – 'has the legal adviser in there, telling him that if the government does nothing to try to stop *Indomitable*, he could personally be had up for war crimes. By the time he gets out he might be a little long in the tooth for the top job.'

They exchanged amused glances. Dawnay was far from respected or liked in the Foreign Office. He wore his ambition too gauchely on his sleeve. And they resented what a Foreign Secretary like that did to them. He might carry the can while their own careers sailed serenely on, but they all forfeited influence in Whitehall if the Office was perceived as weak.

'Where have our ships got to?'

'*Tenacious* has been shadowing *Indomitable* for four hours now. The carrier has detected her, and is tracking her with Merlin helicopters, so the submarine is keeping a respectful distance of around fifty miles. The main task force is bursting their rivets pursuing them, and HMS *Ocean* is on its way from Sri Lanka, with God knows how many marines. When they all converge, *Indomitable* will be well and truly over-powered.'

'But not in time?'

'Looks that way.'

'Has your man finally abandoned the idea of special forces?'

'Yes, thank Heaven. It would have been awful. Any kind of parachute attack on the ship was impossible, of course. They would have seen the plane coming, and put the kettle on for their guests to drop in.'

'What about using *Tenacious*?'

'That was the only alternative, according to the MoD. Get an SBS team onto the sub when it was well away from the carrier, then try to sneak up close at night and release them in something called an SDV – swimmer delivery vehicle. Apparently their normal practice when boarding ships is to approach the stern, fire grappling hooks onto the deck and climb up.'

'Real Schwarzenegger stuff.'

'Rather too much. One of their experts came over to brief us. He said the SDV can only carry four men and it does twelve knots, max. The carrier may be going twice as fast and, even at a gentler cruising speed, will comfortably be doing over fifteen. They say the only hope is to position the vehicle forward of *Indomitable* and hope for the best as it goes by. A bit like trying to jump on a moving bus as it passes. Only in this case the bus is full of marines pointing auto-matic weapons at you.'

'Mmm, I see what you mean. The MoD said a flat no?'

'They were so incensed, even the Defence Secretary worked up the courage to complain. It wasn't only loss of life they were worried about. They say that half of the value of our special forces is the way their reputation precedes them.

If they were humiliated by our own navy, it wouldn't exactly burnish their image.'

Gordon-Booth smiled and looked again at the Foreign Secretary's closed door.

'Do you think I can interrupt? I need to ask him if he's willing to take the risk of warning Tiernan what's coming his way.'

'If I were you, I'd wait. He's probably asking whether he should expect ten years or twenty in prison.'

'Oh dear. It sounds like it's going to be another long night.'

*

Cameron went back to the Ops Room to check for himself. He walked up behind the operator and looked at the screen. The image was being relayed direct from the Merlin.

'Still the same?'

'Yes, sir. She's still about fifty miles south of us, tracking our course and speed. Estimated depth two hundred feet.'

'Good.'

It *was* good. It meant that *Tenacious* was too far away to interfere with the rigid inflatable boat, even though the sound of its outboard would definitely be picked up on their sonar. He made his way to the port side where the RIB was being readied for lowering into the water. It would be a round trip of over two hundred miles – way beyond the normal range of its fuel tanks, and it had two supplementary tanks lashed on and painted in non-reflective paint to stop them gleaming in the full moon. It would be an arduous journey, and it was a relief that the electrical storms were probably over for the night.

Four marines in fatigues, their faces blackened, watched as a leading seaman carefully supervised the lowering process. The sea had become rougher and they had to take care to stop the RIB capsizing as it hit the waves. At last it was down safely. Two of the marines climbed in to keep it under control

167

and looked back up. They could just make out Grace, accompanied by Theresa and Robert, appearing above them. Soon the Captain came out and took a good look at Grace.

She was wearing Theresa's green calf-length wraparound costume, with a life vest over it. Most of her hair had been cut off, and what remained was matted in tight little curls. Removing the soft framing threw her beautiful features into striking relief. Cameron stepped towards the trio.

'Would you mind if I had a word with Grace?'

Young and Theresa stepped back discreetly.

Cameron dropped his voice, 'Remember, if we don't show up, wait in the church till midnight, then try to make your way back to the drop-off point . . .'

She nodded, eyes down.

'For what it's worth, Grace, this is one of the bravest things I've ever seen.'

Her head jerked up.

'*Brave?* Don't you realise that I'm totally, utterly, terrified?'

'I would be too.'

'You should at least know why I'm doing it . . . No, it's not just for Theresa and the Lobus. For some stupid reason that I don't come near understanding myself, I couldn't bring myself to let you down.'

'I can't tell you how much we appreciate it.'

'It's nothing to do with "we". I don't mean Robert, or Wings, or Colin. I don't mean the bloody navy. I mean *you*.'

Cameron hesitated.

'Thank you.'

'Don't thank me. I think you're a manipulative bastard . . . The least you can do is give me a hug.'

Cameron looked over her shoulder, where the others were speaking in low voices. Grace glanced up at him.

'Screw them. Quick, before I change my mind. You've mutinied, fuck it, you can break this rule too.'

Cameron's face softened into a smile. 'I agree.' He slowly enfolded her in his arms. For one lingering moment, she buried her head against his shoulder and closed her eyes. As she turned, she saw Young carrying a waterproof jacket towards her.

'Grace, you'll need this to protect you from the spray . . .'

She put it on. Robert unearthed something small from his shirt pocket. 'More important is this.'

Grace examined it carefully. It was a like a small black pendant on a fine thread, with two recessed coloured buttons on the front. Robert explained.

'There's too big a chance that they'll frisk you and find a satellite phone, so our engineers have made this up specially. Wear it round your neck, and keep it well hidden under your clothes till you need it. The lower button – this red one – switches it on and illuminates the green one. Just press the green once and the signal is sent. Remember, don't press it until Michael Endebbe is out in the open *and* Nabote's there too. If we go in before he arrives, it gives him more chance to reorganise his defences or flee Kindalu. We want to cause maximum confusion.'

Grace looked unconvinced. 'But what if things don't go to plan? What if we need to speak to each other?'

'It's too dangerous. Go ahead, put it on.'

Grace bowed her head and pulled it over. That was her only lifeline gone. She felt like she was being sent into the jungle armed only with a penknife.

'Good luck, Grace.'

She stepped towards the two marines who were still on the deck. They helped her down and got in themselves. The helmsman started the engine, and the RIB swung around on its own length and moved swiftly away.

Theresa stood, waving. Grace looked back but didn't respond. A few yards away, Young was leaning on the railing beside Cameron.

'I know that we twisted her arm something rotten, sir, but I don't know many female civilians who would have done something like that.'

Cameron kept watching until the little boat was lost in the darkness. 'I don't know *any*.'

*

Two of the marines hopped out as the RIB grounded. They swung their short stubby automatic weapons left and right as they advanced up the beach, disappearing behind the screen of low bushes. One reappeared and signalled back to the boat. A single marine was left to guard it while the other escorted Grace up the sand.

It took them forty minutes to reach the dirt road. When they had checked it out, the sergeant looked at his digital watch. It showed 04:23.

'Right, you have six miles to walk and two hours, ten minutes to dawn. Okay? . . . You remember how to work the device? Red for power on, green to transmit.'

When Grace nodded, the sergeant gave her the thumbs-up. She answered with an ironic thumbs-down. He grinned at her, and he and the other two melted back into the bushes. It had gone according to plan. By the time it began to get light, they should be fifty miles out to sea.

Grace looked up and down the road and said to herself out loud, 'What *have* I done?'

*

In the island at the north end of St James's Park the pelicans huddled together for warmth. It had been the coldest night of the winter so far, and it would be another hour and a half before the first watery grey streaks began feebly to illuminate the sky to the east. Thirty yards away, and forty feet up, the yellow lights burned brightly, as they had since the previous afternoon.

Patrick Dawnay had never known such a sense of exhaustion. He'd had sleepless nights before, but never the

170

combination of emotional desolation and physical tiredness which were sapping him so much. He had gone home to his flat in Maida Vale and tried to sleep for an hour. It was impossible. If there was ever a time when he could have welcomed the succour of a wife's kindness, this was it. But his wife was in their draughty constituency home in Grimsby, and, even if she had been around, his stealthy affairs and condescension had gradually squeezed their marriage of any compassion.

When the third nocturnal phone call disturbed him, he'd thrown in the towel and had his car take him back to King Charles Street. The burden felt unbearable. By the end of today his career could be in tatters. And that might not be the worst. If what the Foreign Office legal adviser had told him was true, he might face a nightmare scenario that would make the loss of office seem piffling by comparison. As the Rover swept silently through the deserted streets, he summoned steel to his sinews. He could still avoid being the fall guy. There was nothing – nothing – he had done wrong. If Cameron had behaved like any reasonable man and accepted his orders, none of this would have happened.

It had been four forty-five when he got back to the office, and it was seven fifteen now. Whereas Dawnay had managed a quick shower and electric shave, Gordon-Booth and Adair had pepper and salt stubble peeping through, and the dark-haired naval commodore was looking distinctly swarthy. The door opened and a much tidier looking CDS walked in. Dawnay picked up a copy of the *Post* and tossed it down to him.

'I suppose you've seen that.'

'Yes. Rather fortunate in the circumstances. When their deputy defence correspondent rang our press office and got stonewalled, he tried a shot in the dark, asking whether there could have been a major accident on board. Our man didn't confirm anything, of course, but, rather smartly, he didn't try too hard to put him off that particular scent. Now that the story's appeared, we've denied it, of course, and their editor is hopping mad. It's bought us a little time, anyway.'

171

The Foreign Secretary nodded curtly. 'What's *Indomitable*'s latest position?'

'She continued to slow overnight. They're now sixty-five miles north west of Kindalu. *Tenacious* picked up a sonar signal. Looks like they sent a RIB ashore for two hours.'

Adair chipped in. 'What will it be doing?'

The CDS shrugged. 'Hard to say. It's unlikely that they could get more than four or five men in it as well as someone to drive it. They launched it so far from the coast that it must have been carrying a large load of fuel, which would reduce space even more. The most likely explanation is that they've dropped off a few marines, either for reconnaissance or as snipers.'

Dawnay's grey, drawn face twitched with alarm.

'*Snipers?* For what? Assassinating Nabote?'

The CDS shrugged. 'I'm afraid there's no way of knowing, Secretary of State, and, frankly, not much point in wasting our energy trying. It does confirm that Cameron is planning some sort of active intervention. Mind you, I don't think anyone in this room's been in any doubt on that score since the moment he pulled the plug.'

Dawnay looked profoundly ungrateful for the reminder. From the beginning he had been hoping that it was all a bad dream, that somehow or other the problem would miraculously resolve itself. In the last couple of days he had come to despise everything these navy men stood for. It would take a supreme effort of will to stop that showing through. He took a deep breath before speaking.

'I presume that the various components of the task force are still too distant to be of any use?'

'The gap has narrowed, but the nearest pursuers are five hundred miles away.'

A woman secretary put her head round the door and carried a note over to Adair. They watched while he read it.

'It's the French Foreign Minister. He says that if you won't take his call this time, their President will phone Number Ten.'

Adair looked up at the clock. 'The Prime Minister will be back there within the hour.'

'Shit.' Dawnay didn't need this. He got up, went back to his desk, and picked up the phone. He had to wait for a second before the call was put through.

'*Bonjour*, Pierre. *Comment-allez vous?*'

Gordon-Booth and Adair telepathically compared notes about his accent.

'Look, I'm sorry, I didn't get back to you yesterday . . . Yes, of course. I am very well aware of your concerns . . . No, of course we wouldn't . . . Absolutely. I will definitely call you later today and give you a full briefing . . . Yes, thank you. *Au revoir.*'

He banged the phone down and returned to the table. Adair had more bad news for him. 'On the subject of allies, the American Ambassador has been calling repeatedly since six thirty.'

Dawnay groaned. 'What the *hell* am I supposed to tell him?'

His natural resilience struggled back to the surface.

'Gentlemen, the situation is clear. If *Indomitable* attacks Numala later today, the legal, financial and political ramifications for the government are incalculable. We have done our best to get surface ships to the area in time. We have examined the options with special forces and found them unworkable. What it boils down to is this: the only asset we have within striking distance of the carrier is HMS *Tenacious*. We have no choice but to use her. Her captain must be ordered to disable *Indomitable* without delay.'

The CDS looked horrified.

'Secretary of State, what exactly do you mean by "disable"?'

Dawnay hesitated. Gordon-Booth rode to his rescue. 'Surely you can do a surgical strike? Hit the propellers or something. Aren't modern torpedoes controlled by wire?'

'Yes, they are, Toby. And provided Cameron agrees to

cooperate by keeping his ship on a constant course and speed, there is at least a twenty per cent chance that your plan might work perfectly . . .'

He cast his eyes round the room. 'The reality, however, is that the instant *Indomitable* detects the torpedo's discharge, Cameron will manoeuvre like fury. He may he able to dodge it altogether. If he fails, it could hit him anywhere. Modern torpedoes aren't designed to explode on impact. They detonate a few yards under the hull. The air bubble caused by the explosion throws the ship violently in the air and breaks her back. The ship could sink. Whether she sank or not, the casualties would be horrendous.'

Everyone in the room felt sobered, even Patrick Dawnay.

'We may have no choice, CDS. However, we could give him one last chance. Can you fire a warning shot?'

The CDS calculated. 'Yes, but, if we do, Cameron might depth-charge *Tenacious.*'

Toby Gordon-Booth twisted his face into a superior sneer. 'Surely an "idealist" wouldn't attack his own side.'

'Normally I would agree with you. But we have no idea of his current state of mind. If he is in an agitated state – hardly unlikely in the circumstances – he might confuse a warning shot with a real attack.'

The Foreign Secretary was having none of it.

'We can't procrastinate any longer. Please order a warning shot to be fired as soon as practicable. Let's meet again in two hours. If Cameron hasn't changed his course, we will have a much harder decision to take. And it will be on Captain Cameron's own head.'

16

The XO brought the signal to Lewis, who read it through twice.

'As we feared.'

The XO nodded. 'Couldn't we radio *Indomitable* first?'

Lewis pointed to the signal. 'Not if we follow these orders to the letter.'

The XO pulled a quizzical face. 'So what will you do?'

'Whatever the consequences, there's no way I'm going to do this without speaking with Chris.'

As soon as they had risen to periscope depth so the main antennae would operate, he put in the call. Cameron accepted it without hesitation, but he was painfully aware that, in Owen's own interests, he would have to play this one very straight. He could not know if the radio exchange would be monitored. Lewis sensed the reserve and struggled to find the right words.

'I have received certain instructions. I am not prepared to act on them without speaking with you direct. Please tell me what is going on. Over.'

'I have declined to follow orders over a matter of conscience. I will not attempt to explain, because it would be wrong to try to influence you. You must act on your orders in whatever way you consider right. It is only fair to add, though, that whatever you plan to do, I am not going to deviate from the course I have decided on. Over.'

'I must warn you how serious this is. I have been told to be ready to attack you. Over.'

'And if you do as ordered, I will entirely respect that

decision. However, if we find ourselves pitched against each other, you must understand that I will do whatever is necessary to protect my ship and my people . . . I believe we have said all we usefully can. Good luck. Out.'

Lewis put the handset down. The XO had been standing next to him and had heard the lot.

'So what do we do now, sir?'

'We'd better close distance and prepare. But let's do everything we can to help him work out what our next move is.'

Tenacious progressed at full power, making no attempt to avoid cavitation, the sound emitted by their propulsion unit. Lewis wanted to make sure that *Indomitable*'s Merlin helos knew that they were not trying to hide. As they got close to torpedo range, he picked up the microphone to speak to the crew. He hated having to lie to the men who trusted him implicitly, especially as they might know the truth already.

'As you are all aware, we have been tracking *Indomitable* for seventeen hours. The exercise, codenamed Pandora, is now going to the next stage. We have been ordered to make a synthetic attack. We will fire one live Spearfish torpedo. We will, of course, aim to miss. In order, however, to make the attack as realistic as possible, we will maintain the torpedo on attack course and guide it away only in its final approach. *Indomitable* will naturally carry out realistic anti-submarine operations. Therefore, as soon as we have discharged the torpedo, we will engage maximum angle of dive and practise evasive manoeuvres. For added realism, it is possible that *Indomitable*'s Merlin may release anti-submarine torpedoes primed to pass at a safe distance from us. All the same, we should brace for a significant shock wave. That is all. Thank you.'

The tension in the Ops Room was palpable. Cameron and Young were in their seats, but both had one eye on the PWO, who was surveying displays of the information being relayed by the helo.

'Range is now less than four miles. She's coming shallow. Estimated depth twenty metres.'

Cameron whispered to Young. 'It'll be very soon now.'

The Helicopter Controller spoke into the mike. 'Sabre One. Over.'

They could all hear the crackle from the Merlin. 'Roger, this is Sabre One.'

'Stand by to drop homing torpedoes. Over.'

'Standing by. Over.'

The shock jolted every one of them when the shrill voice of the sonar operator called out. 'Torpedo, torpedo, torpedo . . . Range six thousand yards. Bearing red two five.'

Cameron reacted immediately.

'Officer of the watch, come left, three four five.'

Up on the bridge, the young officer turned to the helmsman. 'Port thirty.'

'Port thirty, sir.' The helmsman swung the little handles sharply left, and the carrier began to heel violently, like a lorry entering a corner too fast and leaning heavily as it tried to get round it.

'Thirty degrees of port wheel on, sir.'

The officer of the watch spoke again. 'Midships, steer three four five.'

'On course three four five, sir.'

Back in the Ops Room, people were gathering behind the sonar operator.

'Range four thousand yards. Bearing red two five.'

From their left the PWO yelled out: '*Tenacious* is going deep. Sabre One is staying directly over her, sir.'

Cameron was glued to the screen. He knew what Lewis would be doing; his only concern was the torpedo. If its bearing remained steady, it was going to hit them. He would have to decide in an instant whether to take the submarine out before it could fire another.

'Range three thousand yards. Bearing red two five.'

Young came up behind Cameron. 'Sir . . .'

'I know . . . *wait*.'

The PWO and helicopter controller were looking hard at him too, waiting for the signal. Cameron stared ahead, muttering under his breath, 'Change, *change*.'

Suddenly there was a flicker, and the digit five turned to six, seven, eight . . .

'Range two thousand yards. Bearing red three zero. Bearing changing, moving left.'

They said nothing.

'Range one thousand yards. Bearing red four zero. Marked bearing change. Torpedo passing ahead.'

Cameron stood up. The helo controller was still watching him.

'Tell Sabre One to relax. Owen Lewis would never miss by that much unless he meant to . . .' He picked up the microphone to speak again to the bridge.

'Officer of the watch, resume original course . . .' He spoke to Young more quietly. 'It's the next one we should worry about.'

When *Tenacious* went into a twenty-five-degree dive, everyone on board clung on to something. As one of the few aboard aware of what was really going on, Simon was experiencing a degree of terror that made his parachute jump seem like a happy memory. Even Lewis and the XO looked clammy. It was the first time in their careers that they had been threatened by a live attack.

It was only when they had levelled out at three hundred metres that Lewis felt the throb of his heartbeat begin to settle down, and he relaxed enough to reach for the microphone and congratulate the crew on a successful exercise. Once he had done it, the XO approached him. They both knew what might lie ahead.

'Sir, what are we going to do if the next order comes? Will we obey it?'

'I don't even want to think about it.'

*

Grace's feet hurt. Theresa's shoes might be an important part of the disguise, but walking the better part of six miles in them had given her excruciating blisters. In the last half-hour clusters of huts had begun to give way to bigger stretches of shanty communities and the occasional ramshackle store in decaying low-rise blocks, some still unfinished, with rusting iron reinforcing rods jutting clear. As it got brighter, through the milky early morning haze, she could make out the sprawl on the hills above the city centre. A few early risers were already going about their business, and the first of the street hawkers were setting up their stalls.

She walked on and saw her first polling station, festooned with brightly coloured Nabote posters which contrasted with the faded, flaking paint of the building itself. There were no pictures of Michael Endebbe. It didn't look as if the station was open yet. She looked down at the scratched face of Theresa's watch. Seven forty-five.

Within the hour the streets were filling with people. Already two men and one woman had addressed her as they passed, and she had sensed, rather than seen, the men turn and watch her as she tramped on. Her skin had prickled hot with alarm. The woman said something – not one of the phrases Theresa had taught her – so Grace offered a mum-bled greeting, muddling the words for the time of day. She passed another polling station, where soldiers in torn fatigues and trainers were marshalling the first arrivals.

For what seemed like ages she'd been looking out for the junction Theresa had described, with the tall brick building and an old Pepsi hoarding. She had walked so many blocks she feared she'd missed it altogether, and if she hadn't been mortally scared of running the soldiers' gauntlet again, she would have turned back by now.

At last a giant Pepsi bottle came into view. Grace turned left at the crossroads and began the long walk uphill. As she crested the rise, she saw the church with its sweet little cross. She opened the door and sat in a pew. A scrappy bunch of flowers flopped out of a plastic vase, a few candles flickered at the base of a chipped plaster statue of the Virgin, a painting of some black saint hung on the wall and there was a tiny crucifix on the simple square altar. A tall, dignified man wearing a white vestment came silently out of a side door by the altar, startling her, and stepped in her direction.

It was fortunate that he had beautiful enunciation, and said so clearly the word for hello that she had learned. She repeated it, but his next phrase was not in her primer. There was nothing for it but to switch nervously to English.

'May I pray here for a while?'

He had already guessed it from her air and her accent. He could see the fear in her eyes, but he had to be careful. Nowadays there was no one you could trust.

'Everyone is welcome here. I will leave you to your prayers.'

He had stepped up to the altar, and was genuflecting before going back to his sacristy, when she took a risk.

'I am a friend of Theresa Endebbe.'

She saw him freeze. Slowly he got up, turned and retraced his steps.

'Sometimes the guards come here, though not to pray . . . Perhaps you would prefer to pray in my study.'

*

The clock struck two chimes for half-past nine as the door opened. They all looked up from the table, surprised to see the CDS wearing full-dress uniform, and accompanied by two naval officers. The Foreign Secretary was too preoccupied to dwell on clothing and, if the thought had passed through his mind at all, he would have assumed the man was off to some official function afterwards.

As soon as the CDS sat down, Dawnay got to the point. 'Well?'

'*Indomitable* has resumed its course. It is now in poise position off Kindalu. I have sent a personal signal to Cameron appealing to him to withdraw. I regret that I have received no response.'

'So he could attack at any time?'

'Yes.'

'Then there is not a moment to lose.' Dawnay took a deep breath. 'Gentlemen, we have now exhausted all our preferred courses. With the heaviest of hearts, I have decided that we must eliminate *Indomitable*'s capacity for offensive action. Whatever the pain, suffering and embarrassment we must endure, when the full facts come out, I am confident that we will be judged to have done the right thing in terrible circumstances.'

All eyes swung towards the CDS.

'I must remind you that there are nearly eleven hundred British citizens on that ship.'

'All of whom have mutinied. They ran this risk knowingly. *Indomitable* must be put out of action immediately. Indeed, the clear legal advice we have received is that if we are in any doubt whatsoever about our success in disabling it, we are obliged to inform the Numalan government to allow them to take whatever defensive measures they see fit.'

The colour began rising in the CDS's face.

'Nabote has attack boats armed with Silkworm missiles. You would let him send those against a crippled British carrier which might not be able to manoeuvre or defend itself in any way?'

'If *Tenacious* does its job satisfactorily, it will not be necessary.'

'If *Tenacious* does its job at all.'

181

Dawnay growled at him.

'What exactly do you mean by that?'

'Secretary of State, while nothing whatsoever has been said in my hearing, I suspect that there is more sympathy in the Navy for what Cameron has done than you would appreciate. I don't doubt that the captain and crew of *Tenacious* will do their duty, but you are pushing their loyalty to the limit.'

'Then you must throw your full personal authority behind the order to attack.'

The CDS took a deep breath. It was vital that he did not lose his temper now, especially in view of what he was about to say.

'I presume you have discussed this with the Prime Minister.'

It was Dawnay's turn to cling to his cool. The fucking nerve of the man.

'You presume correctly. I called him when he touched down at Northolt and again as soon as he got to Downing Street. I advised him that the unanimous view of this committee was that if Cameron carried on, we would have no choice in the matter. I can assure you that I have his full confidence.'

He was still seething, but it seemed that he had finally crushed the CDS. He resumed his seat and looked down the table. 'I presume we *are* still unanimous.'

Everyone nodded except for the CDS and the Navy men. He rose slowly and with dignity.

'Foreign Secretary, you are aware that I have a constitutional prerogative?'

'What are you on about?' Dawnay looked totally baffled as the CDS marched briskly out, with the two officers hard on his heels.

'What the hell did he mean by *that*?'

Crispin Adair, seated at Dawnay's left, dropped his voice to a whisper.

'He has the right to go over your head, direct to the PM. I believe it's called "crossing the road".'

One hour later, all the Foreign Office and Cabinet Office officials were still there, chatting quietly in small groups. Patrick Dawnay was at his desk, signing papers, attempting to give the impression of business as usual. He had tried once to get through to the PM himself and was told he could not be disturbed. As the minutes ticked by, the feeling in his gut was getting worse.

The phone rang in the corner and Adair picked it up. Dawnay put his pen down and tried to listen in. Adair merely nodded a few times, then quietly said thank you. He turned around.

'Secretary of State, I have been asked to inform you that the Prime Minister has assumed personal charge of the situation.'

17

Even by Numalan standards the storm was a bad one. Through the curtains of rain, lightning bolts lit up the bruise-hued clouds and the thunder sounded loud enough to bring the whole sky crashing down. People were huddled in the polling station, trying to avoid the rivulets pouring in through the roof. Two young men made a scurrying run for it from the store across the road, causing much resentful moaning as they crashed, laughing, into people by the door. The official inside had pretty much given up. Water must have got into the box, mushing the papers inside. Now nobody was leaving and nobody was coming. Unless the heavens relented soon, there might not be a lot more voting today.

The view was much the same from the bridge of *Indomitable*. The afternoon was as dark as night. Cameron and Wings were looking out with concern. The giant sheets of rain generated phantom images on their radar and could hide the real thing. Even more troubling was the effect on aircraft. There was no way anything could fly in this. When they saw the storm coming, they'd had to recall the Merlin, and until it abated they were blind. They knew it was only a matter of time before *Tenacious* came again, this time for real. Though he had told no one, Cameron had made up his mind that as soon as the submarine went into an attack pattern, he was not going to sit there to be taken out. If it was kill or be killed, he would hit it with everything his Merlin had, and hope that at such shallow depth most of the men on the submarine would be able to evacuate safely.

But that was when the Merlin were flying. After the warning shot, *Tenacious* had withdrawn to a range of around twenty-five miles, well out of torpedo range. Now she could be anywhere. *Indomitable*'s own sonar was primitive compared with that on the helos, and provided Owen Lewis kept his submarine well below cavitation speed, they would have no means of detecting it. The first they would know of it was when they heard the torpedoes being fired.

Cameron turned to see Billy Ward come in, grinning broadly. 'What's so amusing?'

Billy held out a piece of paper. 'Another signal for you from the CDS, sir.'

'And it's *funny*?' He had expected one last message, either from the CDS or the First Sea Lord, before they sent *Tenacious* in for the kill. He unfolded and read it.

'Well, I'll be damned. Thanks, Ward . . . Wings, take a look at this. It looks like we can stop worrying about our own side for a while.'

The mood of relief lasted no more than ten seconds. The voice of a radar operator crackled over the intercom.

'I've got a small contact six miles south-east, sir. I'm pretty sure it's not rain.'

'What speed is it moving?'

'It's almost stationary, sir. Probably a fishing boat.'

Cameron looked over at Wings. 'We can't put a helo up in this. Let's hope the boat has no radio.'

The fishermen had been caught out at sea in storms often enough. It came with the job. This was one of the worst, though. They were all praying for the fireworks to stop. Sea water coming over the shallow gunwales was combining with the furious rain and slopping violently to and fro as they pitched. If it got much deeper, they'd have to risk their necks on the deck and start bailing.

The youngest of the three men thought he saw something and peered through the gloom. He touched the skipper on the arm and pointed. The skipper reached to a shelf under the screen and pulled out a battered pair of binoculars. He took a good look and handed the glasses around.

The conversation became animated, and for a while they forgot about the deepening water. The skipper picked up the handset of their primitive radio. He had to fiddle with the dials for fully five minutes before getting any response over the swirling static.

*

Bob Tiernan couldn't believe his eyes. It even flashed through his mind that this telegram could be some sort of hoax. It wasn't. *Indomitable* was on her way back, and might show up at any time.

The stark words of the telegram gave no background, no explanation of why this had happened, of why he hadn't been told earlier, of what was the purpose of the mission. They hadn't needed to add that he was now in harm's way, especially after the assurances he had delivered to the Foreign Ministry that the warship was returning to base.

It advised him not to respond to any summons by the Numalan government. In fact, Bob doubted that Nabote would bother with normal diplomatic protocol when he found out; he was more likely to vent his spleen by giving his bully-boy guards their head.

Should he make a run for it in the Land Rover? Not if they were on the lookout for him. What about the Swiss Embassy? The guards were no more likely to respect its sanctity than the High Commission's. So what *should* he do? It all depended on what was likely to happen. Would the carrier's aircraft go into action, and if so when, and against what targets? It seemed clear that no one was going to tell him, and all he could do was try to survive an hour at a time.

Within the High Commission itself, there was only one option, the registry. The steel door had lateral spars jutting far into the walls on either side and a numeric pad for the combination code to unlock it. It should withstand a casual attack. There was no time to lose, and he busied himself with preparations, quickly drawing up a list of what he should take. Biscuits, water, mobile phone and charger, a bin to piss in, his own chair for comfort and sleep if he got that far, a pen and paper in case there was anything to write, if only a farewell note to Alice. In case they turned the power off, all the torches and candles he could lay his hands on. Fortunately, because of the regularity of normal power cuts, the High Commission staff kept a plentiful supply of both, and pressed them into service whenever there was a hiatus before their own generator kicked in.

If the guards broke through into the registry, they would probably torture him, possibly kill him, or conceivably arrange for him to be sentenced for a long stretch in their ghastly jail. Would it be better to commit suicide while he still had the chance? How? He had no gun, no sleeping pills, and if the guards might storm the compound at any minute he could hardly rig a tube up to the car's exhaust. Anyway, these thoughts weren't real. For Alice and the kids he would have to hold on, and take whatever fate threw his way.

He read the telegram again, letting out a hollow laugh at the final paragraph. 'Rest assured that we are doing all in our power to ensure your welfare. Take all possible precautions to secure your situation until help comes.'

Thanks, guys. Maybe a posting in some junior corner of the Paris Embassy would have been a better idea, after all.

*

The rain had eased fractionally, but the roads in the capital drained poorly and looked like shallow rivers. The armoured personnel carrier was kicking off spray like a waterskier, forging a way for Nabote and Julius in his black bullet-proof presidential Mercedes. Nabote had long got into the habit of turning up unannounced. It kept people on their toes, and the lack of formal plans reduced the risk of an ambush, a sniper or an opportunistic grenade. It always amused him to see the reactions when they saw his cavalcade coming. He was not disappointed this time, as they rounded the corner and drew up in front of the forbiddingly ugly prison, its carbuncular face crowned incongruously with a delicate tiara of razor wire.

The sentries jumped up from their shelters and stepped into the still heavy rain, pulling their dirty caps on as they moved. They glanced nervously behind them as they waited for the main door to be opened. Their comrades inside raced to let the governor know. He in turn struggled to get his trousers back on, tumbling over in his panicking hurry and telling the girl to get out the back door in case the President wanted to visit his office.

Fortunately, Nabote had no such intention. As soon as his car swept in to the courtyard, he issued a simple command and, with the governor struggling to catch up, father and son walked single-mindedly to an old stone building in the far corner of the complex.

Rainwater was making its way down the walls of the cell, and for a while had driven the rats and cockroaches into hiding. Endebbe was chained by both arms to rusting iron rings embedded deeply in the wall, and his shoulders had long been dislocated by his body weight bearing down when he lost consciousness. He tried to blink the water away as he heard the clank of the cell door opening.

Nabote and Julius swept in, with two Presidential Guards and the governor in attendance. Behind them, two prison guards hurried in with a lopsided old wooden table, which

188

they set down, as Julius instructed, in the centre of the cell. Nabote was smiling broadly, relishing the moment.

'Ah, my honoured opponent. This is a momentous day for both of us . . .'

Endebbe blinked again.

'I came here because I wanted you to have the chance to participate personally in the democratic process . . . Julius?'

Julius reached into a pocket and pulled out a polling card. He dutifully passed it to the President, who waved it under Endebbe's disfigured face.

'I will leave it there on the table. Do not wait too long to complete it. I see you are not wearing a watch . . .' He looked at his own chunky gold Rolex. 'The polls close in two hours. Soon after that we will both learn the people's verdict . . . You and I will share the privilege of hearing the result first-hand in the stadium. If you win, I will be the first to congratulate you. If you lose, the people will not wish justice to be delayed. I expect the stadium will be very full. Using a firing squad would be too dangerous, so I have broken with our judicial tradition and built a gallows for you. Do you not think it is fitting that a traitor who has betrayed his country to the British should die in the British manner?'

If Nabote expected any reaction, he was disappointed. His expression quickly turned to annoyance as he was interrupted by the trill of a mobile phone.

Julius quickly fished it out and answered it.

'Yes . . . yes. *What?*'

Nabote's irritation was replaced by concern as he sensed a problem. Julius gestured to him to come to a far corner of the cell, and they began whispering urgently. Endebbe observed the anger erupting on the President's face as he grabbed the phone and turned away to make sure he could not be overheard.

'Kim, you are sure? Yes? Then find it and destroy it immediately.'

Julius put his mouth close to the President's ear.

189

'We must kill him now.'

Nabote hissed back. '*No* . . . Then they will say I am a tyrant and a dictator . . . But close the polls early. Bring the rally forward to five. Get that announced on the radio immediately. And have your men at the British High Commission bring their chargé d'affaires to me.'

They all hurried out of the cell. Endebbe had heard nothing of what they said. He suspected, however, that something had gone badly awry. Whatever it was, he feared that it could only speed his own death. Or was there was anything happening out there that could give him the slenderest ray of hope?

The rain had little effect on the speed with which the fifteen Korean sailors boarded the three attack boats tethered bow to stern in the harbour of Kindalu. Ropes were fast uncoiled from the capstans and within another twenty seconds, all three craft were nosing away from the jetty.

They pulled into a column, the leading boat's throttle lever was thrust up, the bows rose and they gathered speed. As they neared the river mouth, the men were out on the deck, urgently pulling canopies clear from the missiles.

In the Ops Room in *Indomitable*, two radar operators peered together. Although the rain was clearly weakening, there were still large patchy green shadows across much of their screens.

One of them started and stuck out a finger in front of him. 'D'you think that could be . . . ?'

'Hard to tell. Better not chance it.' He switched on the microphone on his headset. 'Sir, we may have a new contact. Could still be rain.'

On the bridge Cameron replied, 'Let me know as soon as it's confirmed.'

The operators kept looking. Suddenly the image sharpened in intensity.

'New contacts confirmed. Range twenty-eight miles. Speed forty-five knots. Must be the attack boats, sir.'

Cameron knew that every second they gained by putting more distance between them and the missiles would count. 'Hard a-starboard. Full speed both engines. Steer two six eight.'

'Hard a-starboard, sir. Full speed both engines.'

Cameron looked over to Wings. 'It won't take them long to get us into their radar range. We've no choice but to risk the Lynx . . . And I'd better get down to the Ops Room.'

Two Harriers and two Lynx had been up ready on the flight deck before the storm hit. The rotor blades of the helicopters had been pulled back straight and the fuselages tethered as an extra precaution. That all had to be unravelled at a furious pace before the engines could be started.

In the Ops Room the tension was rising as Cameron arrived and took his seat.

'Range twenty-three miles and closing.'

They hardly noticed the voice of the fighter controller on the loudspeaker.

'Viper One and Two, you are cleared for immediate take-off.'

The controller pressed another switch and spoke to the aircraft handlers. 'And get those Harriers stowed.'

As they whipped across the waves, the commander of the leading boat looked at his screen, then frantically peered through binoculars. In the very far distance he could make out the dots in the sky. He barked.

191

'Switch radar on.'
'Radar switched on.'

Everyone in the Ops Room tensed as they heard the piercing sound of the Electronic Warfare Officer's whistle.

'Threat radar. Racket 4201 by Footbrake 071.'

The Air Warfare Officer grabbed the baton. 'Taking 4201 with Lynx.'

The voice of a Lynx co-pilot came through. 'This is Viper One. We have radar lock on targets.'

Low over the water two Sea Skua missiles slipped clear of the bellies of each Lynx and hung there inertly for a moment, before fizzing down to their cruising height fifty feet above the waves and catapulting themselves forward to maximum velocity.

On the flight deck of *Indomitable*, Demon Three was being manoeuvred urgently to the forward lift.

In the bridge of the leading attack boat a strident alarm rang out. The number two called out.

'Enemy aircraft has lock on us.'

His commander screamed back. 'Get lock on carrier.'

'Lock on.'

'Fire both missiles.'

Simultaneously the Silkworms exploded in a blinding flash from their launchers, propelling a massive shockwave through the hull. The same frantic drama was being played out in the other two boats, but they never got their missiles away. None of the crews saw the Skuas before they hit them. In an instant the boats were fireballs.

The first Harrier was safely down in the hangar, and Demon Four was being manoeuvred onto the lift platform. Seconds later the lift began to descend. In the Ops Room there was no time to welcome the kill of the boats. The EWO was struggling to keep his voice calm.

'Zippo two. Enemy missiles launched. Radar track 4202. Range eighteen miles . . . Range seventeen miles . . . Range sixteen miles.'

The twin Silkworms skimmed across the water, darting left and right to confuse enemy systems, whipping up a tall plume of spray as they flew.

The second Harrier was down now, and the electric tractor was pulling it off the lift platform. They were all listening to the broadcast, willing the lift up and sealed.

In the Ops Room the tension was intense. The missiles were almost on them.

'Range ten miles. Fire chaff.'

From six banks of launchers up above them the chaff was launched, programmed for differing heights and directions. It bloomed like monumental hydrangea.

One of the missiles was fooled. It veered violently left towards a chaff cloud. But the other was heading straight for the ship.

'Range five miles. Brace, brace, brace.'

Everybody in the ship – seamen, stokers, cooks, marines, pilots – grabbed on to something and slid down to the floor. The men in the hangar did the same, all watching as the lift above them rose painfully slowly. The only exception was in the Ops Room, where Valerie Winston, the young Goalkeeper operator, stayed in her chair. Her voice was eerily calm.

'Taking 4202 with Goalkeeper.'

On the deck the forward, aft and starboard Goalkeeper guns roared into life, sending a hail of titanium into the sky. The second Silkworm got within three hundred yards when one of the 30mm bullets smashed through its casing, and, with a bang that could have been heard ten miles away, it exploded in thousands of pieces, flinging fiery debris everywhere, some of it skittering across the flight deck, tearing gashes in the runway, slamming into the superstructure. One huge jagged piece bounced violently twice before ricocheting into the still gaping mouth of the lift. Within seconds black acrid smoke was billowing from below.

In the Ops Room everyone pulled themselves back to their feet. Cameron smiled over at the Goalkeeper operator.

'Good shooting, Winston . . .' He picked up the microphone. 'This is the captain. I need a damage and casualty report.'

As he stood there waiting impatiently, Trish Moore came in.

'Excuse me, sir.'

'Everyone all right in the MCO?'

'Only spilt coffees, sir . . . I'm not sure if this is the right moment, but shortly before the attack we received a signal from *Tenacious*.'

'And?'

'They've picked up an announcement on Numalan radio that the stadium event has been brought forward to five p.m.'

Cameron looked at his watch. 'Holy Moses.'

*

For over an hour Grace had been watching the rain cascade through the sodden graveyard. Blue in the western sky hinted that normal sunny service would soon be resumed, but for now water was still pouring off the eaves, loud enough to cloak the sound of the priest coming back in.

'I believe it is finally stopping.'

Grace smiled uncertainly. Since she had got there, he had offered her a glass of water, some fruit and some ointment for her feet, but had said little else. He had asked no questions and she had volunteered nothing. She had no idea how far she could trust him. What might have happened since Theresa had fled and her husband had been captured and, doubtless, tortured? What was the priest doing when he left her alone? Could he have called the Presidential Guards? Might they be waiting outside?

'If you were planning to vote you may be too late. The radio says that the polls have closed early . . .'

Why was he saying this? Surely he must have realised that she was no local.

'And the announcement of the result in the football stadium had been brought forward to five o'clock. That's only thirty minutes from now.'

'Thank you, Father.'

'I will not go to the stadium myself. However, I need to visit a sick woman nearby. If you are thinking of walking that way, perhaps you would permit me to accompany you.'

'Thank you.'

'If we are going, we should leave right away.'

18

The final preparations for the banquet were all but complete.
The ballroom in the Presidential Palace was draped in the
national colours of white, blue and amber. In the President's
study, Julius was sitting with Kim. Julius seemed as cool as
ever in his dark glasses and freshly pressed uniform. Kim's
own uniform was showing damp signs of anxiety around the
armpits. He was finishing a conversation in Korean on his
mobile phone as Nabote came in. He glared at Kim.

'Well?'

'The attack on the carrier has been carried out, Excellency.'

'Was it successful?'

'Yes.'

'Good.'

'However, our boats were also destroyed. The crews are all
killed or missing.'

'Your government is well paid for the risks your men
take . . .' He stepped closer to Kim. 'If they were all killed,
how can you know our attack was successful?'

'A fisherman reported a great explosion and smoke in the
vicinity of the carrier.'

'Did it sink?'

Kim hesitated. 'It must be crippled, at minimum.'

Nabote went very quiet and leaned forward till Kim could
smell his hot spicy breath.

'Are you *sure* it is completely disabled?'

Kim felt his hands trembling. What choice did he have?

'Yes, Mr President.'

Julius turned the screw on him. 'Colonel Kim, your men at

the airport have shoulder-launched SA-7 anti-aircraft missiles. If you are not one hundred per cent sure, you should order them to bring them to the stadium.'

Militarily, it was obviously the right option. But it was a trap too. It would prove that he was in doubt and he was in mortal fear of how Nabote would react.

'No, it is not necessary.'

Nabote looked searchingly at him one more time before turning to Julius.

'Where is the British diplomat? I told you to bring him to me.'

'He has locked himself inside the High Commission. The guards have broken down the front door. They will capture him very soon.'

'I want to question him *before* I speak at the stadium.'

'I understand, Excellency, but it may not be possible unless we use explosives and risk killing him.'

The President's temper cooled a few degrees. 'It is true he is no use to me dead. Bring him to me as soon as you have him . . . Very well, it is time we got ready.'

*

Grace felt only fractionally safer walking with the priest. As soon as they made it down to the main street, Kindalu seemed to be full of curious eyes. One crazed-looking man accosted them and it took all the priest's persuasion, and maybe his height, to shoo him away. At least her feet had been soothed by the ointment, and sore as they still were, they were less of an impediment.

The stadium had been visible in the distance as they came out of the church, but it dipped out of view as they descended. Now the tops of its high walls came into sight again between the buildings in the foreground, and the nearer they got, the more the streets were thronged. People were spilling off the sidewalks into the streets, and it was

197

becoming difficult for cars to get through. Why were so many going there? Was Nabote less unpopular than she'd thought? Were they really so keen to witness his apotheosis, or was it the prospect of a public execution that attracted them?

She saw a line of policemen in the middle of the street challenging some of the drivers and pedestrians, and she felt a new chill. Shortly before they got to the line, one policeman yelled at a driver and banged violently on the roof of his Toyota. Grace kept her eyes down as they passed, and managed to resist the instinct to look up when she heard one of them speaking sharply to the priest. Whatever answer the policeman got seemed to satisfy him. They walked on. When they'd got within a quarter-mile of the stadium, the priest turned into a side street, looked behind him and stopped.

'Whatever your intentions, it will be more dangerous if I am with you. There will be no Lobus inside there, and I am one.'

Grace nodded her understanding and whispered her thanks. He walked on down the side street, turned another corner and was gone.

*

Astonishingly, there had been no fatalities and only two serious injuries. The bad news was the damage the ship had sustained. One of the gashes in the flight deck was right in the Harrier launch path, and feverish efforts were underway to patch it up. However, much more worrying was the chaos in the hangar. Cameron was down there with Wings, Young and Dewar, in earnest discussion with the Chief Engineer. They were all shouting to make themselves heard as, with worried looks, they watched the frantic work on the huge hydraulic shafts that powered the lift. Behind them, a posse of men in white firefighting gear continued to spray foam on the tangled, smouldering wreckage of expensive machinery. The Chief, his face coated with grime, shook his head.

198

'Considering we hit their missile, they got bloody lucky. The shrapnel's taken out three Harriers, damaged two helos pretty badly and buggered this lift.'

'How long will it take to fix it?' It was all Cameron cared about.

'If you mean properly, twenty-four hours.'

Cameron looked at his watch. 'We've got around fifteen minutes. What about the aft lift?'

'It's working, but the damaged helos are the problem. We won't be able to move them out of the way fast enough to get any Harriers up there.'

Cameron gestured to the damaged lift. 'Any chance at all with this?'

'Your plan requires four Harriers, right? The most we can hope for is one, and I can't guarantee that. We can raise maybe three Merlin up the aft lift in the same time.'

'Thanks, Chief, I'll get back to you in a sec.'

Cameron gestured to the others to follow him away from the deafening noise. They stepped a few yards into the nearest passageway.

'We'll have to change the whole plan. Wings, if we've only one Harrier, how long could we keep it in the stadium?'

'You know it can't land, or all its weapons systems will disengage automatically.'

'I mean in the hover.'

'Eighty seconds, tops. Any more than that, and it'll use too much fuel and coolant to get back here and land safely.'

'Who's your best man?'

'Shane Black. No question.'

Cameron nodded, went back to the hangar, and yelled into the Chief Engineer's ear. 'Chief, make it Demon One. And get the Merlin up too.'

He stepped back out to where Young and Dewar were waiting. Wings had left to brief Black.

'Colin, for now we'll have to forget about securing the airport, the army barracks and the Guards HQ. If we're down to

199

three Merlin, we can only take around thirty of your men in the first wave. The odds aren't great. Theresa reckoned the great mass of Presidential Guards would be concentrated in and around the stadium. There's also the little matter of up to ten thousand of Nabote's supporters.'

Dewar grimaced. 'Don't tell me, sir, your new plan's to surround them.'

Cameron smiled. 'Can you do it?'

'Piece of cake.'

'Good . . . Robert, which volunteers from the MCO did you get to help at the radio station?'

'Ward and Moore. They wouldn't hear of anything else. But if they're going, so am I, sir. I've left a note for my wife in my cabin, just in case.'

Cameron nodded. He knew that some of the marines and pilots were doing the same.

'Okay, it's ten to five. Robert, can you please let Wings know that as soon as the Merlin are up on deck, they should be burning and turning in the hope we can get Demon One up too. If we can't, we'll have to abort.'

*

Tenacious was lying at periscope depth within four miles of Kindalu. Owen had followed with alarm the missile exchange, and he was mightily relieved that their sonar showed that *Indomitable* was still moving under power. Simon had picked up the short-wave radio signal from the fishing boat reporting an explosion in the area of *Indomitable*, so it sounded like the carrier must have sustained some damage. If they were unable to launch aircraft, surely Cameron would have to abandon whatever plan he had made. If he *was* going ahead, the very least that Owen could do was to follow the drama as closely as possible on the off chance that, without any flagrant breach of his orders, he could find some way to help.

200

In the meantime, he and the XO had a pressing local problem. The line that this was an exercise had worn very thin. The crew had all known the circumstances of *Indomitable*'s departure from Numala, and when they realised that it was now approaching the same coast they must have worked out that something was up. When the attack boats came out of harbour, they would have realised that a confrontation was likely this time. Then missiles were flying, two of the attack boats were sunk and a third was dead in the water, probably no more than a smoking hulk.

The men weren't fools. The ones Owen passed in the passageways looked away or wore strange, quizzical looks. He knew he was forfeiting their trust by not levelling with them, yet was still under specific instructions not to. However, he was damned if he would actively mislead them again. This was patently no exercise. If he pretended that what might now unfold was a normal authorised mission, he would probably be unmasked as a liar by midnight. On the other hand, saying nothing at all was now clearly untenable. He reached for the microphone.

'This is the captain. You will all have realised by now that *Indomitable* has come under attack from Numalan fast boats. As far as we are aware, she has successfully repulsed this attack and eliminated the immediate threat. It is likely that *Indomitable* will launch a mission against Numalan targets on land. Our orders are to continue to observe the situation. I will advise you when I have further information.'

By his side, the XO nodded. Neither of them was enjoying this, but in the circumstances it was the best they could do.

*

'Ninety-eight per cent.' The Minister of the Interior was standing beside the President as he prepared to step into the black Mercedes. Julius was already in the other rear seat, his uniform bedecked in medals, with Kim in the front passenger

201

seat. Various members of Nabote's extended family were sitting patiently in the two cars behind. Armoured personnel carriers would escort the motorcade.

Nabote, dressed in a magnificent white costume embroidered with gold and blue thread, pondered. 'That is too greedy. Make it ninety-two. No, ninety-four. But not precisely, you understand.'

The Minister of the Interior bowed as the driver closed the door and the dark glass hid the President from view. As soon as the cars had driven off at speed, the Minister went back into the palace and dialled.

The empty beer cans were mounting up under the tables in the town hall. Rain had been a problem there too, and the officials had dodged the areas where the broken panes in the ceiling had afforded no cover. Fortunately the worst of it was over before the trucks had delivered the first sealed ballot boxes and the soldiers began stacking them in a corner. Even with the foreshortened polling hours and the much reduced time to collect the boxes, there must still have been hundreds of thousands of cards in those boxes, and it would have been an impossible task for the thirty-five men, all wearing badges saying 'election official', to count them in less than an hour. It was as well that they didn't have to bother.

The oldest of the group got up and answered the phone. He must have been close to seventy and wore a clean white shirt, a tie with a floral pattern done tightly up to the collar, a dark grey suit, very shiny at the elbows and seat, and glasses with a small crack in one lens. Using his free hand to pull from his shirt pocket his most treasured possession, a Parker fountain pen, he wrote in a very precise hand 94.3, then, with an unhurried, dignified gait, walked out to where a car was waiting.

Two of the Merlin were already burning and turning and the aft lift was steadily moving the third one up. About ten marines had clambered into each of the first two, and another similar size group, plus Young, Ward and Moore, were ready to go. All three aircraft had been equipped with machine guns protruding from their port doors. A few minutes before, the two Lynx had landed on safely, and their aircrew were making a beeline for cold beer to celebrate their kills.

Down in the hangar, the engineers had finally managed to clear enough space to manoeuvre Demon One into position on the platform of the forward lift. They withdrew, turned to the Chief, and gave the thumbs up. When he pressed the large green button there was a groaning and whirring, and the contraption heaved itself upwards. They all had their fingers crossed.

Less than twenty seconds later, sparks flew and the lift abruptly stopped moving. There was no need to listen to the curses: the Chief's face told the whole story.

*

Grace's pulse quickened as she neared the steps up to the stadium. The crowd was getting very vocal, some picking up a spontaneous, threatening chant, as they jostled and shoved. From the agitated voices she guessed that they were fretting about the time. It was three minutes to five. The early start must have caught them out, and they were concerned that they wouldn't be there to hear the result, to hear the President speak, and to see Endebbe swing.

She was carried forward by the human tide to the bottle-neck where the Presidential Guards were checking all who were trying to get in. Twenty yards away now, fifteen. The crowd pressed forward and it was more like seven or eight. For a moment she felt her feet leave the ground. Over the heads she saw a guard raise a whip to beat some unfortunate. The crowd lurched to the right, then back, then she felt a tidal wave behind her and she was pushed almost into the face of one of the guards. He took one look at her, clearly surprised, and barked in Mendé.

'Where are you from?'

Grace understood nothing, and blurted out the word she had learnt for hello.

The guard slapped her face and repeated, 'Where are you from?'

She tried good evening.

The man grabbed her and frisked her, squeezing her bottom and breasts tightly. He felt the pendant.

'What is this?'

Grace shook her head, only able to guess the meaning.

'Show me.'

He made a move to put a hand down her chest, but she beat him to it, pulling the pendant out and waving it about, trying to make light of it, implying it was a meaningless, valueless trinket. The guard grabbed it and with one powerful yank tore it from her neck. He took a careful look. She could only watch in mute horror as he jabbed a finger at one of the buttons. It was the red one. He was about to try the green when he was distracted by a commotion – another guard had discovered a long-bladed knife in some man's pocket, already had him on the ground. The pendant fell, forgotten, from the guard's hand as he went to join in the kicking.

Grace grabbed it up and seconds later was through the dark gateway and into the stadium's terracing.

*

They had coaxed the lift up another ten, eleven feet when it seized again. *Shit*. Now they would lose another three minutes replacing the wiring and the fuses, and trying to free the obstruction. Of its twenty-five feet of travel, the lift had only managed sixteen, and the Harrier was marooned in a useless no-man's-land. It was four minutes past five. If the ceremony started on time they might be too late, even if they got the plane airborne.

Up on deck, Shane Black was waiting impatiently. At twenty-eight he was the calmest, sharpest and most annoyingly good-looking pilot Wings had ever had under his command. Black hadn't felt particularly nervous before he got his gear on. He'd treated it like another mission. With the hanging around, though, there was plenty of time for the caterpillars creeping round his stomach to turn into big flapping butterflies. People would be shooting at him. He would be pretty vulnerable there in the hover. He tried very hard not to think of his kindly mother and proud father, or his sweet, sexy girlfriend. If he got unlucky, let it be a fast death.

*

Grace was still shaking, and tried to take her mind off her terror by forcing herself to estimate the size of the crowd. Six, seven thousand, maybe, and still they were coming in. There was a marked contrast in the two structures that stood at either end of the pitch. To her left was an open-sided marquee, gaily striped in the national colours, containing three long rows of wooden seats. In the centre of the front row were five much grander chairs, the middle one adorned with an insignia of interlinked shields and spears. In front of all this was a dais covered in red carpet, and in the middle a tripod supporting an array of microphones. Grace's eyes swung back to the right end of the pitch, where a gibbet stood on a crudely nailed platform.

The hubbub hushed as a figure emerged from the tunnel, supported under each arm by a guard. The crowd craned to watch, and Grace realised it was Michael Endebbe. As he made his way falteringly down the ground, the audience's hesitation passed and the jeering began. When he reached the foot of the steps up to the platform, his legs seemed to lose all strength and he had to be dragged up like a dead weight. When he got to the top, he looked like he was summoning his last reserves of energy just to stay standing.

Grace felt the pendant in her hand at her left side. The crush was so tight, it would be hard even to raise it without attracting the attention of the people around her. What if they saw her and shopped her to the guards? She fingered the buttons, wondering if she could press them in the correct sequence without looking. Was the red one on the top or the bottom? She tried to twist her hand and glance down, but when her knuckles rubbed against the next guy, he said something sharp, and she backed off. It wasn't time yet anyway. She looked across to the far side of the terracing and her eye was caught by a canvas-covered box way up at the top of the terraces, with a sign saying NBC. She could make out two men sitting in front of microphones.

Owen had joined Simon to listen to the broadcast.

'We understand that the President has left the palace and his motorcade is on its way. Shortly we will go over to the National Stadium for a live relay of the official ceremony.'

As the cars made their way through the still wet streets, Nabote felt a flash of annoyance that his Mercedes would get so dirty. He quickly dismissed the thought from his mind. Nothing should be allowed to spoil the proudest moment, indeed the crowning moment, of his life. Perhaps he should have permitted the EU observers to stay. His doubts about his popularity in the country had been washed away by the exhilaration of his victory over the British, and he now felt confident that he would have won – truly won – by a handsome margin.

As they drove on, he reflected on the battle. It was without doubt the greatest African military victory over the British since the Zulus annihilated them at Isandlwana. It would be remembered and celebrated for centuries. It would guarantee him a leading place in the pantheon of African warrior chiefs and propel him to the forefront of African politics. For students, idealists and lovers of democracy worldwide, his name would be a watchword for courage and audacity and as a scourge of neo-colonialists.

Neither Kim nor Julius had dared interrupt his reverie. As they came within sight of the stadium, Nabote turned to his son.

'Julius, I have entrusted you with all the arrangements. I hope everything is in order.'

'I have done as you directed. The ambassadors will be in the VIP box. The cabinet will be with you on the podium, plus the judiciary and the highest-ranking officers of the Guard. You instructed that General Mbekwe should not be invited.'

'Nor any other army officers.'

'Security will be tight but discreet. Three hundred guards will be there, some of them manning four machine-gun positions. I have also ordered my men to place armoured personnel carriers on either side of the platform.'

'What about the broadcasting station? I told you to make absolutely sure that nothing is done to sabotage the relay.'

'It is taken care of, with my men and some of Kim's. The building is impregnable . . . And the banquet tonight will be the most magnificent in the history of our country. No expense has been spared.'

Nabote nodded, satisfied.

'Ah, here we are.'

The rear end of the leading personnel carrier rose up as the vehicle dipped into the tunnel under the stadium.

19

'The members of the cabinet are coming out now to take their seats, along with the honourable judges of the Supreme Court, and the Chairman of the Electoral Commission . . .'

Lewis looked over his shoulder to where his radar operator sat. 'Still nothing airborne?'

'Nothing, sir.'

'We're sure they got the time change?'

The XO nodded. 'Unless they were asleep. Maybe we guessed wrong. The ceremony might not be their target after all. They could be waiting for darkness.'

Lewis shook his head. 'That doesn't make sense. Cameron wouldn't be bringing her in at full speed if he didn't plan to attack right away.'

The comms operator came up. 'Any more signals for Fleet, sir?'

'Send saying *Indomitable* is still making twenty-eight knots, heading due east. Current position is twenty-three miles west of Kindalu. No aircraft aloft.'

*

Tiernan had completed his barricade. Every desk, filing cabinet, chair, indeed anything weighing more than a few pounds had been pressed into service. He doubted that bullets alone would displace that lot. Obviously, if they went for grenades or explosives, his defences would be blown to pieces. So would he, most likely.

He could hear occasional muffled sounds through the thick

walls. They'd hammered on the steel door for a while with
what might have been rifle butts, and there had been one
short burst of gunfire. What would they do next? Try to cut
through the walls or the floor above his head? It would all
depend on whether they cared any longer about harming
him, and he supposed that this would turn primarily on
whatever the hell that bloody carrier was going to do.

His lifeline was the mobile, though in the basement the
reception was poor. As he'd expected, they'd cut the landline,
and probably shot to pieces the array on the roof. Sod's law
had decreed that when the warning came through from
London, his phone battery was running low. He'd got it on
charge for less than an hour when the Guards cut the power,
plunging him briefly into darkness.

He'd spoken to the head of the Central African Department
at the Foreign Office to let them know what was happening.
He wanted to scream at the man, to tell him what he felt
about the way he'd been treated. Even now they wouldn't
level with him, wouldn't say what the game plan was, claiming fear of electronic interception. By the Numalans? What a
joke. The Koreans maybe, but he doubted that. He suspected
that they didn't trust him, didn't want to risk him bleating to
the Guards if they got into the room. He might die at any
moment and would go to his grave still at the wrong end of
a 'need-to-know' ordinance. If Roger Fairfax had been here,
they would have told him, all right.

Oh well, there was nothing much he could do except put in
a call to Alice at her mum's in snow-peppered Wiltshire. The
Office had already been on to her. However hard she tried to
be strong for him, her voice choked with worry. He'd wasted
valuable battery power persuading her not to ring someone
senior – Gordon-Booth or whoever – and give him a piece of
her mind. It simply wouldn't help. By the time he got her off
her high horse, the battery indicator was down to one bar out
of five.

A candle toppled over, and he had to move fast to catch it,

getting a dollop of burning wax on his hand. He cursed colourfully.

*

Up on Flyco, Wings was beside himself. Ten past five. The three helos had been ready for minutes. He stared out at the forward lift. He could just see the tail of the Harrier, but nothing more. It hadn't moved for thirty seconds; the lift must be jammed again. There were several figures gathered round the edge of the mouth looking down, including Shane Black in his flying suit and Cameron, dressed unfamiliarly in fatigues. He saw Cameron hurry back towards the superstructure and soon a voice came over the intercom.

'Wings, if we don't get the helos on their way soon, we'll be too late anyway. It'll take them ten minutes to cover the twenty-five miles. Our only chance is to launch now and recall them if we can't get the Harrier up.'

'Roger.'

'Okay, I'm off. See you later.'

'Good luck, sir.'

He watched as Cameron walked across the flight deck and clambered into the second of the helos. As soon as they were aloft, Wings went briskly to the hangar.

'Chief, how are we doing?'

The Chief shook his head despondently. 'The lift's still twelve feet below the deck and it's blowing every time it moves three feet. Sorry to say this, Wings, but I don't think we'll make it.'

'Just keep trying, eh? We haven't had the signal from Grace yet. They may be running late.'

The Chief turned away and called out more instructions to his team.

*

210

'Three aircraft aloft, sir. Helos. I think.'

'Good . . . Get a signal off to Fleet right away.'

Simon felt the tension rise too. He would never have expected it, but he was on the edge of his seat. This was more exciting than any subjunctive.

*

Grace watched as Julius came into the stadium. Having heard about him from Theresa, she guessed it must be him from his swagger, the medals and the dark glasses. When he sat to one side of what was clearly the President's seat, it was confirmed. Nabote must be due to arrive any moment. If she could switch on the gizmo now, she could have her finger poised over the green and press it, unseen, the instant he appeared. She glanced to either side, checking that the people around her had their eyes firmly on the pitch, then stealthily brought her left hand round in front of her stomach and with the index finger of her right hand pressed the red button. The green one lit up.

There was a sudden commotion behind her. As she turned round, she felt a powerful hand clamp down on her shoulder and out of the corner of her eye, saw long black fingers and a flash of a gold ID bracelet. Oh, Jesus Christ. Two guards.

While one spoke, quick-fire, into his radio, the other grabbed her left wrist and forced it back, trying to prise from her fingers whatever she was holding. Grace wriggled and twisted.

The stadium erupted with cheers as the President emerged into the soft late afternoon sunshine. The PA system blared the national anthem and the crowd at the back surged, shoving Grace and the guards five or six teetering steps forward. The force knocked the pendant clear out of her hand. It fell, bounced off an unseen foot, and it toppled down the steps of the terracing. It came to rest three or four yards away, the little green light dimly visible through the forest of legs. The

211

guards angrily wrestled bodies out of the way to get to it. As a space formed, Grace watched in horror as she saw a rifle raised in the air. The butt crashed down right onto the buttons, crushing both them and the casing.

Phil McManus half jumped out of his chair in the MCO and he grabbed the microphone. 'That's it, sir. The signal from Grace.'

Wings clenched both fists involuntarily. He was standing with Shane Black in the compartment beside the flight deck. 'Call Sabre Two and pass the word on to the Captain.'

'Yes, sir.'

Wings pressed another button on the intercom.

'Chief, we've got the signal. How're we doing?'

He listened, muttered an oath under his breath and got the Ops Room to patch him through to Cameron.

'This is Wings, sir. They've got it to eight feet below. Chief says they need another five minutes.'

The voice crackled back. 'We're out of time. Can Black jump down and try to take off from where it is?'

'That's bloody risky. If he doesn't do a perfect vertical, he could clip the rim, and you know what that would mean. Even if he made it, he'd burn up so much fuel it would cut his hover time by too much.'

'Please just ask him.'

The gap behind the two guards had been filled by the swaying waves of bodies. By the time they turned back, she had vanished. In a fury they began shoving their way through. Which way had the bitch gone? They couldn't see her at all.

Grace had gained only ten yards, crouching, half crawling, squeezing past midriffs and legs. She stumbled and got a few kicks, and one nasty stamp on her blistered foot. She hardly noticed; she had to keep moving. Having made another twenty, she took a chance on rising to take a look. *Shit*, they had seen her. On, on, on, now no longer bothering to crouch. Anything to put more distance between them and her. She looked back again.

What had happened? They seemed to have stopped their pursuit. The one with the radio was talking into it. Were they being ordered not to risk disrupting the ceremony? They could always pick her up on the way out. Grace continued to move, taking care to look ahead too, and make sure she didn't simply run straight into another of those dreaded blue uniforms.

What was she supposed to do now? The plan had been for her to try to slip back out of the stadium and make her way back to the church, or to the drop-off beach if the boys never made it at all. She'd have to think of some other way to get out of here. As she kept squeezing past people, she was only vaguely aware of the old man in a dark suit stepping up to the dais. His frail voice soon echoed round the stadium.

'As Chairman of the State Electoral Commission, I will now announce the result of the Presidential election . . . I am pleased to report that the election was fairly and freely contested and well over eighty per cent of those eligible voted.'

The excitement was clear in the radar operator's voice. 'A fourth aircraft's up, sir. A Harrier.'

The XO's face gleamed. Simon tried to punch the air, hitting grey steel instead. He hopped around whimpering. Lewis stood behind the radar operator, watching the screen as one fast-moving blip pursued three slower ones. He whispered to himself.

'Go for it, boys.'

He broke off the vigil to go over to Simon, who was still nursing his wounded fist.

'Can you leave the official broadcast to the others now? I want you to concentrate on the guards' VHF system. Let me know right away if you pick up anything useful. I'm going to signal Fleet that the operation is imminent.'

The old man had all but concluded his introduction.

'I particularly want to congratulate my staff for the impressive speed with which they counted the ballots . . . I now come to the result.'

There was a hush, and many eyes turned to Endebbe, still half-propped up by two guards. Everyone knew this would be his death warrant.

'Excluding a small number of abstentions, the proportion of all votes cast which were received by Michael Endebbe was five point seven per cent . . .'

Grace saw Endebbe's head slump.

'The incumbent, His Excellency President Nathan Nabote, received ninety four point three.'

A vast cheer went up, both from the people and from the PA machine. Nabote, still seated, was beaming.

'I therefore have the honour to announce that Nathan Nabote has been elected to serve as President for a term of ten years.'

The crowd went wild, and the cabinet, the judiciary, the top-ranking Presidential Guards and the ambassadors in the VIP box stood up and applauded. Nabote remained seated, soaking up the acclaim before getting to his feet, stepping forward and throwing his arms out dramatically. The cheering went on for another two minutes. Nabote had to gesture to them to fall silent.

He stepped to the microphone.

'Thank you, thank you . . . Today I feel honoured, and I

feel very humble. Yes, humble, that you, my children, have chosen me to lead you forward . . . I tell you, I see a glorious future for our country. But we must be prepared for what it will take to accomplish this. We must be sympathetic where sympathy is merited, harsh where harshness is due. I will not shirk this challenge . . .'

He let the cheers die down again.

'Nor, I am sure will you. In recent days it has been an inspiration to see how the whole nation has risen to counter the threat from the British. Now I can tell you of an even greater triumph – the greatest victory for this nation since we threw off the imperial yoke, and one of the most magnificent in the long, troubled history of our continent . . . You, like me, thought that the British had retreated. I believed their official representative when he confirmed that. But he was lying. *Lying.* It was all a trap. While their dishonourable government was hoodwinking us, the reality was that their aircraft carrier – that most hated symbol of the aggression and oppression – was, like a devious wolf, sneaking back here.'

He paused to gather his strength for the climax.

'The British hoped that on a day when we were occupied with our democratic process, we would not be watching out for them. They were wrong. Our forces were vigilant and detected the threat. Last time we were merciful and let them run away with their tails between their legs. But not a second time. I gave the order to crush them and crush them we did . . .'

Grace's hand flew to her mouth. Had their missiles destroyed *Indomitable*? Were they all dead? Robert, Colin, Christopher?

'Yes, within the last hour, Numalan sailors hunted down the British warship and destroyed it. If it were not for their courage and skill, who knows what might have happened? Who knows what villainy has been thwarted? As it is, my children, you can celebrate this momentous day free from fear.'

The crowd went delirious. The man beside Grace was working himself up into a frenzy. Then over the cacophony she thought she heard a faint drone. The man let go another piercing scream of jubilation, and she only just stopped herself shushing him. There it was again. She was sure she wasn't imagining it. In fact it was getting slightly louder. Nabote continued.

'The only thing which sullies this happy day is the need to deal with a despicable act of treachery. But good justice is swift . . .'

There was another great cheer. At a prearranged signal, the two guards holding Endebbe forced him a few steps forward until his face touched the noose. The hangman moved to pull it over his head. Grace saw Endebbe try to turn round behind him. Had he heard it too? My God, it *was* getting louder.

Her eyes flicked back to the podium. She could make out a sudden movement from Julius and the Asian in the uniform. Nabote himself was still in full flow.

'Endebbe is a traitor, one of the rankest villains in Numala's history. The sentence which the court passed . . .'

He faltered. The noise was now getting loud, so much that the ground was beginning to shake. All other eyes in the stadium were looking away from the dais, pulled as if by magnets to the end from where the noise was coming. Nabote stood stock-still, his mouth hanging in horrified disbelief, as over the rim of the stadium, silhouetted against the yellowing western sky, came the bringer of war.

When they saw the Harrier descending, the crowd panicked. Some people stood transfixed, only to be knocked over and trampled by those desperate to escape this diabolical vision as it swooped slowly on over the gallows and towards the dais. Nabote had turned and was fleeing towards the tunnel with its promise of safety. Kim was desperately shouting orders, Julius caught between fury and fear. The guard on one of the armoured personnel carriers had the presence of mind to man his machine-gun. The driver of the other one panicked. As the jet settled into its hover facing the fast emptying podium, he slammed his vehicle into reverse, crushing the legs of a cabinet minister whose long tribal costume had betrayed him with a trip. Tearing on backwards, the personnel carrier bounced off the shallow wall behind the goalmouth, and toppled over.

The gunner in the other vehicle was dead now, and his friend beside him, and Black turned the Harrier's cannon on to the fixed machine-gun positions. The men guarding Endebbe held their nerve and were emptying their cartridges into the rear of the Harrier, many of the bullets raking the fleeing crowd. The coolest of all was the hangman, reluctant to miss his payday. He yelled at the guards to force Endebbe's feet over the trapdoor. But the dim ray of hope had given the victim a new burst of desperate energy, and he was now willing to struggle to his very last breath. The noise was so great, the struggle so intense, that none of the men on the scaffold noticed the huge shadow of the Merlin arriving above them.

As Grace saw it settle, she suddenly realised it was her best chance too. But getting down to the pitch was like swimming against a rip tide, as the stampede continued. She glanced back behind her and saw the guard with the radio fighting his way towards her. He raised his rifle and tried to take aim. There were far too many people streaming past her, too little chance of a clean hit. He had no choice but to get closer.

Sixty feet above the gallows, two long, heavy ropes flopped down from Sabre One, and marines came flying out of it. Go, go, go, *go*. In six seconds there were eight men down, Colin Dewar in the lead. One marine down took a hit on the shoulder and fell. A second took out one of the guards on the gallows; they all rushed up the steps just as the other managed finally to kick the legs from under Endebbe. With a yell of triumph, the hangman yanked the lever. Dewar flung himself bodily forward and tackled the body back to the platform as it fell. As he wrenched the noose off Endebbe's neck, another of his men shot the guard through the midriff and used his rifle butt to swipe the hangman clean off his feet.

But the defences were pulling together. Though Black had taken out the two machine-gun posts in front, the others were firing at him, the helo behind and the marines on the ground. Two more men took hits and fell. The Merlin had come down close to ground level now, and was swaying left and right, trying to make itself a harder target as Dewar dragged a half-conscious Endebbe back and flung him inside, before turning back to help recover their three wounded. Inside, Young and Ward were standing by to help lift them in.

Demon One was in big trouble. Black had held his position for sixty-five seconds. His canopy was crazed, the fuselage was being hit time and again. Any second now, the thing might explode.

'Sabre One, I've got ten seconds left, max.'

'Roger, Demon One.'

Whatever the risk from the gunfire, the Merlin pilot had to hold his aircraft steady, or they'd never get the wounded men in. As Dewar helped shove the first one in, there was a shout from Young. He pointed urgently. Wasn't that Grace, clambering over the low wall by the side of the field, going arse over tit, then back up? Yes, it bloody well was. Billy dashed off to tell the pilot.

In the cockpit, Black's voice came though again. 'Sabre One. Three seconds and I'm out of here.'

'Hold on, Demon One. Give us another ten.'

'You must be crazy. You've got five.' A bullet smashed through his canopy, grazing his helmet, sending his head spinning.

They could see that the long dress was making it almost impossible to run, but they couldn't move nearer her until the last of their wounded was in. Dewar saw a guard raise his rifle to shoot her, and lunged for the machine-gun to cover her, forcing the guard to dive below the wall.

The last wounded man and his two rescuers were almost there. Yelling to Ward to concentrate on helping him, Robert levered himself past so he could reach out for Grace. He gestured to urge her on. She was no more than twenty-five yards from them. The guard's head was popping up every few seconds. He fired wildly, the bullets tearing great dusty gouges in the pitch, then ducked again.

'Right, I'm gone.' Black pressed the throttle forward.

Robert turned his head and saw the Harrier scream over the podium, up towards the rim and with an almighty roar accelerate clear of the stadium.

Now the Merlin became the main magnet from the one surviving machine-gun position. If the aircraft crashed in a fireball, it would take the whole mission with it. Somehow, they got the last man in. Everyone was aboard except Grace. The pilot knew he had a tough call to make.

Robert yelled out. '*Hold on, hold on.*' Grace was ten yards away. It was a miracle none of the bullets had hit her. Run, you can make it.

And then she tripped.

The helo rushed forward, as if to greet her, then stormed right over her and skywards. The last thing Grace saw was Robert Young looking down at her as it flew up and out of sight.

As quiet began to fall on the half-empty ground, she looked up to see the guard clamber over the wall and begin walking towards her. She curled up into a ball.

20

There was pandemonium in the tunnel. Hundreds of people, including most of the VIPs, had taken refuge there and were running round crazily, unable to decide whether to get to their cars or stay where they were.

Nabote was in no doubt at all. As he jumped into the Mercedes, Julius and an ashen-faced Kim tried to do the same. Nabote yelled at Julius.

'No. Go to the broadcasting station. They will take Endebbe there. If you can kill him, we are still safe.'

The fear was etched on Julius's face. 'Let Kim do it.'

'I want him with me at the palace.'

'Father, if they attack, the palace will be hard to defend. We only left twenty men there. You should not go.'

'Wait.' Nabote dialled a number on his mobile and got the answer he was hoping for.

'It is still secure, though I do not know for how long. I *must* collect something first, and then I will go immediately to the Nigerian Embassy. Send the family there.'

Julius nodded. 'I will order some guards to the embassy to protect you, and tell the rest to regroup at our headquarters.'

'*No.* That is what they will expect. It is too easy a target. Send them to the British High Commission instead. With their diplomat there, they will never attack it . . . Now, *go.*'

He pulled the door closed. The driver thrust his foot down and the big car barrelled out of the tunnel and swung right, fishtailing, knocking one young woman clean over the bonnet and scattering the fleeing crowd.

Kim knew he had to break the silence.

'I do not know what to say, Excellency. The fishermen must have been mistaken. But I promise you we will soon recapture Endebbe and recover control.'

Nabote said nothing. As the car bounced and bucked down the road, he reached into a walnut-capped compartment in the door and withdrew a mother-of-pearl-clad 9mm pistol. The driver caught a glimpse of it in the mirror and slowed enough to make sure a bump did not damage the President's aim.

Kim slumped forward, as if lulled to sleep by the drive.

*

Bob Tiernan was pretty sure he'd heard the sound of an aircraft. That could only mean one thing. Now he'd be lucky if they left it at killing him with grenades. He picked up his pen, pulled a candle close to him and began writing a note to Alice. Locked in the safe, it might survive the initial explosion and be overlooked in the looting. If they burned the place to the ground, of course, nothing much would remain. He would try to inhale enough smoke to be asphyxiated before the flames reached him.

His mobile rang. Who the hell . . . ? He pressed the little button.

'Is that Bob Tiernan? This is Toby Gordon-Booth in London . . . We've just received a signal from our submarine off Kindalu. They have advised us that *Indomitable* has launched an operation against several targets in the city. They have no idea yet of the outcome. One Harrier appears to have returned safely to base, but other helicopters have now taken off and are heading landwards.'

There was a pause.

'I know you are in a very difficult position there, Bob, and I don't want to hide from you the possibility of reprisals. We'd like to offer practical assistance, but for the time being that is difficult. We will of course endeavour to ensure that the captain of *Indomitable* understands your predicament. All we can suggest is that you try to hang on as long as possible. The situation will obviously be very volatile for a while. If a hostage situation develops, we will use all possible channels to ensure that you are released unharmed. Now, is there anything you want to ask me?'

'No.'

'Then good luck. We will be back in touch if we have more news. Goodbye.'

Tiernan looked at his battery indicator. The last bar was blinking. That double-barrelled tosser had used up more of his precious power, and told him nothing whatsoever of any use.

Sabre Two and Three had long made it to their objectives. Sabre Three had overwhelmed the guards outside the town hall and then hovered directly over the glass roof. The officials, happy on beer, took time to realise what the terrible noise was, but threw themselves under the tables as shards of glass began to rain down. When they looked out, they saw big black boots thump down on the floor. One of the officials couldn't help noticing how beautifully polished they were. A marine corporal bent down and looked under a table.

'Right, you lot, let's be 'avin' you.'

They crawled out and picked themselves up. One of them was more confused than afraid.

'Who are you?'

The corporal smiled. 'We're international observers . . .'

He used the muzzle of his automatic weapon to indicate the sealed ballot boxes.

'So you'd better get counting.'

*

As the car neared the palace, Nabote tried again. This time he got through.

'General Mbekwe? This is the President. General, you must be aware that the capital has come under attack by the British. They have captured the rebel, Endebbe, and may try to destroy our democracy. This is the opportunity you have waited for, to show the people that our glorious army can protect our freedom and institutions, including the person of the President. It is vital in the interest of the nation as a whole that you move decisively . . .'

The car had entered the palace gates and pulled up outside the main door, where two guards stood sentry as usual. For Nabote it was a hugely reassuring sight. It looked like he still had enough time to gather his box and get to safety. Some of its contents might be his only convertible currency in the critical hours and days ahead. The driver leapt out to open the door, but the President barked at him to wait while he finished the call.

'I wish you to gather all your available men and weapons. Come as fast as possible to the Nigerian Embassy. That is where I will set up an interim headquarters until the crisis is over. And, General, I will not forget this. It is time for us to strengthen the army and make sure that its leading officers are well rewarded. In your own case . . .'

The line went dead. Nabote looked at the phone and threw it down on the seat. As he got out and made for the steps up to the door, he yelled back to the driver.

'Wait here. I will be leaving in five minutes.'

As he dashed in the front door, he failed to notice that the guards didn't salute. With no clips in their rifles, and powerful guns trained on their heads from hidden positions only yards away, they were too scared even to twitch.

By the time Julius got close to the broadcasting station, he could see a helicopter hovering over its roof, and hear the

223

sound of automatic fire. This was no place for him. He grabbed a radio from one of his guards and spoke to the lieutenant inside.

He then radioed his second in command, who was charged with arranging the regroup. They quickly agreed to switch their radio exchanges to Mendé, in case the British were listening in. The report the man provided was a relief. It seemed that they had lost forty or fifty dead and wounded at the stadium, and some others – possibly as many two hundred – might have fled in disorder. However, over three hundred had already made it to the British High Commission, and more were arriving all the time. As Julius had ordered, they had left only a token presence at the Guards HQ and told them to protect the rest of the equipment with their lives. The girl that they had captured at the stadium had now been taken to the High Commission. She had admitted being from the carrier, but was claiming to be a journalist. They would get the truth out of her easily enough, and whatever she turned out to be, having a woman hostage could strengthen their hand greatly.

Julius and his number two tried to calculate. The British had aerial power, but they must surely be outnumbered on the ground. As he left the stadium, Julius had told his men to get word to the Koreans at the airport to come nearer to town, bringing their SA-7s. That should put an end to the flights by the enemy aircraft. Julius looked up again at the roof of the building, and saw the helicopter swing away. Had it been beaten off? From the street he aimed his gun up at the sky and let loose a volley.

As they approached the roof of the broadcasting station, Sabre One had again come under fire. There were four Koreans up there and they were serious about defending it. The marine manning the machine-gun was hit through the temple and had to be dragged away from his post by Billy Ward next to him, so Dewar could take his place. The scene inside the helicopter was grisly even before that. Two of the wounded were bleeding profusely and one was close to losing consciousness. In the four-minute flight from the stadium they hadn't been able to do more than try to apply tourniquets and stab the men with morphine shots. Endebbe was struggling to understand Robert Young's terse, shouted explanation of what was planned next.

Even when the first two Koreans went down, the others kept fighting. The Merlin gyrated; they were taking too much fire. Dewar yanked the ring-pull on a tangerine-shaped grenade, and the lever on top of it flew up. On cue, the helicopter swooped down towards the defenders to help Dewar get close, then flared up and away to avoid the explosion. As they looked back, the firing had stopped. With relief Dewar saw that the radio mast was undamaged.

The helo hovered a few feet above the scarred roof and Dewar and the other marines jumped down. As soon as they had double-checked, Young helped Endebbe out. Next Ward and Moore clambered out too, carrying bulky blue kitbags. The pilot took off immediately. They were sitting ducks if they stayed there, and if the wounded men were to have any chance, they would have to get them back to the ship fast.

As Dewar had guessed, there was only one way into the building, a door at the end of a concrete hut-like structure which jutted inelegantly from the roof. A corporal crept forward and gingerly tried it. Locked. Dewar had a hurried confab with his sergeant. They were sure that there would be more Koreans inside, their guns trained on the door, prepared for the frontal assault. If the marines blew it off its hinges and piled in, they would be cut down in seconds. The sergeant took a quick look at the sidewall, and worked out where the defenders were most likely to be bunched. A few urgent words later and two privates were assembling a shape charge, a wooden square with conical charges at each corner and four detonators. They stuck it to the sidewall and retreated, covering their ears.

They had guessed right. Under the rubble they could see the twisted remains of machine-guns and sandbags. Amazingly, one of the defenders was still moving, covered deep in dust and dazed. His colleagues' bodies must have shielded him from the main impact. One marine took pity and dragged clear the heavy lump of concrete that was pinning his leg down, but there was nothing they could do about his shattered left arm.

They got down two flights unopposed before running into more resistance.

Owen Lewis could not tear himself away from the WTO. The state broadcaster was still playing the anthem. They were getting some sort of wider picture of what was going on by eavesdropping on the sparse radio exchanges between the *Indomitable*'s people. It seemed that a multi-target mission had been launched, but there was no reference to places. All that they could be sure of was that Sabre One had succeeded in the first part of its mission, though not without casualties, and Cameron had reacted with clear concern about someone they'd obviously had to abandon on the ground.

Simon was adding to the sum of their knowledge through fragments of Mendé exchanges between the guards. A struggle seemed to be underway for control of the broadcasting building. In the last two minutes, Simon had heard the guards' commander ordering his man to put out a positive statement on the radio. When he heard a comment about their plans for the diplomat, Simon's heart went out to the guy, barricaded alone, and with more firebrand guards arriving every minute, drunk with desire for revenge. Surely it wouldn't be long before they winkled him out. Simon silently thanked his lucky stars for the snug safety of *Tenacious*.

A few seconds later, he pulled down the headset and turned round to Lewis.

'There's something they were just saying that makes no sense. I wonder if I mixed up the words.'

'What is it?'

'I *think* they said they've got a second Brit captive at the high commission, a woman.'

'A *woman*?'

'I can't be sure.'

'Keep on listening. We need to be sure before telling London. If by any chance you're right, this crisis just got even worse – if that's possible.'

Number Ten was being briefed by the minute. To the American President – and him alone – the Prime Minister admitted the truth by telephone. The President agreed to tell only the National Security Advisor, the Defense Secretary, the Secretary of State, the head of the CIA and his own Chief of Staff. There was no other country the PM was willing to trust. Knowing that word of the attack would be breaking, European governments had been told that after the withdrawal of the *Indomitable*, the government had picked up intelligence that the Numalans were planning to infringe the diplomatic sanctity of the British mission. As a result, the UK had ordered the carrier to return to within easy striking range of Kindalu in case any British hostages were taken and military intervention was necessary. The line wouldn't hold for long, but it bought them time.

Nathan Nabote was in such a hurry to get to the safe in his study to recover his precious box that he hadn't noticed the absence of servants. With trembling hands, he worked the combination and took out the small heavy box. He had got out to the hall, carrying it by its delicate gold handle, when it struck him.

'Where is everyone?'

He hurried through to the ballroom. As the light faded outside, the room glistened all the more brilliantly, the gold-rimmed crystal glasses catching the light from the chandeliers. But it was empty. There was something horribly wrong. He must get out of here, fast. He went as quickly as his ageing legs and long costume would take him back to the main marble hallway.

A man in uniform was sitting there. Nabote gasped.

'Who are you?'

The resistance was serious. The marines had wanted to avoid using explosives inside, for fear of damaging the gear. It looked like that was hard luck. One floor below them, six guards and two Koreans pointed weapons at the head of broadcasting as he spoke into the microphone.

'Order is now being restored. The foreigners are retreating in disorder. Six helicopters and four jets have been brought down by our heroic forces. The death sentence on the traitor Endebbe has been carried out by firing squad. Following his glorious victory in the election, President Nabote—'

He broke off when he heard the dull crash of an explosion overhead, followed by the muffled sound of firing and shouts. The guard in command looked up too, but gave the broadcaster a prod with his gun.

'His Excellency President Nabote has assumed personal command of the army, the Presidential Guard and the navy, and is . . .'

This bang was closer and very much louder. The guard was getting more worried.

'You, carry on with the broadcast . . .' He gestured to the

Koreans and four of the guards to follow him. To the other two he said in Mendé: 'You stay here. If they get close, destroy the equipment.'

'Where are my guards?'

Cameron's voice was calm. 'They are in the garden. They are intelligent men and have worked out what will happen if they move one muscle.'

'This is an outrage, a flagrant breach of our sovereignty. We will censure your government in the United Nations, in the International Court, in every international forum. Britain will be an outcast, a leper.'

'Frankly, I don't give a damn.'

'What possible legal justification can you offer for your conduct?'

'None that you would be interested in.'

'At least you can tell me your intentions. I presume that Britain has not sunk so low as to assassinate a democratically elected head of state.'

'We're not sure how democratic it was . . . My men have dropped in on the town hall. It appears that *your* men over-looked a few votes. Like all of them. We've now instituted a proper count.'

Nabote looked beyond him to the front door. Two British marines stepped into fuller sight. He sat down on a chair opposite Cameron, clutching his box, wondering how to play his next moves. Could this man be bribed? Before he could try, Cameron spoke again.

'While we are waiting for the result, there is something you can tell me. Your guards at the stadium took captive a British woman civilian from my ship. I want to know where she is.'

Nabote looked thrown. 'I have no idea.'

Cameron took out his pistol and stepped to the chair.

229

'I said I want to know.'

'And I said I have no idea.'

Cameron put the muzzle against Nabote's thigh. 'If you don't tell me now, you will have a very sore leg.'

The President was sweating profusely, and his pleas were becoming falsetto. Cameron concluded that the man was either a consummate actor or telling the truth. Slowly he pulled the gun away. It did not take Nabote long to spot an opening.

'If you will let me make a phone call, I will find out for you. I will ask my son, the guards' Commander-in-Chief. Please bring my mobile phone from my car.'

Cameron was desperate to discover Grace's whereabouts, but if he let Nabote phone, it would alert his son to her significance, which could make things even worse for her. And letting the guards know that the President had been taken could prompt an immediate attack of the palace. With only ten marines, and one of them wounded, he was in no position to repel serious numbers.

The guard left in charge at the broadcasting station had sent the Koreans and his own men ahead to try to stop the attackers getting near to the studio. Soon his ears were telling him it was a losing battle. His only hope of getting at Endebbe was through stealth. There was only one way for the enemy to reach the studio, down a long corridor. He trotted along it and chose one of the many doors leading off it. He pulled the door carefully to, so that it stood open only one inch, and stood silently behind it, pistol in hand.

He didn't have to wait long. The last defenders were beaten back, and Dewar and two of his men burst down the corridor, past that door, and on into the studio. The gunfire in there was soon silenced. Dewar came back to the corridor and gestured to the others to follow. The guard bided his time. Ward and Moore dashed along, heads down, dragging their bags. Two seconds more. Then, *yes*. Michael Endebbe was hobbling along, one of his arms round Robert's neck.

The guard flung the door open, pointing his pistol straight at the heart of the traitor. Young threw himself forward, taking the first bullet in his shoulder, the second in his chest, the third in the side of his head as he went crashing down. Endebbe collapsed as his legs gave way. The guard stepped closer. As he raised his gun to take more careful aim, footsteps thudded behind him, and the great hams of Billy Ward's arms came around him from the rear, swinging him so violently that the weapon flew clean out of his grasp and clattered to the floor. Wrestling himself clear, the guard lunged for it, but Billy kicked him in the face so hard that it knocked the fight and half the consciousness out of him.

When Billy looked back where Robert lay and saw the pool of blood and the smashed temple, he let out a yell and flung himself at the dazed guard, and tore into him with fists and feet. Dewar had got back to the corridor now too. He went over and knelt by Robert's shattered body, then got back up and put a hand on Ward's shoulder.

'Billy, you're needed in there. I'll let the Captain know.'

Billy pulled himself to his feet and administered one last rib-crushing kick before going through to join Trish in the studio, wiping hot angry tears from his cheeks as he went.

21

Nabote listened carefully as Cameron answered the bleep on his radio.

'Yes. Oh *no* . . . And you've heard nothing about . . . ? Okay. Thanks, over.'

'Bad news, I hope?'

'For me, yes, very bad. But for you too. My men took the liberty of searching your house for a radio. As you see, I have set it up over there.'

Cameron went over and switched it on. It was playing the national anthem. He sat down again, buried in his own thoughts.

They waited impatiently for the national anthem to end. One of the operators had alerted Lewis as soon as the previous broadcast was broken off. Simon had been picking up ever more worrying signs. There had been some sort of shoot-out near the airport. The Koreans manning the defences were pinned down there, but it sounded like one of *Indomitable*'s helos had crashed. The better news was that the guards seemed to have lost radio contact with their own headquarters. However, they had now managed to muster around four hundred and fifty of their number at the High Commission. The guards might be bruised and off balance, but they were still numerically far superior to the marines.

There had been no more mention of hostages. Could the British chargé d'affaires be dead? The music stopped abruptly and there was silence. Lewis put his ear nearer the speaker. Simon pulled his headset off to listen.

'People of Numala, this is Michael Endebbe.'

Simon threw his arms out exultantly. 'They fucking well did it.'

Lewis smiled. 'Let's not count our chickens. But so far, so fucking good eh?'

Nabote listened calmly till the end of the speech. It had been in the circumstances a measured affair. Endebbe was not even claiming victory yet. He looked over at Cameron.

'Before you congratulate yourself, you should consider, have you achieved anything? Oh yes, you have saved a traitor from the gallows. Endebbe is a worthless person. Attractive in the eyes of people like you, perhaps. A country like Numala needs a strong leader who understands his people and knows what is good for them. All that man can do is slavishly copy you. He is a third-rate white man in a black man's skin. Take him with you. Do not leave him here, because if he stays here as your puppet, I will overthrow him in a month.'

'You will find it hard to overthrow anyone from a prison cell.'

'Endebbe will lose the vote, and then what will you do? Unless, of course, you cheat. If on that basis he were to win, I presume you would arrange transport abroad for me and my family. That is standard international practice, I believe. From exile I will plan my return at leisure.'

'I'm not a big fan of standard practice. And I'm sure your judiciary have their own standard practice for cases of murder, rape, corruption, and conspiracy to commit genocide on your own people. You and your son will be handed over to them.'

Nabote smiled. What did it matter what the judiciary did,

even if Endebbe appointed new judges? A proper trial would take *months*. He cared not one hoot if the army supported Endebbe; they would not be able to resist the guards once the British had left. In the meantime, the guards held the diplomat, and, by the sound of it, maybe one other hostage. That should be enough to block any idea of summary justice. He felt his confidence begin to flow back. A crushing victory was still possible. All he had to do was to hold his nerve. In fact, he should not demean himself by attempting to bribe this loathsome captain.

The CNN team were finally ready to transmit, but they still weren't sure what to use as a backdrop. All they knew was they didn't want to venture very far. The best would be the Parliament building, right round the corner. They would have to hope the floodlights stayed on. The day had worked out very differently from what they'd expected. They had been steered firmly away from the stadium event, probably because the government had calculated that the image of the opposition leader's dangling body might not play well on US and European screens. Instead the correspondent and cameraman had been cooling their heels in a downtown hotel, waiting for the call to come to the palace to record the speech the President would make at the banquet.

The first evidence of a change of plan was when they heard aircraft overhead, followed by distant gunfire. In the hotel there was chaos, with the few residents locking themselves in their rooms, and the casual visitors not knowing whether to stay put or run for their lives. There was no information about what was happening. First there was the broadcast announcement of Endebbe's death, followed quickly by the dead man's own voice. Even two hours later, the dust had not started to settle. There were claims and counter-claims everywhere, with rumours that Nabote had fled to the north, others that he was in the Nigerian Embassy, yet more that he had taken over the British High Commission and that the Presidential Guard were rallying to him there. For the first time in months, they had seen men from the army, as one ancient Soviet tank rolled by, tearing up the remains of the tarmac.

There were no other foreign correspondents to check with, and now they had no more choice: get on and do something over the satellite phone, or lose their jobs for ducking one of the biggest stories in ages.

*

High in Canary Wharf, fifty people were gathered round the TV set. The earliest word had come half an hour ago over the wires. CNN was showing the first pictures.

'Night has fallen in Kindalu, leaving the city in confusion. Behind me is the Parliament building, but which party will control it is far from clear. A coup d'état appears to have been launched by the Numalan army, who are believed to have rescued the Opposition leader, Michael Endebbe, from execution at the eleventh hour. British forces operating from the carrier HMS *Indomitable* have been involved, but it is not yet known what was their role or objective. Rumours that President Nabote has fled the capital have been dismissed by a government spokesman, who accused the army and the British of trying to overthrow by military means a democratically elected leader.'

Peter Mayhew, standing next to the editor, permitted himself a chuckle.

'Some accident, eh, John?'

The rest of the group stole looks at Jason. A wicked smile even played around Debbie's lips. The presenter interrupted a pundit to announce that the Foreign Office had just issued a statement. She read it out. 'The action by British forces in Kindalu follows the capture of the chargé d'affaires, Robert

Tiernan, who was taken hostage in the High Commission building. Efforts are continuing to secure his release.' The editor shook his head. There had to be more to it than that. If they were going to get any half-decent comment for the first edition, they'd have to hit the ground running.

'Peter, pull out all the stops at the MoD and the FCO. Jason, you concentrate on the women. Try to track down the wife of this Tiernan fellow and see what you can find out about him. If you can't raise her, get hold of the High Commissioner; he must be around somewhere. Now at least we know why Grace wasn't allowed to communicate. When they release her from it, she should have one hell of a story to write.'

Jason pulled a face. 'Really? She's probably drinking a gin and tonic in the wardroom.'

*

Tantalising though it had been, they hadn't laid hands on her. They had touched her up just a little, shoving their hands up her dress and down her front. Nothing serious, though. None would have dared strip her – let alone take her – before *he* arrived. So they'd tied her up in a chair, and a few of them entertained themselves by standing inches in front of her, making graphically lewd body movements, and laughing uproariously at the cowed reaction. One pulled his dick out and pissed all over her dress, then quickly thought better of it and threw a bucket of water over her. The boss wouldn't want her to smell of anything except fear.

When Julius got there, the woman wasn't his priority. It was to secure their defences. If he put guards all round the perimeter compound, it would be too easy for snipers to pick them off. Better convert the main building into a fortress. With the diplomat there, the Brits would never risk storming it. He gave the order, and all the men on the gates and the fences were summoned back inside. He decided not to switch the mains power back on, and stick instead to the lamps they had rigged up using car batteries. This would keep the hostage Tiernan in the dark, and in the rest of the building, the low light inside would make it harder for any snipers to see what was going on.

He was assuming that Mbekwe had gone over to Endebbe. That wasn't too worrying in itself. In recent years the army's numbers had shrunk to three or four thousand men, and an ill-armed, poorly disciplined rabble they were. As long as they hadn't got hold of the arms at the Guards' HQ, they would have little more to shoot with than some rusty old rifles, a couple of field guns that would probably explode if they were fired and at best one serviceable tank lacking shells. Even if they did get hold of newer weapons, they were no match for the guards as a fighting force. Provided, of course, the British had gone.

How many soldiers must the British have? One hundred, two hundred? He couldn't risk a straight shoot-out with them. That was why he must keep hold of the High Commission until they were gone. It was good that they now had two hostages. If they needed to show they were serious, they could kill or mutilate one and still hold the upper hand. International opinion would put pressure on the British to sort out a solution quickly and leave. It would not matter what deal he or his father agreed to as long as they were gone: it would take no more than a week to get control back.

Since his father hadn't made it to the Nigerian Embassy, he must have been captured. It was his poor judgement that lay at the heart of the problem. Endebbe should have been killed days ago. And going back to the palace – presumably to gather his stash of diamonds – had been stupid. Worst of all, depending on Kim had been a fatal mistake. If the British had got them, they would feel the need to observe the rule of law. Mbekwe and Endebbe might kill him while they could. It was what he would do in their place.

One way or another, his father's stature was fatally diminished. It was unlikely that he could regain his authority. If it was proved that the votes had not even been counted, no one abroad would take him seriously again. The reaction wouldn't be much better at home. They would detect the vulnerability and move against him. The time had come to act decisively. His father had groomed him as his successor. If it hadn't been for British interference, he would have been forced to endure another ten years of waiting. This could be his moment. Unlike his father, he would not need to consult some witch doctor before striking.

It was time to concentrate on the hostages. The diplomat was still locked in his chamber. He had arrived just in time to stop the idiots using grenades to blow it open. They might well have killed him, and what use was a British corpse? He told them to continue with axes and picks. It should not take more than a couple of hours. In the meantime there was the girl. This he would enjoy. He went through and slumped down in a chair opposite her and examined her with amusement.

Grace looked away when she saw him coming. She felt desolate, betrayed. She had risked everything, and they had left her there in the stadium, to be killed or to face an ordeal that might be far worse than death. The most bitter pill was that Cameron had abandoned her.

Julius pointed his gun casually at her crotch.

'So, you're a journalist?'

'Yes.'

She had already told his men everything. Everything except the mutiny, and only that because they hadn't asked, and she wasn't convinced they'd believe her. They had scared her so horribly. Not even that had prepared her for what she now felt seeing those evil eyes. In the semi-darkness, he looked terrifyingly sinister. When he moved his hands, she couldn't stop herself looking at the long thin fingers, silhouetted in the weak lamplight, that had carved initials on Theresa's breasts. What would he carve on hers?

'You went to the stadium in order to tell white men when to attack your own kind.'

She stayed silent.

'Are you sorry for your actions?'

'Yes, I am very sorry.' Her only hope was to be servile.

Julius nodded. His voice seemed to go softer. 'Tell me, Grace, how many men there have been?'

'What?'

'How many men have had you?'

'I don't know.'

'So many that you can't remember? Are you a journalist or a whore?'

'Eight or nine.'

'Are you married?'

'I am engaged.'

'To a black man?'

She shook her head.

'So, how many of this nine were white?'

'Four.'

'Ah . . . So you are not choosy. That is good, because by this time tomorrow you will have added four hundred and sixty-six black men to your list of conquests. That will give you something to write about. It will be an interesting experience for a nice professional woman from England . . . Many of my men are HIV positive, which is why I always insist on being first. To get AIDS from a woman would be unfortunate, but to catch it from the body fluids of my own men would be revolting.'

She retched. Tied as she was, the vomit went all over her dress. One of Julius's men came in. They both rocked with laughter.

Julius stood up, still laughing. 'I am busy now. I will leave you to enjoy your own stench. My men will hose you down before I come for you.'

*

London was anxious for more news. They were still dithering on whether to send a Foreign Office junior minister on

Newsnight. Apart from CNN, the only source of information was *Tenacious* monitoring the radio waves. Numalan radio was continuing to report that a recount was underway and that the result would be announced as soon as possible. With London's backing, *Tenacious* had tried to communicate directly with *Indomitable*, asking if they had captured Nabote. There was no response.

On board the submarine, Lewis was getting worried about Simon. This was exhausting work even in shorter stretches, and he'd been at it now non-stop for over nine hours, with not a lot to sustain him beyond gallons of coffee and barrels of biscuits. He'd brushed away the XO's suggestion that they tape some of it, and let him listen to it after he'd rested. He was thinking, but didn't point out, that the hostages couldn't ask for a break.

Lewis's eye was caught as Simon's hand shot up.

'What is it?'

'They've just said it again. It *is* a woman. A journalist.'

Lewis turned to the XO. 'Cameron has a correspondent from the *Post* on board, doesn't he? Surely he wouldn't have brought her in with the attack, though. It's more likely to be some journo working locally. I didn't think there were many left. We'd better let London know, all the same. And *Indomitable*.'

22

Colin Dewar had finally made it to the palace. Having stayed at the broadcasting station until Sabre Two came to evacuate the casualties and Robert's body, he'd had the helicopter drop him off, together with four unscathed marines from Sabre One. Sabre Two had brought some reinforcements too, and he calculated that in total he had twenty-two men in the city and five more near the airport. Of those in the city, six had been deputed to stay with the army platoon guarding Endebbe's impromptu base in the Ocean Hotel.

Dewar and Cameron got down to business. They were acutely aware how precarious their situation was becoming. They'd anticipated that the bulk of the Presidential Guards would go back to their HQ, where they could be attacked from the air. That had not happened, and now the element of surprise had been lost. Flying was becoming increasingly hazardous, their only form of ground transportation was cars they could commandeer, and, as time went on, their lack of local knowledge and small numbers would tell against them. Although the army had come over to Endebbe, they would not be able to rely on them if the Presidential Guards came out fighting.

Time was of the essence. The cold light of morning would reveal with hideous clarity how poorly things stood. If their handful of men at the airport couldn't hold out, they might lose more than the one aircraft and, far from being able to use helos and Harriers on the offensive, might be holed up here, prey rather than predator. Whatever they were going to do, it would have to be tonight. There were three options.

One, withdraw now, and leave Endebbe and the army to take their own chances. Two, take Endebbe with them. Three, go on the offensive. If so, they would have to work out the dispositions of the guards, even if that meant risking helos with night-vision gear. Whatever they were going to do, they needed to get away from their vulnerable position in the palace. With its sprawling layout it would be impossible to defend with such small numbers.

They said little about Robert. Right now talking about it wouldn't help. Their exchanges about Grace, too, were limited to the stark facts. Colin was deeply affected by what had happened to her. Had they shot her there and then? If she was alive, he shuddered to think what they were doing to her. He didn't think he could ask how the captain was feeling about it. Did Cameron blame them for not staying the extra seconds to save her? Or did he consider her just another casualty of war? Colin didn't have the faintest idea.

The radio bleeped. Cameron grabbed it.

'This is Wings . . . We've just had another message from Wales. Over.'

Cameron smiled at the reference to Owen Lewis.

'Roger.'

'They have picked up intelligence that they are holding a second hostage at the High Commission. A woman journalist. Over.'

Cameron's hand tightened on the radio. 'Do they have any estimate of numbers there? Over.'

'Yes. They think four hundred plus. Over.'

'Have you looked at the possibilities? Over?'

'We've downloaded the large-scale satellite images. The residence of the Swiss Ambassador is directly opposite the target and seems to have a back garden big enough to land a Sea King if we needed to. Over.'

Dewar had found the High Commission on the map and pointed.

'Yes, we have it. I think we have enough cars to get us

there. I don't want to advertise our arrival or risk a helo until we have to. In the meantime, can you get the engineers to knock me up a "special" radio set? Do you understand? Over.'

'I understand. I'll get them working on it. Out.'

Cameron put the radio down beside him.

'Did you get all that? . . . Okay, let's get moving.'

'What about Nabote?'

Cameron glanced out towards the hallway, where the President was still under guard. 'He comes too.'

'I don't suppose the Swiss Ambassador will appreciate us dropping by uninvited.'

'Don't worry. We'll let him stay neutral.'

*

The convoy was a weird sight. It had been a squeeze getting all the men into the few cars at the palace. There were large calibre Barrett guns, too big to get inside, poking out of the windows, and boot lids flapping up and down like butterfly wings: with all the gear crammed in, it was impossible to get them closed. Cameron and Dewar were travelling in the big Mercedes, and had taken Nabote with them, forcing his chauffeur to drive. It was just as well that they had him: street lighting was intermittent, and alone they would have got hopelessly lost. Before getting into the front passenger seat, Dewar had to pull out Kim's body. The upholstery and dashboard were still smeared with his blood.

Nabote felt smug. Though this captain had said nothing about their destination, and his own driver was too frightened to answer the question he had himself posed in Mendé, from the route they were taking he could guess where they were going. That had confirmed that the tide was running his way. Julius must have consolidated his men at the High Commission, and would be readying his proposition in return for the lives of the hostages. Presumably he would deliver his demands to the captain when they arrived. Surely then the British would have no choice but to retreat. He smiled thinly at the prospect of a second ignominious withdrawal, and a resounding phrase occurred to him that he could use tellingly in his speech when the army was crushed, and his election was reconfirmed. It was a pity that he had been forced to sit behind his driver, and not in his usual seat. He might have been able to ease open the side compartment and slip out his handgun. He looked out and saw they were entering the street where the High Commission building was situated.

Cameron told the driver to stop two hundred yards away. The other three cars braked to a halt behind them. Dewar jumped out and ordered six of his men to go with him on foot. His reconnaissance took less than five minutes. As far as he could work out, the guards must all have retreated within the High Commission building. The gates appeared to be unmanned. They managed to get to the Swiss residence unchallenged. When they knocked on the door and marched right in as the servant opened it, the ambassador emerged from his dining room, looking astonished and unsure whether to be relieved or outraged. With all the activity across the road, he had been in a state of anxiety for some hours, hoping fervently that the drama would shift to some other part of town. Dewar left it to one of his men to deal with the protests, and got on with radioing the captain. The other cars came up the road at speed, swung in through the residence gates and decanted their cargoes without a single shot being fired at them.

They embarked on a quick survey of the house, finding a useful couple of cellars, one of which could be used for locking up Nabote. Dewar sent two of his men to the master bedroom on the first floor, from where they would have a good view across the street.

*

Their arrival did not go unnoticed. When Julius was alerted to the sound of the cars, he ordered his men at the upper windows to hold their fire. This was not the time to start a fight. In fact, it was a good sign that they had come.

Having found the British Foreign Office switchboard number in a directory on the reception desk, he had dialled it on his cellphone and got through at the second attempt. The operator quickly transferred him to someone senior. He had dictated his catalogue of demands, and the man had read them back to confirm and rang off. Julius doubted that much would happen for the next few hours. His men were making good progress chipping away round the security door and would have the diplomat out well before the first deadline. If they had to kill one of the hostages, it would be him.

He was relieved that the nervousness among his own men had begun to subside and their natural swagger was coming back. He had played a large part in that, going round the building, cheering them up. The girl would help too. He was looking forward to kicking things off with her, but there was no hurry. It was good to get in the mood to savour a woman. He had a joint, which helped him relax. Considering how bad things had looked at half-past five, it was remarkable how much they'd recovered by eight forty.

They had been guests of the Swiss for less than ten minutes when Wings came through to Cameron on the radio.

'Wales has received a signal from London. They are in receipt of a set of demands from the Presidential Guards. Will you take a call direct from him to describe? Over.'

'Yes. Out.'

It took only the shortest time for the radio to bleep again. Cameron went straight to the point.

'Hello, Owen. What do they want? Over.'

'The demand is from the Commander-in-Chief of the

Guards, Julius Nabote. He is in our High Commission building and claims to be holding the journalist from your ship as well as the chargé d'affaires. He requires the withdrawal of all UK forces from Numalan territory by dawn, plus a formal promise not to return or intervene in any other way. If they do not receive our agreement by midnight, they will kill one of the hostages. The other will die at six a.m. After that, they will begin an offensive and will take no British prisoners. Over.'

'Understood.'

'There is also a personal message for you from the Prime Minister. In the exceptional circumstances, he recognises that they have no one else on the ground in a position to negotiate, and asks if you are willing to assume this role. He adds that he hopes that you will bear in mind that the safety of hostages is paramount, and that loss of life on all sides should be avoided if possible. Over.'

'If I accept, how am I to contact them? Over.'

'They have provided a radio frequency for you to use. Finally, you should be aware that London still has direct contact by cellphone with the first hostage. However, they fear this may not be available for much longer. Over.'

'Roger. Give me both. Over.'

Cameron scribbled the numbers. 'Tell London I'll negotiate my own way. Over.'

'I expected nothing less. Over.'

'Owen, this is very important. Do you have any equipment on board which could be used for very-short-range listening? Over.'

'I believe we could rig something up. Over.'

'Then I need to borrow it. And I gather you have someone on board with the gift of the local gab? Over.'

'That is correct. Over.'

'I want him too. If I send a helo, can we pick both up? Over.'

'There's a snag. My man's a civilian, and I don't know how keen he will be, but I'll try. Over.'

246

'Thank you. Over.'

'Good luck. Out.'

Dewar had heard the lot as he sat checking his automatic. Cameron squatted on his haunches beside him.

'What d'you reckon, Colin?'

Dewar gave himself a moment to reflect. 'Well, sir, after all the whole ship's company has been through, and the casualties we've taken today, I don't think any of us will feel particularly thrilled about buggering off now, with or without Endebbe. I'm sure he's a decent guy, but surely we didn't come all this way only to save his skin.'

'If we leave, how d'you rate the chances of the army holding out?'

'They haven't fought in years. Even with what they've scavenged from the Guards HQ, they have very little equipment. I think it'll be all over by tomorrow night.'

Cameron nodded quietly. 'Did you ever study Nelson?'

'I read a book about him a long time ago. Can't say I remember much of it.'

'Never mind the details, from what you generally recall of the man, what d'you think he would have done here?'

Dewar clicked the magazine back into place. 'I don't think he would've gone a bundle on murderers and rapists like the Presidential Guards. I reckon he'd have done something about them.'

Cameron clapped him on the shoulder. 'Thanks, Colin; that's what I think, too.'

He reached for the radio.

'Wings, is that special radio ready? Over.'

'Yes. Over.'

'Good . . . Can you send it here via Wales? I need a few things picked up there too. Over.'

'No problem. Out.'

*

One of Julius's men came in carrying a radio. He said they had been contacted on the frequency they'd given the Brits by some guy saying he was in the Swiss Embassy and claiming to be Cameron, the captain of *Indomitable*. Julius smiled with satisfaction and took it.

'Good evening, Captain. I hope you find this a pleasant neighbourhood. I presume you have heard my demands. What is your response?'

'My government is still considering its substantive response. However, we have an interim offer for you.'

'What is that?'

'I am willing to exchange myself in return for your two hostages.'

What was this shit? Julius couldn't work it out . . . He needed time, and told Cameron he would radio back on the same frequency.

What should he do? It could be a trap. But what if it was a genuine offer? The situation in London or Washington might be moving fast. The British might be coming under intolerable pressure. They might need to agree a deal faster than he'd expected, and be keen to keep him sweet in the meantime. The government could have ordered Cameron to do this. Imagine if he, Julius Nabote, captured the commander of the hated *Indomitable*. In propaganda terms, this man would be worth fifty diplomats or journalists. Imagine the war crimes trial. Cameron would be tried and executed. Or imprisoned for life, as a symbol of Western double standards. No other trophy would guarantee more completely his succession as President.

But again, it could be a trap. He would be a fool to release both. Let him have the diplomat. That would be a good exchange. They would keep the girl. It would be a tragedy to let her leave without experiencing their hospitality. He would, however, hold that detail back till the last minute.

He picked up his radio. 'Captain Cameron? Very well, I accept.'

'Good. I will radio back soon to let you know when I am ready.'

*

'Is that Tiernan?'

'Yes.' The voice sounded shaky, and there was a muffled sound of hammering in the background.'

'This is Cameron of *Indomitable*. What is your situation?'

'I'm still in the registry in the basement, but they'll break through before long.'

'When?'

Bob aimed the torch at his watch. 9.46. 'Ten thirty, latest. By the way, this phone's almost out of juice.'

'Okay. I'll call again later.'

*

This wasn't even remotely funny. Getting excited about the mission was one thing, but being nearly swept overboard in the dark, swaying sickeningly as he was winched aloft, then flying into the danger zone over Kindalu, hearing gunfire, never knowing when a bullet or a rocket would take them out. Why had he been dumb enough to agree? It must be the exhaustion addling his brain. The engineer who had come along from the submarine with him, bringing the listening gear, looked distinctly nervous too. Simon decided to close his eyes, and only opened them again when he felt the helicopter swooping down. Below he saw the lights that the marines had laid out in the back garden of the residence. The pilot didn't mess around landing, and they bumped hard onto the lawn. Simon and the engineer scrambled out and, with heads down, ran into the back of the big house.

Cameron was there to greet them. After all he had heard, Simon couldn't stop himself being in awe of the man.

249

'Thanks for coming over. Specially you, Simon, as a civilian. I appreciate it . . . I'm afraid we haven't got a lot of time to chat now. Can you get the gear working in the bedroom upstairs?'

A marine showed them the way. Although the Captain had said little enough, there was something in his manner that had instantly brushed away Simon's fears. In three seconds he had made him feel part of the A-team. His chest swelled with the wish to do his best for the man. Back in the kitchen, the helicopter co-pilot came in, and held a small package out to Cameron.

'Sir, I was asked to give you this.'

Upstairs, Simon was in business within three minutes. The engineer had hooked the gear up to the heavy-duty batteries, positioned the directional antenna so it pointed horizontally across the street, tested it, and handed the headphones over. As Simon pulled them on, he could hear from the next room the Ambassador's wife doing her Swiss nut. Toblerone flashed through his mind and was forcibly expunged. No time for that now. It was nine fifty-eight.

By ten past ten, he'd got nothing useful. Cameron had come in three times already, getting no more than rueful shakes of the head.

Thirty seconds later things changed. Simon waved his arms furiously, trying to attract attention without stopping listening. The engineer ran off and yelled down. The Captain took the stairs three at a time. Simon waited to catch another sentence, then pulled one of the earpieces away.

'They're not going to give you both, only one.'

'Do you know which?'

'The man. They're going to keep the girl.'

Cameron nodded and pressed the button on his radio.

'This is Cameron again. I'm ready to come over to you now.'

250

Julius's voice came back. 'You will walk across to the High Commission, alone and unarmed. When you are safely inside, we will release the hostages.'

Cameron pulled a wry face. What did this idiot take him for? 'No way. We'll make the switch in the middle of the street. Bring them out.'

'Impossible. You must come inside. You have my word of honour.'

'Nothing doing.'

'Okay, we'll do it outside, but if that's the case you only get one.'

'That wasn't the deal.'

'I don't trust you. Unless you come over here, we're only willing to exchange one for you. Take it or leave it.'

'Okay, but make it quick. Which are you offering?'

'Tiernan.'

Just as Cameron had expected. 'Right, bring him out now.'

'We'll bring him in twenty minutes.'

Good. They meant they hadn't got Tiernan out yet, and they would have to release Grace. 'Why?'

'He's ill. We're giving him medicine.'

'Balls. It's now, or the deal's off altogether.'

'I'll make it fifteen.'

'It's right this minute. Or nothing.'

Inside the doorway of the High Commission, Julius hesitated. What was the big hurry? He was in the driving seat. Why not call this man's bluff? On the other hand, what if, for whatever reason, he backed off? The chance might be gone for good. He hated to lose the girl, but then maybe he didn't have to.

'Okay, but we don't do it in the street. We do it inside the gates here, in front of the building. That's my best offer. Otherwise we kill one within the hour.'

'Very well. I'll be there in two minutes.'

Julius turned to his second in command, told him how to brief the two men who would accompany the woman to the

251

switch, then went to where Grace was and told the man guarding her to untie the rope.

Grace started to shake. Were they going to kill her now? Or was the raping about to start?

'What are you doing?'

'You're being exchanged. For another hostage. Less pretty, but a bigger fish.'

'What? *Who?*'

'The captain of the carrier.'

The astonishment barely had time to register on her face. He grabbed her wrist and yanked her to the door.

As he stood by the front door, Cameron could just make out the shape of one of the six marines who were slithering on their stomachs across the road yards away from the High Commission gates. From behind, he heard the clatter of heavy boots on the stairs, and turned to see Dewar running down the hallway towards him.

'The translator's just heard them say they're going to try to grab her back as soon as they have you.'

Cameron pulled a wry face. 'Surprise, surprise.' He looked at his watch and punched the button on the cellphone they'd borrowed from the Ambassador.

'Tiernan. It's Cameron again. Is there anywhere impact-proof where you are?'

Tiernan shone the torch around. 'Only the safe.'

'Can you get inside it?'

'Doubt it. Even if I could, I'd never breathe . . . That's my phone bleeping. It's about to die.'

'Listen. Do you have a watch?'

'Yes.'

'It's ten twenty-four. In five minutes, try to get as much of your body as possible inside it. You may not . . . *Damn.*'

Tiernan's battery had gone.

Cameron made his final preparations and had a private word with Dewar. He left him with one final order.

'Remember, whatever happens – whether I'm in there or not – don't abort the ten-thirty run.'

'I understand, sir. Good luck.'

When they saw Cameron entering the gates, two guards came out towards him and another pair brought Grace out of the building. Her legs were shaky and she could only manage one step at a time. She looked up and saw him coming. Her eyes caught his. Despite all she had felt and thought in the last five or six hours, she wanted to find some word to say. But what? Even a simple thanks was out of place. He said nothing either, only smiled. He seemed strangely calm.

She watched the guards step forward to take his arms and saw him lay his radio down on the ground, and, for some reason, reach up to touch his ears.

The last she remembered of the exchange was seeing something small flying over the wall. Six stun grenades went off simultaneously, ten times louder than thunder, fifty times brighter than lightning. Grace went down like a sack of potatoes. Even with ear plugs and closed eyes, Cameron staggered and fell. The four guards were on their knees, dazed out of their skulls. The grenades were bouncing about like jack-in-the-boxes from hell, exploding again and again.

From the upstairs windows across the way two long-barrelled Barrett guns opened fire, punching huge half-inch bullets right through the upper façade of the High Commission. Marines wearing ear defenders and goggles raced in through the gates and sprinted forward to drag Grace away and help Cameron back to his feet. One of them deftly side-footed Cameron's radio, sending it skittering forward, unnoticed. Before the defenders could recover, Grace and Cameron had been spirited, unhurt, to safety.

Inside the building Julius had fallen to the floor. There was a crazed look in his eyes. From his prone position he yelled. 'Kill that other hostage. *Now!*'

As Grace came to in the kitchen of the Swiss residence, she opened her eyes and saw Cameron.

'You bastard. I thought you were really going to swap yourself for me.'

Cameron smiled and pulled out his ear plugs. 'Sorry, can't hear a word.'

She couldn't hear him either. The stun grenades had temporarily deafened her. Cameron glanced at his watch. Ten twenty-eight.

Bob had tried it once already. If he took his shoes off he could nearly fit in, but he couldn't get the door closed. His digital watch said ten twenty-eight and forty-five seconds. He was squirming, trying to get a better angle, when a hand grenade went off, blowing the registry door right off its hinges and through the air, sending debris flying like shrapnel. Pain whipped through him like an electric shock. He had taken a hit on one calf. His torch was shattered. There was cloudy light coming from the far side, but in that contorted position, and with all the choking dust, he was struggling to see, breathe or think. Was that why Cameron had told him to get in the safe? Was he supposed to come out now? As he pushed his one good leg out, it bumped into something solid. *Shit.* The remains of the door had come to rest over his half-open safe, trapping him. He strained again. It was useless. He heard angry voices getting closer.

Shane Black had volunteered to fly one more mission. Even if Demon One had been serviceable, he wouldn't have flown it. This was a job for the heavy mob, the Harrier variant with wider wings and bigger engines.

As he crossed the coastline, the red blinking light came on. Good. The smart bomb's homing device was working. He hoped they'd placed the frigging thing in the right place.

Cameron's radio lay where it had come to rest, just below a window in the front of the peppered High Commission facade, silently sending its Judas signal. All the marines and everyone else in the Ambassador's house had taken refuge in the cellars. Nabote had been forced to share his cell. Cameron watched him struggling to work out what was happening. All smugness had vanished from his face.

Black liked punctuality. Bang on the stroke of twenty-two thirty he pressed the button, laid his thousand-pound egg and banked sharply away. The bomb flew down and detonated right on top of the radio.

*

The marines did what they could themselves, and got Mbekwe to bring many of his men to help. There was very little equipment to be had, and they used their hands and primitive tools to clear the wreckage, and for the first hour at least had no more illumination than car lights and torches. It was grisly work with all the corpses and body parts. Plenty of the guards had simply ceased to exist. There was a deep crater where the facade had been. Towards the rear a little more had survived including remnants of walls, and, amazingly, a couple of smaller rooms.

It was past midnight when they found Bob Tiernan, the last of twenty-six survivors. When the world had stopped collapsing, he'd managed to crawl out of the safe, which had been knocked right over by the impact, and drag himself a couple of yards, finding by touch a small space where falling girders had created a natural air pocket. He went in and out of consciousness, hallucinating at times. At other moments he was lucid enough to work out how fortuitous it had been that the registry door had lain where it did. It must have protected him from some of the direct blast. However, even in his cogent moments, he could not fathom what had happened to the building and why.

As they gingerly lifted him on to the stretcher, he managed a weak smile. The only thing on his mind was asking them to get a message to Alice. A medic took a note of that before giving him some morphine to deaden the pain of the helicopter ride. Back on *Indomitable* the ship's surgeon had been busy much of the evening, and when he had finished operating on one of the wounded marines, he started on Bob. He was quite a mess, with a badly crushed leg, one perforated lung, sundry broken bones, damaged eardrums and severe concussion. Along with a number of the other casualties, they would have to get him to a proper hospital as soon as possible. However, he would live. When Wings came to check on his welfare, Bob even ventured some dry remark about negotiation techniques.

*

By half-past midnight, the firing was only exuberance. Another forty or fifty guards who had not been at the High Commission had been rounded up by the army. Most had given up without a fight. The best guess was that around a hundred and fifty had fled the capital, taking some guns and ammunition. While these would be dangerous bandits, hopefully there were too few of them to pose any serious risk. Several government ministers had done a runner too. Nabote was still under guard in the cellar of the Swiss residence, clutching his little box. Now that the immediate danger had

256

passed, the Ambassador seemed less than interested in politics; it was the devastation of his antique porcelain and glass collection that was most on his mind. He was insisting on reparations from the British government.

State broadcasting had spread the word of what had happened, and people were pouring triumphantly onto the streets. Escorted in person by Mbekwe, Michael Endebbe had been driven from the Ocean Hotel to the town hall. Cameron had judged it safe enough for Theresa and Sasha to be flown in there.

As the counting approached completion, the excitement was growing. Though they would have to wait for the Talu count to be sure, the preponderance of Lobus in that region left little doubt of the result. Endebbe consulted with his aide and his wife, and decided to chance it. He knew that the situation was still shaky, and uncertainty could be harmful. When Cameron let Grace know what was going on, she insisted on being there, and a helo brought clean clothes for her. Outside the town hall the chanting was growing deafening. The CNN team had been given pride of place opposite the makeshift platform which had been erected outside. More than fifty soldiers were there, in their tattered uniforms and bearing some doubtful-looking weapons.

Finally, around one thirty, Endebbe came out grinning broadly, flanked by his wife, daughter and seven or eight of his key supporters. Theresa had pulled Grace out into public view with her. Cameron made sure that he and Dewar kept inside, well out of sight. They heard the roar of the crowd and watched the old man in the dark suit walk slowly past them holding a sheet of paper, and go through the door to join the group on the platform. Through the open door, they listened as he spoke in his grave, measured way.

'As Chairman of the Electoral Commission, I am glad to report that the Presidential election was conducted in a free and fair way. However, we discovered some irregularities in counting, and will now announce an amended provisional result, subject to confirmation tomorrow . . . Of all votes cast, excluding abstentions, Nathan Nabote received approximately thirty-four per cent. Michael Endebbe received sixty-six per cent. I therefore provisionally declare . . .'

He was drowned out by the raucous cheering.

Cameron and Dewar waited patiently as Endebbe made his speech, every sentence cheered to the heavens. Eventually the group came back inside. Cameron stepped forward.

'May I offer my congratulations, Mr President?'

'Thank you, Captain Cameron. I will now try to speak with your Prime Minister, if he is still awake at this hour.'

Cameron smiled wryly. 'I have no idea of his sleeping habits, but tonight I think you'll be in luck. You may get a surprise.'

'About what?'

'I'll let him tell you in his own words.'

'Very well. I intend to ask if you can stay on for some time as my guests.'

'That's very kind of you, but we will go back to our ship at first light. We have interfered enough in Numalan politics. With Nabote in custody and his son dead, you and General Mbekwe should have the situation under control. However, there is one thing I want to ask of you.'

'Anything.'

'Do not become a monster.'

Grace laughed. Theresa, smiling, stepped between the two men.

'Do not worry, Captain. If he breaks his word to you or to God, I will make him wish he had never been born.'

Still Cameron did not smile. He was staring at Endebbe with a fierce intensity. 'I am not joking. Many sacrifices have made to secure your position. If you betray the trust and become like Nabote, I will find you and kill you.'

Endebbe nodded gravely. 'Captain, what you and Theresa have said will concentrate my mind wonderfully. I will try to avoid needing to worry about either threat.'

Cameron allowed his face to relax. Outside the chanting was still going on. Endebbe and Theresa went to take another bow.

Grace looked at Cameron. 'Are you happy?'

'I'm glad, but not even close to happy . . . Grace, there's something I haven't told you. I wanted to give you a chance to recover first.'

'What?' She could see from his expression that this was not going to be any jest.

'Robert.'

'What about him? Where is he, anyway?'

'He died.'

Her face started to crumple.

'He was hit by a bullet that was meant for Michael Endebbe. He threw himself in harm's way.'

Her eyes brimmed and broke their banks, and her whole body shook gently with the sobs as she sank to the ground.

23

A fine sight lay beneath them as they flew back in the clear dawn light, *Indomitable*, *Tenacious* and the warships of the task force.

As soon as Cameron helped Grace inside, Wings met them with a warm handshake, and a signal from *Tenacious*. Cameron read it and nodded. Owen Lewis had been instructed to deliver a signal in person.

'Okay, we'd better send a helo for him. It can take Simon back too . . . On seconds thoughts, no. I'd like to invite him for breakfast in my harbour cabin. How about you too, Grace?'

'If you don't mind, I won't. I feel like I want to stand in a shower for an hour.'

Wings left to get the helo organised while Cameron escorted Grace to her cabin.

'Mind if I come in for a minute?'

'If you like.'

He followed her in and closed the door. She turned round.

'What is it?'

'Are you okay, Grace?'

She thought about it for a while. 'I'm not sure. It'll take time before I know. . . . Why are you looking at me like that?'

'Can I give you a hug?'

'If you want.'

She stayed right where she was, eyes down, as he stepped forward and he enfolded her in his arms.

'I'm so very glad you're safe.'

'I'm glad you are too.'

He kissed her on the forehead and squeezed her tighter. She looked up at him.

'What do you do now?'

'I go to my cabin and write to Robert's wife and the other wives and parents.'

'I understand. But that's not what I mean.'

'I had a signal sent to Fleet last night saying I and all the ship's company would surrender to the commander of the task force as soon as I returned to *Indomitable*. I imagine I'll be put under arrest, and will sail back on one of the other ships.'

There was a knock on the door and a junior officer came in.

'Excuse me, sir. The Sea King's on its way with Commander Lewis.'

Cameron greeted his old friend warmly, and Lewis handed over a sealed envelope. Cameron opened it and read it carefully. He shook his head in mystification, pocketed it and invited the submariner to join him for breakfast.

Simon, Wings and Colin were already in the harbour cabin. Cameron took Wings and Colin aside to brief them privately, and then they all settled down for a good old fry-up. Towards the end of the meal, the Captain flicked an eye at his steward, who disappeared and re-emerged carrying a silver tray, held aloft so they couldn't see what was on it.

'Simon, can I tell you an old, old story?'

Chewing on a piece of toast, Simon nodded.

'When I was in the Falklands twenty-odd years ago, the captain of the carrier I was on had an unusual custom. If some member of the ship's company had done something truly remarkable, he called him to his cabin and gave him a Crunchie bar.'

Simon took a sip of coffee. 'Did you get one?'

'After a fashion. He gave me one, but only after he had given me the most painful bollocking I've ever received, and as Owen here will probably tell you, I've had more than my share . . . I kept my Crunchie for ten years until it had well and truly disintegrated. After that, I kept the wrapper.'

Owen Lewis smiled warmly. The Crunchie story was famous. Simon dunked the last corner of toast.

'So?'

'Last night you made a vital contribution. You showed plenty of guts coming to Kindalu. More important, what you did when you got there was of huge importance . . . I think you deserve a Crunchie bar.'

He nodded to the steward, who lowered the tray.

Simon reached forward, took the bar and examined it carefully.

'Thank you.' He quickly unpeeled the wrapper and bit into it. Wings, Dewar, Lewis, Cameron erupted with laughter. The steward had a hard time suppressing his own giggles.

Simon looked utterly nonplussed.

'What? What's so funny?'

Soon after Lewis and Simon had left, Cameron was back knocking at Grace's cabin door.

'What's happened?'

'They want to authorise the action in Kindalu retrospectively, to treat it as if we were acting under orders. Believe it or not, around now, Patrick Dawnay is holding a press conference, taking credit for a successful example of our ethical foreign policy.'

'What does that mean for you?'

'*Indomitable* is to sail back to Portsmouth under my command. They want me to speak to the ship's company again, to ask them all to keep the mutiny to themselves.'

Grace snorted. 'Bollocks. They'll never get away with it. Too many people know about it.'

'That's what I think.'

262

'Even if the ship's company agree, surely some of them or their families will blab.'

'Most likely. Although if anyone does, we'll all face court martial. And if it got known who did it, I wouldn't like to be in his shoes.'

'What about the refuseniks, the ones who went over to *Fort George*, plus the crew of that ship?'

'They are being spoken to separately.'

'Does the same apply to everyone on the submarine?'

'I suppose so. Mind you, Owen Lewis says only five knew for sure.'

'What about the task force?'

'Sealed orders, apparently.'

'And all the civil servants in Whitehall?'

'You're dead right. Far too many people know.'

'Are you seriously suggesting that this can be hushed up?'

'Not at all. Frankly I think it's inconceivable that at some stage someone won't say something. If not immediately, then over the next ten years.'

'Oh, I get it. By then, the waters will have closed over the truth.'

'Something like that. At least everyone in the know is a government servant, and subject to the Official Secrets Act.'

'Except for me, right?'

'Right.'

'If I tell the truth, the whole gaff will be blown.'

'Correct.'

'I will have the biggest scoop for decades.'

'Without doubt.'

'And you'll go to jail for God knows how many years.'

'Perhaps.'

'So you're asking me to give up something that would make my career.'

'No, I'm not asking you to give up anything.'

'While you go on to be First Sea Lord, or whatever?'

Cameron's laugh was hollow. 'After this, you really think

they'll trust me to command a dinghy? No, dear girl, whatever happens, I'm finished. I expect I'll be quietly pensioned off in a few months' time. I'm not qualified to do very much else, sadly. Maybe I'll learn to be a carpenter.'

'So why do you want to gag me?'

'To protect my people – the ones on this ship.'

Grace paced up and down the cabin.

'I can't believe it. You've done it again, haven't you? I really have no choice.'

Cameron smiled. 'Look on the bright side. Even without the mutiny, you've still got a pretty good story to write.'

*

Patrick Dawnay got away with the press conference by hiding behind a veil of operational confidentiality. He majored on the rescue of the two British hostages, although saying that he did not yet have information on how Grace Parsons, the journalist covering the mission, had fallen into the hands of the guards. Normally, the press would have shredded him. This time, however, criticism was muted. The editors knew how well the action had been received in the country, and judged it smart to avoid looking grudging, especially with Christmas only three days away.

Crispin Adair and Toby Gordon-Booth had watched the performance with some relief. There had been a chance that it was going to be a fiasco on such a scale that even officials would feel the draught. Now it looked like their careers would go serenely onwards and upwards after all. Dawnay would be a different matter. Nothing might happen for the next few months, but, however feverishly he tried to mount a rearguard, come the next reshuffle he would be cut adrift.

Over the next days, including Christmas itself, none of them got much rest. It was taking time to work out the ramifications of the cover-up, let alone implement it. The powers that be decided that *Fort George* should rendezvous with

Indomitable and the crew who had opted out should be transferred back across. Otherwise, how would their absence be explained to their families when the ship arrived back in Portsmouth? The navy was furious about the subterfuge, and the MoD generally had been naturally nervous about how this would be received in both ships. They only finally convinced themselves when Cameron undertook to offer them a warm welcome back and to make sure that everyone on the carrier did the same.

They didn't doubt that at some point in the future questions would emerge. Hopefully it would be far enough down the track that the fallout would be limited. The COBRA Committee remained unanimously of the view that no British interest would be served, and plenty would be damaged, by admitting the whole truth.

*

Boxing Day wasn't easy for Jason. He hadn't realised how keen on him the poor girl had become. Did she really think they were in a relationship? Of course, he could have strung her along on the side for weeks or months. But that wouldn't have been fair. He so regretted the whole thing. If he hadn't been at such a low ebb when Grace flew to Gibraltar, or if Debbie hadn't come on so strong, it would never have happened. It was more unlucky timing than anyone's fault.

At least he'd ended it decently, not by email or fax like some arsehole. As soon as he got back from Christmas with his mother, he called her up, suggested they meet for lunch, and told her right out. He'd reasoned with her. It had been fun, they'd had some great times. They could stay very good friends. But he was engaged, for Christ's sake, she *knew* that.

Debbie threw a glass of red wine over him and walked out without another word. As Jason wiped his face with his paper napkin, he was relieved that they were in a dark cellar wine bar, and that in the lull before New Year it was all but

265

empty. It was lucky too that he was dressed all in black. The stain wouldn't show. Thank God it was done, anyway. Quite apart from the guilt, she had been far too close to home. Never again. Would he tell Grace about it? Of course, he would have to, for all sorts of reasons. Surely she'd understand that it was only disappointment at losing his dream assignment that had knocked him temporarily off balance, and laid him open to temptation. In picking the timing to tell her, he should be careful not to be selfish. *He* might feel better getting it off his chest immediately, but would Grace want the elation of her homecoming destroyed?

He took a cab back to the flat. Tomorrow first thing he'd be driving to Portsmouth. He'd checked that the nearest and dearest of those on board would be allowed into the naval base to welcome them home. He couldn't wait to see Grace. After three weeks away, she'd be gagging. And whether she knew it or not, she was going to be quite a celebrity now. The editor was planning a huge spread for her story. All sorts of chat shows and magazines were keen to get hold of her. Handled well, this might turn out to be more than fifteen minutes of fame. With looks like that, there was no knowing how far she could go. She could become a genuine celebrity. *Hello!* might offer a shedload of loot to cover their wedding.

She would probably feel like some rest. Where could he take her for New Year? . . . Paris, of course. He logged onto the Internet. It looked like train tickets were no problem. Now, what was that cute hotel Grace had found near the Louvre? . . . Yeah, there it was, the Hôtel Thérèse. Perfect. She'd love that. He filled in the dates on the site and clicked.

Fuck, it was full.

*

The last night on board, Cameron invited Grace to dine with him in his harbour cabin. In the intervening days, he'd been frantically busy – especially with the odd business of taking

Tom, Tara, and all the others back. In the circumstances, Tom had been remarkably gracious about it, and had some kind words for Grace too. Tara was withdrawn and sulky. When Grace had tried to be friendly, Tara had ignored her completely. Cameron had spent a long time talking with Tom, and they had agreed that it would not be appropriate or comfortable for either of the returning officers to resume normal duties.

There were so many other things too which the captain had to attend to during the six-day voyage home, and he had not had more than the odd snatched conversation with Grace. Even now, apart from the occasional jovial exchange with the steward, the conversation was subdued. The mulligatawny soup was supped in near silence. Cameron finished and put his spoon down.

'Will Jason be waiting for you in Portsmouth?'

Grace nodded. 'That's what his email said.'

'I never asked if you've set a date.'

'April fifteenth. Will you come if I invite you?'

Cameron tried his best not to let his face express his feelings.

'That's very kind of you, but I'm not very good at weddings.'

They relapsed into silence. It was Grace's turn to break it.

'This is almost as bad as the first time we had dinner.'

They both smiled.

'Are you getting much sleep?'

'Not a lot, even with the pills. And when I do, I get horrible dreams . . . Apart from that, it's hard to say. In some strange way, I feel changed.'

'I know what you mean. I feel it too. I'm sure the navy can arrange some counselling, if you want it.'

'Thanks. I'll think about it.'

'At the very least, you should get Jason to give you plenty of TLC.'

'Yeah.' She hoped he couldn't read what she felt when he said that.

'Grace, can I tell you something I've never admitted to anyone?'

'Sure.'

He looked to make sure that the steward wasn't in the room. 'When I made my attack run in the Falklands I was terrified. I was so desperate to get away, not to get shot up or captured by the Argies, that I nearly bogged the whole thing. I was ashamed. And, you know, that private sense of shame never left me. I always compared myself to my hero, Nelson, and I knew he would never have been so weak. Ever since, I hoped I'd be given another chance to see if I could conquer my fear.'

She waited, unsure where this was going.

'When you were taken, the only thing I could think about was getting you out. When I walked across that street, I knew I could be killed or captured, yet I didn't feel a single ounce of fear – all because of you.'

There were things that Grace, too, badly wanted to say, but she was afraid it would only make it harder. She just reached out and squeezed his hand, pulling it away only when she heard the steward's footfall.

'What about TLC for you? Will Charlotte be there, do you think?'

'I don't think so. I wondered whether I would find an email when we hooked the system back up.'

'Nothing?'

'Nothing. There'll be other people waiting for me, though.'

'The heavy mob?'

'A few of them. They've promised to let me off with a quick debrief tomorrow. The real stuff will start after the holiday period. What I meant was the families of our dead. Some of them will be there to collect the bodies.'

'Of course . . . What about New Year? Do you have family or friends to stay with?'

'I'll just stay in Lymington. I'm not sure I feel very social.'

It wasn't until they were within sight of the south side of the Isle of Wight that Grace's mobile snapped back into life. There were so many voice and text messages, from family, friends and colleagues. As she listened to all the familiar voices, she felt a wave of comfort at the thought of being home. On to the text messages. Twenty-four of them. Even a bubbly one from the editor. She didn't realise John *knew* how to text. She smiled at the thought that he'd probably called Karen Stelling in to do it for him. She pressed the button to take her on to the next. Oh – one from Karen herself.

She was glad she was alone in her cabin when she read it.

*

There had been many sad farewells to the pilots, especially Shane, as, one by one, the aircraft took off for their resting places. The ship felt somehow soulless without them. Grace walked around the decks saying goodbye to her many other friends. Lots of email addresses and phone numbers were exchanged, together with lots of solemn promises to meet again. Billy Ward threatened to come and embarrass her at her posh office if she didn't catch up soon for a drink with him, Trish and their mates.

For the final approach up the Solent, the sky was cloudless and sapphire blue. *Indomitable* saluted the flotilla of small boats that had come out to greet her. Despite the bitter north wind, the bulk of the ship's company, all dressed in their best uniforms, lined the flight deck to wave at the astonishing numbers of well-wishers at the mouth of the harbour.

Grace was on the bridge as the great ship came alongside. Wings, standing next to Cameron, spotted Millie on the jetty, then cajoled Colin into joining him in gently teasing Grace, trying to guess which one was Jason.

If this took any longer, his bollocks would be frozen right off. That was the problem with Paul Smith coats. They might look good in London, but they were useless at dealing with the freezing provinces. He checked his pocket again to make sure the ring hadn't slipped out. How long could it take to tie up a boat? He hopped about, trying to get some feeling to his toes.

Up above, Wings had got him in one, and Grace wasn't sure that was a compliment. Jason's continuing jig was prompting more grins. She looked again. Why was he doing that? Didn't he know what a prat he looked? And that Paul Smith coat might look great in the right clubs, but when you compared that and his skinny black jeans with how the men around looked in their finery . . . Wings, Colin – they both looked great. As for Chris . . .

She looked over at the Captain again. There was something in his expression that concerned her. She went close and whispered. 'Are you okay?'

'Sure.'

'Is Charlotte there?'

'I don't see her.'

'Well, I hope she is.'

'Thanks.'

'Look, I'd better go and get my bags.'

'They've already been taken . . . Can I escort you down?'

She said her farewells to Colin and Wings, and she and Cameron walked together in silence, stopping when they reached the top of the gangway.

'I guess this is it, then, Chris. We *will* meet again, won't we?'

'I promise. Have a happy New Year.'

'You too.'

She wanted to give him a hug, but it didn't seem right. They just shook hands.

As she got to the bottom of the gangway, he saw Jason step

forward and thrust a big kiss on her. The sight of it cut deeply. Soon the pair disappeared through the crowd. As Cameron glanced to his left, he was amazed to see Charlotte right at the back. He went down the gangway and over to see her. The crowd parted to let him through. As he approached, her smile was very kindly. He kissed her on the cheek.

'Hi. I didn't expect you to be here. How *are* you?'

She nodded. 'I'm okay . . . You?'

'I'm okay . . . Listen, I won't be able to get away for a few hours. I have to see some families and so on. Why don't you go on ahead and I'll . . .'

'Chris . . . That's not why I'm here. I wasn't planning on coming at all. After all you've been through, I didn't want there to be no one to welcome you home. I'm so proud of you . . . I also decided you deserved more than a note at the flat.'

'I see.'

'I'm sorry I never called back. I needed to do some thinking.'

'Have you gone back to Tim?'

She paused for what seemed like an age. 'I haven't moved in. I'm living at my sister's. He and I are taking it slowly.'

'I'm glad for you. I hope it works out.'

'Thank you . . . I'm truly sorry.'

'I know I have only myself to blame.'

'I'd better be going.'

'Thanks for coming . . . You were right. It *was* good to have someone here.'

She kissed him, gave his hand a tender squeeze, and, with one last long look, turned and went.

Only two of the families had come, both parents of young marines. He and Colin saw them together. Cameron, who had never cried since childhood, had to cling to his composure. After that, the debrief felt profoundly prosaic, and went on far

271

longer than promised. It gave a mechanic the chance to put the E-type's battery on charge to make sure it would get him home.

When he finally got out, Cameron let the engine warm up before driving to the Unicorn Gate. As he slowed for the security post, he saw a figure standing under a lamppost beyond. He drove the few yards, stopped under the corona of light and stretched to wind down the window.

'What the hell are you doing here?'

'Freezing to death. Can I get in?'

He pushed the door open, grabbed her bags and stowed them behind with his own.

'Jesus Christ, I'm cold.'

He took her right hand. She had no gloves and it felt like cold stone.

'How long have you been there?'

'Bloody ages.'

'Where's Jason?'

'Probably back in London shagging some tart.'

'Is that what he did while you were away?'

She nodded. 'A girl from the office. I got a text message from the editor's secretary warning me.'

'Did Jason confess?'

'Eventually. Under torture.'

'Will you give him another chance?'

'Not in a hundred years.'

He had to struggle to stop the glee showing. Grace blew into her hands to try to warm them.

'Is Charlotte waiting for you somewhere?'

'No, she's not. She came, which was good of her, but only to tell me she was leaving. Had left, more like it. She's back with her ex.'

'Sorry to hear that.' It was Grace's turn to suppress a big grin.

'Don't take this the wrong way, Grace, because I'm truly delighted to see you, but what's the plan now? D'you want me to drive you to London?'

272

'I don't have anywhere to go there. Jason and I shared a flat . . . That's not why I'm here. I only stayed on the off-chance that Charlotte hadn't come. I hated the thought that there might be no one there for you. I know how tough you are, but even Superman gets TLC from Lois Lane.'

'What about you?'

'I need some TLC too.'

She smiled. Chris took her hand.

'Does that mean we're starting something?'

'I don't know . . . No, that's a lie. Of *course* that's what it means. It's also a lie that I'm so upset about Jason. I've been wanting you for what seems like the longest time.'

'I've been wanting the same. So badly. Was it too painfully obvious?'

'I wasn't sure. Until last night, anyway.'

'Doesn't the age difference horrify you?'

'Not particularly. It'll give my friends who worry about the race difference even more to gossip about.'

'Think about it. If we stick together, I'll be a retired carpenter or whatever when you're still in your prime.'

'Then let's take it a day at a time, eh? I won't spook you. I know what you're like. I solemnly promise never to mention the "m"-word.'

Chris laughed, let off the handbrake and pushed the gear lever forward. The throaty sound of the straight-six engine bounced off the walls and the sodium glare of the street lights picked out the sinuous shape as the car accelerated crisply away.

They had fallen into a long silence when, twelve miles out of Portsmouth, the car began to slow and ground to a halt on the hard shoulder. Grace looked alarmed.

'What's the matter? Have we broken down?'

Cameron shook his head. 'Listen, I can't deny that for me

committing's a problem. But that's partly because there's never been anyone I cared enough about losing. You're risky for me, Grace: my gut tells me that before long I won't be able to bear the thought of you leaving.'

Grace tried to hide her disappointment. 'Fair enough. You want to back off.'

'No, I don't. I want to marry you.'

'Chris, you *cannot* be serious . . . Or, if you are, you must be mad. We haven't even . . .'

'That bit we can take care of in the next hour . . . So? Will you?'

Slowly Grace shook her head. 'I got engaged in haste and repented at leisure. Never again. If you're still keen in a year, ask me then . . . Come on now, let's get going.'

He didn't move. 'In a year I may have lost my nerve.'

'Nine months, then. That's my best offer.'

Cameron's eye was caught by something in the mirror. Headlamps and blue flashing lights were coming up behind them.

'Police. Quick – it's illegal to stop here. Six months – deal?'

'You manipulative bastard . . .' The lights were getting brighter. '*Okay.*'

Cameron pushed the door open as the patrol car rolled to a halt and two officers got out. They walked towards him as he stood by the Jaguar.

'Spot of trouble, sir?'

'Overheating. I had to let it cool for a while. Should be all right now.'

They wandered around the car, admiring the shape and stopped beside the passenger door. Grace rolled the window down as one policeman put his hand on the roof above it.

'You've got to be careful with these old ones, miss. They have style all right, but they're always letting you down.'

Grace turned and caught the eye of Cameron. He shrugged. She smiled, dazzlingly.